PROMISES TO KEEP

READ MORE ABOUT THE THOMAS FAMILY IN THESE
NOVELS BY DEAN HUGHES:

PROMISES TO KEEP

Diane's Story

DEAN HUGHES

DESERET
BOOK

SALT LAKE CITY, UTAH

Library of Congress Cataloging-in-Publication Data

Hughes, Dean.
   Promises to keep : Diane's story / Dean Hughes.
      p.   cm.
   ISBN 978-1-59038-987-4 (paperbound)
  1. Single mothers—Fiction.   2. Problem children—Fiction.   3. Ogden (Utah)—Fiction.   4. Mormons—Fiction.   5. Religious fiction.
6. Domestic fiction.   I. Title.
   PS3558.U36P76 2008
   813'.54—dc22   2008024938

Printed in the United States of America
Sheridan Books, Chelsea, MI

10   9   8   7   6   5   4   3   2   1

For my granddaughters,
Carrie Hughes and Katie Russell

CHAPTER I

"Mom, can you take just a minute to talk to me?" Jenny asked.

"Sure." Diane Lyman set her red pencil in her textbook and closed the book on her lap.

"I want to ask you something, but will you please not say no until you've heard the whole story?"

Diane smiled, but she was wary. Jenny had just come in from the kitchen, where she'd been talking to her dad on the telephone. Diane had picked up on some of the conversation. She knew that the two of them had been planning something and she could pretty well guess what Greg had said: "Your mom's going to say no, but get her to listen to you before she makes up her mind."

"Go ahead," Diane said. "I'll listen. But don't take forever. I've got a lot to do tonight."

"You've got a lot to do *every* night."

But that was a little annoying. Jenny knew that Diane was in grad school, taking night classes. They had talked it all out, and Jenny had agreed that it would be hard for both of them—but worth it. Diane had finished her master's degree; now she was going on for an administrative certificate. She wanted to become a principal. She had been teaching Special Education and running resource rooms for a long time, but she had been telling Jenny that she needed a change. Even more, she needed more income, and Jenny certainly agreed with that. "This *is* a busy time," Diane said.

Jenny dropped onto the couch, across from Diane. It was the same old flowered couch they'd had since Jenny had been little, and Diane winced as she saw the sudden motion pull at a rip along a seam in front. "Okay. Here's the thing." Jenny paused, lacing her fingers together on her lap. For a girl not yet sixteen, she could look very composed, and she knew how to sound reasonable. "Dad is going to London. Marilyn can't go, so he could take me and it wouldn't cost him any extra for the hotel room. He can even use Frequent Flyer miles to buy my ticket, so taking me wouldn't cost him very much at all. He really wants me to go with him, and you know how much I've always wanted—"

"When is he going?"

"It's in about three weeks—the first week of November—I know I'd have to miss some days of school, but—"

"How much school?"

Jenny suddenly stood up. "Never mind. There's no use talking to you. You've got your mind made up already. I told Dad you'd never let me go." Tears were starting in her eyes, but she stood tall, took on a hurt look, and then she turned and started toward her room.

"Wait a minute."

Jenny stopped and turned back, tragedy still in her face. Diane could see Greg in that look. Jenny's hair had darkened over the years to a walnut brown—rich and shiny—almost as dark as her father's, and she had his bone structure, too, the same carved, clean look. But she had Diane's eyes, big and smoky blue. And the combination was striking. Boys had discovered her in the last year or so—even though she was skinny as a stick—and she had begun to recognize the power her pretty face gave her. She had also picked up some of her father's skill at manipulation, and that bothered Diane.

"I've never been anywhere, Mom. I just thought it would be a

2

chance to see something new, for once." Now the tears were working their way down her cheeks.

"Explain this to me, Jenny. Your father won't send us your child support so we can save up and take a trip of our own—but now he wants to be the hero and whisk you off to London to see the queen."

"Okay, fine. I'll call him back and tell him I can't go."

Diane stood up. She wanted to touch Jenny, wanted at least to let her know that she understood her disappointment, but she was furious at Greg for putting her in this situation. "Honey, I don't think it's good to miss school that way, and what about cross-country? You can't just run out on your team like that."

"We don't have a big meet that week. I already looked at my schedule. It's just a practice thing that doesn't count in any of the standings."

"But you'd lose a lot of conditioning. How long does he want you to be over there?"

"It's a week—six days, really. I'd only miss one week of school and one cross-country run. And what I could do—Dad even said this—I could run in Hyde Park every day. We'd be staying right close to that area."

"Oh, yes, Greg'll certainly be staying in a fancy hotel. Don't you realize, Jenny, half the reason we have to live the way we do is that he doesn't come through for his own daughter. I'm tired of it."

"But he's had all those problems with his business. He's really sorry he doesn't help us more. That's why he wants to do this—to make up for some of that. And he has to go. He's got a deal going over there, and if it comes through, he told me he would catch us up for all the months he's missed. He really does want to—"

"He really does *lie*, Jenny. By now you ought to know that about him."

Diane watched Jenny's face lose all its composure, collapse into that little-girl brokenheartedness that Diane had been trying to relieve all her life. Jenny broke into sobs and took off again, taking long-legged strides down the hallway and on into her bedroom. She shut the door firmly behind her.

Diane was tempted to give Jenny what she wanted, but the truth was, she didn't like the idea of Jenny being around her dad for that long. Greg claimed that he was still active in the Church, but she had heard from people who had watched him do it that he drank sometimes at social events—and she knew that he was connected to people who were considered shady by legitimate businesspeople. Morality, for Greg, always seemed to be whatever he could get away with, and if it served his purpose to seem a "good Church member" in certain circles, he presented himself that way. But Diane knew the truth about him: The only thing that mattered deeply to Greg was Greg himself.

Still, she had to watch how much she said to Jenny. The girl had always wanted to believe in her father—which was only natural. Diane had divorced Greg when Jenny was still a baby, back in the early seventies, and it was 1985 now. Greg had abused Diane, had actually beaten up on her, but in all these years, Diane had avoided telling Jenny that, and she didn't plan to tell her, ever. She had to be careful about being too critical of him. For one thing, it only made Jenny take his side.

Diane sat down in her chair and shut her eyes. She took some time to calm herself—and to let Jenny calm down too—and then she finally walked down the hall and opened Jenny's door. Jenny was stretched out on the bed facedown, crying into her pillow. Diane wondered if maybe the trip was something Jenny needed. It would be a chance for her to feel that she had done something interesting, just once. She had friends at Ogden High who had been to Europe with their families and who loved to talk about their travels. Diane and Jenny had never really suffered, partly because Diane's parents helped them at times, and partly because she and Jenny had learned to stretch their money in every way they could. Still, Jenny wanted to see the world, and she had only rarely even peeked outside the state of Utah.

Before Diane could say anything, Jenny suddenly sat up and twisted around. "You *hate* Dad. That's the trouble. You're just afraid I'll love my own father."

"No, Jenny, that's not true, but—"

"I know some things, Mom. I've always heard your side of the story. But I know more about it now."

"What's that supposed to mean? What did he say to you?"

Jenny looked a little "found out" for a moment, but she looked away and said firmly, "He doesn't have to say anything. I know how you do things. And I can just tell that the problems weren't all his fault."

"I've never said they were *all* his fault."

"But you let me believe it. You've said plenty of things."

Diane was seeing another side of Jenny now—a quality that had started to appear only lately. She liked to take on a tone that implied that she knew her way around, that she knew more about the world than Diane did. "Jenny, I think you *should* love your dad. But I don't think it's right if he's making a case against me."

"I didn't say that he was." Jenny got off her bed. She was wearing jeans and an old gray sweatshirt with a stretched-out neck. She liked to let it hang over one shoulder—the "Flashdance" look that so many girls had gotten into—even though she knew that Diane didn't approve. "But I know how uptight you are about everything. I'm sure that's how you were with him, too."

"I don't even know what you're talking about."

"You hate everything he ever buys for me."

"The only thing I *hated* was that red skirt—and you know why."

"There was nothing wrong with it."

"Jenny, let's not go through this again. We talked about that."

"No. You talked about it."

"And did you want to go around looking like that—in a skirt that hardly covered your backside? You looked like a little tramp."

"That's how *you* see it. I don't."

"So I'm the one who's uptight?"

"Yes. A lot of good Mormon girls—as you always call them—are wearing skirts that short."

Diane wasn't going to do this. She took another breath and placed her hands on her hips. Jenny had always been stubborn, even defiant when she was little, but for such a long time, the two of them had been close—and now this. The animosity in Jenny's voice cut Diane more than the words.

Jenny seemed to know that she had Diane on her heels. She stepped closer. "Dad said I can come and live with him anytime I want."

Diane was suddenly frightened. Things could easily get out of control if she weren't careful. She looked at the floor for a time, trying to get command of her voice, and then said, "Is that how you feel, honey? That you don't want to live with me anymore?"

Jenny didn't answer. She looked away, and a little of the hardness left her face. She sat down on her bed again. It was an amazingly organized bedroom, with Monet prints on the wall—not posters of Prince or Michael Jackson—her desk neatly arranged, her clothes all hung up. "I'm going to be somebody, Mom. I'm going to get a scholarship for college, and I'm going to be a businesswoman. I'm going to have my own company."

Diane wasn't sure what Jenny was trying to say at the moment, but this had been Jenny's theme lately. She was smart, a very good student, and she was driven to get perfect grades. She was going to make her own way, she liked to say, and she wouldn't marry until she was thirty—if at all. Diane hadn't paid much attention to the talk; she knew Jenny hated having less than her friends. But always before, this whole notion had seemed the fantasy of a fifteen-year-old; now her firm, Greg-like jaw seemed set on it.

Diane sat down on the bed next to Jenny. "Honey, I know how you feel. I've done the best I can, but I know—"

"I know what you're going to say. *Dad* hasn't given us enough money. Everything is always *his* fault."

"I'm sorry. I shouldn't harp on that kind of thing so much. I'll try to be careful about that." She put her hand on Jenny's. "More than anything, I want us to be okay with each other. I may seem uptight to you, but I'm the one who has to teach you what's right. I have that responsibility."

Jenny pulled her hand away, slid back a little, and turned toward her mother. "A lot of parents have the same responsibility, and they aren't worried about their kids' clothes half as much as you are. You ought to see what some of the girls are wearing—and the grades they're getting. Tracy calls me 'Little Miss Perfect' because I never do anything wrong."

"You are a good girl, Jenny. I know that. And maybe I hover over you more than I should. You're my only child, so I probably do worry more than some parents. But it's only because I love you so much."

"And Dad doesn't?"

"I didn't say that." Diane was getting weary of all this. She just wanted the fight to end. "But do you really want to go live with him? Are you that mad at me?"

"I don't see why it would hurt for me to go to London. You're just afraid I'll get to do something that you've never done. Dad told me exactly how you'd react."

Diane stood up and looked down at Jenny. "He's telling you a lot these days, isn't he? Maybe you need to ask yourself who's being fair and who isn't."

Jenny stood too. The two of them were almost the same height now, and they were standing so close that Diane could feel the heat coming off Jenny's face. "Maybe when I talk to him, he *listens*. And maybe he understands me better than you ever will." She pushed past Diane, knocking against her shoulder, and headed down the hallway.

"Come back here," Diane was saying. "You're too old to throw tantrums." She hurried after her.

But Jenny reached the front door to the apartment, jerked it open, stepped outside, and slammed it behind her.

Diane hurried to the door, thinking for a moment of running outside after Jenny, but she knew better. They both needed time. There was nowhere for Jenny to go, and it was cold outside. She wouldn't be gone long.

So Diane sat down. She told herself she would go back to her studies. She really needed to do that. It was a Friday evening, and she didn't have her evening class until the following Tuesday, but she was way behind on her reading. She'd promised herself she would study Friday night so that she would have time to clean Saturday morning and then maybe do something with Jenny in the afternoon. The two of them hadn't spent much time together lately, and they needed to do that. Maybe that wasn't possible now, with Jenny so mad, but it didn't change the fact that Diane needed to study. She needed good grades too—so she could reach her own goals.

But her mind wouldn't take in the paragraph she tried to read. She was wondering what, exactly, Greg had said to Jenny. It was maddening to think that the man who had thrown Diane into a wall, choked her, and knocked her down could be telling Jenny what was wrong with the woman he'd treated that way.

Diane let her textbook drop to her lap and leaned back in her chair. A realization had been growing in her lately. Jenny was a sophomore in high school. It wouldn't be that long before she would be going off to college. And then, what would Diane do? Her whole life had been devoted to raising her little girl. Now all this independence was raising its head, and before long Jenny would be gone. And once she was gone, Diane would come home every night to an empty apartment and the loneliness she was feeling right now.

Diane was thirty-six, which sounded way too close to forty to suit her. She had gained a little weight these last few years, and she was always telling herself she needed to exercise more, eat better. She hated that she was buying size ten dresses, not the sixes she'd always been able to wear. She knew she could still turn heads. That wasn't even the issue. She just didn't like the sense that she was heading toward middle age, and she was going to be alone. Life hadn't turned out the way she had expected; she had accepted that and done her best. Still, the logical conclusion was about to play out. Jenny would go after her own dreams, maybe become all she wanted to be, maybe bring back grand-kids, or maybe not—but her life would be her own, and Jenny's life had always been Diane's reason for living.

Diane had dated off and on over the years, but she had always had lots more bad experiences than decent ones, and nothing had ever worked out. There were plenty of divorced men out there who had taken a look at her and decided she was just what they wanted, but most of them were needy and usually far too eager. So she had pulled away from all that. She didn't let people line her up anymore, and she didn't go to singles events, where she felt like a minnow in a pond of hungry, fat carp. Whenever she *had* dated in the last few years, she'd sent out all the wrong vibes. She had expected the worst and resisted closeness—not just touch, but even the honest talk that went with real courtship. Even the men who might have been interesting to her asked her out only a time or two after they experienced her practiced aloofness.

The other problem with dating had always been Jenny, who didn't like the men who came for Diane and let it be known. Diane had come to realize that little Jenny—now, nearly grown-up Jenny—had contin-ued to fantasize that somehow Greg would come back into their lives. Even after he had married this time—which was the third time—Jenny had talked about Marilyn not being right for him, as though she could wish the woman away and then the fantasy family she dreamed of would magically congeal. The idea of bringing any other man into their lives clearly bothered her. What was clear to Diane was that even if she met someone she really liked, that would only create bigger problems.

But Jenny was already breaking away, and this little apartment—bigger than her first one, but still in the neighborhood close to Mom and Dad—would be Diane's "home," and she would have to discover something new that would keep her going every day.

Diane did finally raise her book again. She read carefully, making sure she understood, and she underlined crucial passages, but the longer Jenny was gone, the more Diane worried. She was about to call her mother, to see if Jenny had stopped in there, when the door finally opened and Jenny stepped in. She looked a little subdued now, but firm. "I'll call Dad in the morning," she said. "I'll tell him I can't go."

"Honey, why don't we—"

"I don't want to talk right now." She walked to her room again.

Diane was still wondering what she should do. She could give in, and that would soften the feelings between them. But the thought of it was repulsive to her. Greg had been trying to swing Jenny to his side for a long time now, and he was finally making some headway. It wasn't just a contest to see who could win Jenny's love. Greg was dangerous. He could teach things to Jenny that would change her, ruin everything Diane had tried to build. Diane decided that she couldn't give in on this one.

Jenny hadn't been in her room long before the telephone rang. Diane was sure she knew who it was. Her mom called her almost every evening.

Diane walked to the kitchen and picked up the receiver from the wall phone. "Hi, Mom," Diane said, without waiting to hear her voice. She stretched out the cord and sat down at the kitchen table.

Bobbi laughed. "Who else?" she said.

"Exactly. I'm thirty-six and the only person who calls me is my mommy."

"Did Jenny tell you she was over here?"

"No. But I thought maybe that was where she'd gone. At least I hoped. I guess that's when I really have to worry—when she *doesn't* go talk to you."

"Well, yes. That's about right." Bobbi had turned sixty-six this year, but she never seemed to change. She was getting to look a little older, when Diane actually thought about it, but she acted as young as ever. She was still the feisty Democrat in a neighborhood of Republicans, and still as likely as ever to say exactly what she thought.

"Did you two have a good talk?" Diane asked. She folded one arm around her middle. Her kitchen was cold. She had complained a dozen times to the landlord that the window by the table needed caulking around the frame. A stream of air came through it like a wind. The landlord always promised, but never showed up.

"Yes. I guess so. At least it ended up that way," Bobbi said.

"Well . . . I wish I could say that. She wouldn't talk to me when she got back."

"She's punishing you for being so unreasonable—but you know what? She knew she wasn't going to London before she even asked. That's half of why she's so mad."

"Or in other words, she had no hope that her hard-nosed mother could be moved to grant her wish."

"Well, yes. But you know what else? I think she knows it's not a good idea. She does worry about school and running and all that—but I also think she suspects more about her dad than she wants to admit."

"She's been trying to love him all her life, Mom. He comes into her life, buys her something or tries to win her over in some way—and then he's gone again. She doesn't hear from him for long stretches, and then he waltzes in, all full of charm, and she wants to be around him in spite of herself."

"I know. She wants a dad. I guess every kid does."

"I criticize him too much. I know I do. But he's been telling her all kinds of things about me, and that's not fair."

"Honey, you can't make her a pawn in your struggles with Greg."

"I know." She got up and moved her chair farther from the window, stretching the telephone cord nearly to its end. "What else did you two talk about?"

"Well, she was mad. You know that. She came in ranting about you not letting her go to London—and she started in about you going to school these days, always with your nose in a book. It took me a while, but I tried to give her some perspective about all the years you've worked to provide for her. I think I got her to a point where she understood that, but you know what her problem is, don't you?"

"What?"

"It's called 'fifteen.' You had a bad case of it yourself once."

"She's almost sixteen."

"Yeah, well, some would say that sixteen is just a worse case of fifteen. I'm not sure. It's a tough call. Right now, she thinks the world revolves around her, the sun rising over her beautiful face and setting just behind that cute backside of hers."

Diane laughed. "She is pretty, isn't she?"

"She's gorgeous. And that's not an easy thing to be. You ought to know."

"But Mom, I may study a lot these days, but she's watching TV or on the phone anyway. It's like she has to make up some reason to be mad at me."

"Like I said—fifteen. But I talked to her about that. I told her how you managed to hang on after the divorce, get through college when it was so hard to keep going—and all the time you've given to her. That's what you've done your whole adult life, Di—look after that girl."

"Did she buy that?"

"The way any teenager does. They think that's what moms are for. What's the big deal?"

Diane laughed again. "I'm glad I wasn't like that."

"Let's choose to remember it that way."

Diane really couldn't remember herself at that age. She wasn't sure what she had been like then—except in love with herself. She had spent half her life looking in a mirror. Jenny wasn't half as bad in that regard. "I'll tell you what's different about Jenny. She's got her mind made up that she has to be a millionaire to be happy."

"I know. We got into all that."

"She doesn't care one thing about the Church."

"I don't think that's quite true, but I will admit, I said the wrong thing to her. I told her that Church members sometimes make single people feel out of place—just to explain some of the things that have been hard for you. She jumped right on that. She started in about how she may not be active in the Church once she's on her own. I think it's just more teenager talk, but it does worry me a little how worldly all her goals seem to be."

"If you called me to make me feel better, you need to know, you're not doing a very good job. You're just confirming some of the things I've already been worrying about."

The two chatted for a while after that. Bobbi was worrying about Richard, Diane's dad, the way he seemed lost since he'd retired, still reading a lot but seeming to long for more people to talk to about the things he read, and about her mother, Grandma Bea, who was eighty-eight now and starting to get forgetful.

There were always so many hard things in life, Diane decided. They never ended. But after she hung up the phone, she decided to try one more time to talk to Jenny. She walked to her door, waited for a moment, then heard that Jenny was listening to her Madonna album—something else Greg had bought for her. Diane didn't like anything about Madonna, including her music. She decided she couldn't even try to talk to Jenny with that voice blasting through the room. She supposed that Jenny may have put the music on for exactly that reason. So Diane sat down in the living room, gave up on her own studies for the night, and tried to find something to watch on TV. She watched *Dallas* for a few minutes, only to be reminded how stupid the show actually was, and then she checked the other two networks and found nothing better. For a long time, she and Jenny had wanted to get cable television, but they just hadn't been able to afford it. So she wandered back to her bedroom, where the dim, gray light only made her feel the loneliness of her life again.

CHAPTER 2

Diane got up early the next morning, not long after six o'clock. She made herself finish the chapter she had given up on the night before, and she actually concentrated pretty well. She had housecleaning to do, and she still hoped she could do something fun with Jenny before the day was over, but she knew Jenny would sleep in, and she figured she had better study while the house was quiet.

As it turned out, Jenny got up earlier than Diane had expected, but she walked through the living room in her bathrobe, said good morning rather stiffly in answer to Diane's own greeting, and then headed straight to the kitchen. She made herself some toast and carried it back to her bedroom. Just as Jenny reached the door to her room, Diane asked, "What are you going to do today?"

"I've got a paper to write," Jenny said, sounding distant more than angry, and then she walked into the bedroom and shut the door.

Diane knew, of course, that this was all a kind of manipulation. Jenny certainly understood how much Diane suffered when Jenny shut her out this way, and she knew that Diane would usually work hard to get back into her good graces. But Diane wasn't going to do that this morning. She had refused Jenny something she wanted; that was what mothers had to do sometimes, and she wasn't going to apologize for it. But Diane still ached.

She finished her chapter and then studied a journal article she had been assigned to read. That took over an hour, and still there was no sound from Jenny's room. If she was writing a paper, she wasn't using her typewriter yet. Maybe she was reading—or maybe she had actually gone back to sleep. Diane kept glancing at the closed door, wondering how long Jenny would stay in there.

Diane eventually went to her own bedroom, next to Jenny's, discarded her bathrobe, and put on a pair of jeans and a sweatshirt, along with her old Keds. She had a house to clean and clothes to wash. If Jenny didn't plan to help, Diane wasn't going to beg her, but that meant Diane had a lot to do. She picked up a few things lying around the living room, dusted, and got the vacuum cleaner from the hall closet. She vacuumed the living room and then, knowing full well she was sending a message, she vacuumed the hallway all the way down to Jenny's door.

On most Saturday mornings Jenny helped with the cleaning, and Diane thought she might now step out and offer to vacuum her own room, but nothing happened. So Diane shut off the vacuum, gave a little rap on the door, and called, "Jenny, I'm going to start the wash. Do you have some things you want me to throw in?"

"I'll do it myself. Don't worry about it."

"I know. But I want to put in some colored things first. If you have—"

"I'm working on my paper, Mom. I'll do my own wash later. And I'll clean up my room."

Her voice was neutral, even a little edgy, and the door still didn't open.

So Diane got her own wash going, dusted and vacuumed her bedroom, and started on the kitchen. Diane wasn't one to leave dishes in the sink, and Jenny was actually quicker to start the dishwasher than Diane was, but they had both let the dishes go the night before, hadn't even cleared the table.

Diane spent the better part of an hour on the kitchen, even

mopping the floor, and still Jenny stayed in her bedroom. Then, just as Diane was starting on the bathroom in the hallway by the bedrooms, Jenny's door finally opened. "Can I use the bathroom for a minute?" she asked. She still sounded reserved, which was bothersome, but Diane felt the sense that she was working at it, that she was willing herself to hold onto her moodiness. The act was getting tiresome, and it fired Diane's temper a little, but she didn't say anything. Leaving the mirror half covered with glass cleaner, she turned and walked past Jenny.

"I didn't mean you had to stop right in the middle—"

Diane shut the door behind her, rather firmly. She didn't want to argue with Jenny again, but she didn't need this today. Life was hard enough all week, dealing with school kids who liked to challenge the boundaries Diane set.

Diane didn't know whether Jenny was going to shower right then, or what she had in mind, but in only a few minutes she came out and returned to her room. The standoff was going to continue. Jenny hadn't said anything, hadn't even let Diane know the room was free again, the way she would have on a normal morning.

So Diane went back, cleaned the mirrors and the sink and counter, and scrubbed the toilet and the bathtub. And by then she was making a case against Jenny. The girl had no idea what kind of man her father was, the kind of influence he could be. Jenny was still a little girl and she thought she wasn't. Diane had made everything way too easy for her in her life, and she was spoiled by all the attention, all the work Diane did for her. Diane was thinking it might be time to tell her that she needed to clean her own room, and do it now. She wasn't sure that Jenny actually had a paper she had to work on. Diane had heard no mention of it before today.

Then Jenny came out again, and she walked down the hall to the kitchen. Diane glanced to see that she was wearing her sweatshirt and jeans, but no shoes. At least she wasn't heading out the door. Diane wondered what she was up to, but in a moment she heard Jenny's voice and knew she had called someone on the telephone. "I'm glad I caught you early, before you took off for the day," she was saying.

It was after ten o'clock. That didn't seem "early" to Diane.

"Listen, Dad, I'm not going to be able to go to London. Mom said I can't." This was all said in a voice louder than necessary, surely so Diane could hear.

"I know. You told me that. But I guess that's just the way things are. Anyway, there's no use fighting about it. She's not going to change her mind. I talked to Grandma, and she told me that herself."

What was that supposed to mean?

For a time Jenny seemed to be listening. "I know," she said a couple of times, and then, "I'm not fighting with her." And a few seconds later, "I know that, Dad, and I appreciate it. It's something I need to consider."

Diane knew what that was about, and the words made her livid. She stood in the door of the bathroom, her hands on her hips. She wondered whether she shouldn't walk out, grab the phone, and tell Greg to leave Jenny alone.

"I know. Don't worry. I will," Jenny said, and then in a sweet voice, "Dad, I love you so much. Thanks for asking me anyway." Jenny hung up the phone and retraced her steps, heading back to her bedroom. Diane didn't pretend that she hadn't been listening. Surely Jenny knew that anyway. But when Jenny walked past Diane without looking at her, and seemed ready to return to her room, Diane said, "Okay, that's enough."

Jenny glanced around. "What's enough?"

"This little show you're putting on."

"I don't know what you're talking about. I just called Dad to tell him what you told me. That's all."

She stepped on into her bedroom and began to shut the door. Diane moved quickly, caught the door with her hand, and pushed on into the room. "Jenny, do you think I just want to be mean? Is that why I won't let you go to London? Is that what I've been doing all my life, being mean to you?"

Jenny didn't answer. But she took a breath that raised her chin a little and made her look defiant.

"Here's the truth. I don't like the idea of your leaving school, and I don't think you ought to run off in the middle of your cross-country season. But if it were just that, I'd probably let you make your own decision. My real objection is that I don't want you to spend that much time with your dad. I've tried to raise you with certain values—and I hate to say it, but Greg doesn't have values. He does whatever he thinks he can get away with."

Jenny stood for quite some time, her face as inscrutable as ever. Finally she said, "He told me that's the kind of thing you'd say about him."

"Maybe so. But that doesn't mean I'm wrong."

"He made some mistakes. He knows that. But you've never forgiven him, and you don't think he can change. What kind of *values* does that show?"

"Jenny, he knows how to twist things around. He's trying to turn you against me."

"And what are *you* trying to do?"

That stopped Diane. "Okay," she said, after a moment, "you're right. I shouldn't say things about him. But if you ran in the street when you were a little girl, I went after you. That's how I feel now. I don't want you—"

"I'm not a little girl, Mom. I don't think you'll ever understand that. But Dad does. It might be better if I go live with him for a while."

"I won't let you. And the judge won't either. I'm not going to let that happen, Jenny. I love you way too much."

"Is that what you call it? Love? It sounds more like *control* to me."

Diane put her hand to her forehead and looked down. She tried to calm herself before she said, "I know, honey. It does sound like that.

And that's not what I want. But you're not as grown up as you think you are. Every kid your age thinks the same thing. I was like that myself. But there are still lots of things you don't understand about . . . life. I can't just let you make decisions that will hurt you in the long run."

"Mom, I'm going to be making *all* my decisions pretty soon. Even if I make mistakes—and it sounds like you made plenty—that's how I'm going to learn. That's just how it is."

There was something so firm in all that, so clear to Jenny, and Diane knew she wasn't actually wrong. But Jenny still *was* a little girl, whether she knew it or not. And her dad was more dangerous than she could ever imagine. "We need to have a long talk, Jenny. We need to think things through together when we're not mad. Why don't we get out of here, do something fun, and then when we get back we could sit down and—"

"I have a paper to write."

"Since when? You haven't said anything about that until this morning."

"Mom, I always do my homework. I don't tell you everything I have to do. And I don't ask you to help me anymore. But check my grades. If I'm so immature as you think I am, how come my grade point is about twice as high as yours *ever* was? I know all about your study habits when you were in high school."

Diane had just lost this little battle and she knew it. But she knew it in the same way she'd always known that Greg had won. Jenny sounded so much like him that it frightened Diane.

"Okay, Jenny. Work on your paper."

Diane heard the defeat in her own voice, and clearly Jenny heard it too. "Mom, I'm just saying, you didn't study hard in school. You've told me that. But I do."

"I know. Work on your paper." Diane went back to the bathroom and finished her cleaning. Then she put in some more time on her own studies. She was suddenly feeling more motivated to get an A in her class. Jenny hadn't inherited all her brains from her dad, and Diane hoped that Jenny understood that.

But Diane had wanted to spend the afternoon with Jenny, and the time alone with her books didn't give her the satisfaction she wanted. The only thing she was sure of was that she couldn't go back again and beg Jenny to talk with her—or give in and let her go to London.

At about three that afternoon the doorbell rang. Diane couldn't think who it would be until she opened the door and remembered that her visiting teachers had called earlier in the week. Diane had put them off until Saturday and then had forgotten entirely. "Oh, hi," she said, trying to cover her surprise.

"Busy day?" Terri asked. Terri Smoot had been Diane's visiting teacher for several years. She was a little older than Diane, and the two, in truth, had next to nothing in common, but they liked each other. Diane had told Sister Smoot more about herself than she'd admitted to anyone in the ward, certainly including their new bishop. Terri was a soft-looking woman, not heavy, but seemingly layered with extra padding, and she was going gray without bothering to do anything about it.

"Well, yes. All my days are busy, I guess. But Jenny's decided to pout all day, and stay in her room, so that's freed me up a little more than usual. We might have actually done something fun if she didn't hate me quite so much." Diane looked at Carla Pritchard, a younger woman who had been partnered with Terri the last few months. "How are you, Carla?" she asked. "Come in."

"I'm happy anytime I can leave my kids with Jerry for an hour and get out of the house," Carla said. But actually she always seemed happy.

She and Terri came in and sat on the couch, where they always sat, and Diane took the chair across from them. Diane was usually conscious of the tear in her sofa, the tattered state of her living-room curtains, the worn carpet, but Terri and Carla had seen all that before, and Diane didn't worry about it anymore. "I like to include Jenny when you two visit, but I think I'll leave her alone today," she said.

So they talked about that, softly, Diane deciding not to tell about Greg and London, and only mentioning "a little disagreement" between them. Then they talked about Terri's son who was on a mission, and Carla's three little girls. And they talked about Diane's goal to get her administrative certificate. "I'm tired of teaching," Diane told Carla. "I need a change."

"But I know you're a good teacher. I almost hate to see you leave the classroom. We *need* good teachers." Carla was a cute, dark-haired woman with big dimples. She had dressed up in a pretty, rust-colored pantsuit, even though she must have known that Terri would show up, as usual, in an oversized sweater and an ancient pair of pants that were stretched out of shape.

"But no one is willing to *pay* good teachers—even *your* beloved president. Reagan resists every attempt to put any money into education." Diane watched the two of them, and then she laughed. "I'm sorry. I just spoke ill of the great Ronald Reagan. I shouldn't do that. I'm sure we'll reelect him by acclamation in this state. We'll all just raise our hands—at church—and the ward clerk will walk around and take a count."

"No," Terri said. "Someone has to vote for Geraldine—so she gets one vote."

Geraldine Ferraro was running for vice president with Walter Mondale, the Democratic nominee, and the elections were only about three weeks off. "I just wish she were running for *president*," Diane said. "She says what she thinks. She's got more guts than Mondale will ever have."

Terri was smiling by now. "We love you, Diane. *And* Bobbi. Every ward needs a couple of Democrats, just to teach the rest of us patience and understanding."

But they were both laughing, even if Carla did seem a little uncomfortable. Carla had told Diane that for ten years, since her first baby had been born, she had hardly watched the news—and didn't know much about what was going on in politics. That seemed her way of avoiding some of the questions Diane liked to raise, but it actually seemed more likely that she had *never* paid much attention to the things going on in the world.

"I will say this," Terri said. "Every time I talk to you about what's going on, I start thinking maybe I'm half a Democrat myself. I go home and tell Jay the things you say, and he starts in on how wrong you are, but I end up arguing your side."

Diane sort of liked that. But she wished she were more like her dad. He expressed his opinions gently, and people hardly noticed that he differed with them. Diane was too much like Bobbi—usually popping off before she considered how she ought to express herself.

"Let me ask you this, Diane," Terri said. "As a test of your convictions."

"All right. Ask."

"Would you go out with a handsome, prosperous, really nice man—even if he did tend to lean toward the Republicans?"

"What's this? A lineup?"

"It could be."

"No, thanks. I've been there and done that, and I have the T-shirt to show for it."

"And I'll bet you look cute in it, too."

"Not really. My cute years are behind me."

"That's not true," Carla said, taking the words more seriously than Terri would have. "I think you're the most beautiful woman I know."

"For an old lady."

"You're not that much older than I am, Diane. Four or five years is all."

Diane looked back at Terri. "So who's the guy?"

"Remember the cousin I told you about? The one who lost his wife?"

"Yeah. I remember you saying something about it."

"Oh, Diane, it's been really hard for him." Terri had as soft a heart as anyone Diane knew, and she could hear the pain in the woman's voice. "They had a good marriage. And then she got cancer. It took her two years to die, and he stayed home most of that time and took care of her."

The idea of that was touching to Diane, but she felt her usual sales resistance building up. Life was complicated enough right now without thinking about dating anyone.

"He really is nice looking, Diane, and he's got a lot of money. He's got businesses and everything. But when Celeste was sick, he just stepped away from his busy life and gave full time to her."

"I hate to tell you, Terri, but you're not doing a very good sales job. Who would want to fill the shoes of someone he loved that much?"

"But he's got to move on now. Celeste passed away almost a year ago. I told him way back last spring, I'd give him a year, and then I knew a beautiful woman who would be perfect for him."

"To which he responded . . . ?"

"Well, he wasn't willing to talk about anything like that then. But he still has kids at home, and they need a mom. He—"

"Oh, yeah. You're really trying to close the sale now. That's just what I need—someone else's kids to raise. I'm having enough trouble with Jenny today. I don't want to take on any more. How old is this guy? Are his kids all teenagers?"

"Well, some are grown, and some *are* teenagers. He has two kids in high school. Ogden High, actually. Jenny might know them."

"What's his name?"

"Spencer Holmes. He's got a *beautiful* house. You'd love it. But he's such a nice man, and he's interested in all kinds of things, just like you. I know you'd like him."

"I think I'll pass."

"What if I talked to him and just said—"

"No. Really, Terri. I've been that route before. They all want you to be exactly like their first wives. And when you start trying to figure out how to mix families together, it's just a mess. Right now, Jenny has enough trouble with a dad who gives her a big rush and then disappears again. She doesn't need a stepfather to add more confusion to her life."

"She's almost grown up, Diane, and then what are you going to do with your life? You need someone."

"No. Actually, I don't. That's something almost everyone believes about single people—that they're miserable and spend every minute of their days feeling sorry for themselves. I see so many bad marriages, sort of hanging together by a thread, that I figure I'm better off just dealing with Jenny and myself."

"I don't think you really mean that, Diane. I think we all need someone special in our lives."

"That's why I teach Special Ed. I've got lots of *special* people in my life."

"Wouldn't you even—"

"No, Terri. I really wouldn't."

And that ended that. Carla presented a little lesson, and then the two hugged Diane and left. Diane went back to the kitchen table and continued her studies. But she didn't last long. She was tired, actually sleepy, which was not common for Diane, and she really wanted to get out of the house for a while. She decided she wanted to give one more try at patching things up with Jenny.

Diane walked down the hall and knocked quietly on Jenny's door. It took a second knock before she heard a muffled, "Yeah?"

"Can I come in?"

There was no answer, but in a few seconds Jenny was at the door. Her face was creased, her hair messy. Diane knew she'd been sleeping. "Did you finish your paper?"

"No. I just took a rest for a minute."

"That's okay. I just—"

"The paper's not due until next Friday. I was just trying to get the reading finished. I've got a lot going on this coming week."

"Sure. I understand. I was just wondering, maybe we could go get some pizza or something. Or check whether there's a movie we want to see."

Diane could see Jenny struggling with herself, not sure how to answer, but she finally said, "No, thanks. I'm not hungry."

"You haven't eaten all day—just that toast this morning."

"I know. I'll make a sandwich or something."

"I can do that. But I thought it might be good to get out of the house for a while."

Jenny shrugged. "I don't know. I don't feel like it, I guess." But she was changed a little, not as firm as she'd been earlier in the day.

"Come on. Let's just clean up a little and grab something to eat. I don't feel like making anything."

The firmness was suddenly back. "No, Mom. I said I don't want to."

"We need to talk, honey. We could—"

"There's nothing to talk about. You made your decision and I've accepted it. What else can we say about it?"

"I don't know. I just don't like what's going on between us. We need to clear the air a little and see if I can't explain a little better why I feel the way I do."

"You explained just fine." And now the ice was back. "My *father* is too dangerous for me to spend time with."

"Jenny, please. Don't do this."

"I'm not *doing* anything. I'll make a sandwich after a while. Right now I'm going to read some more."

Diane knew better than to push things any further, but she was devastated. She nodded, and then she walked out. She went back to her books, sat down for a minute, realized she couldn't study productively, and then walked in and pushed the button on the TV. The *CBS Evening News* was on, but Dan Rather, the anchor she liked so much, didn't do the weekend news, and all the coverage was election news even though everyone knew already how the presidential race was going to turn out.

Diane got up, walked back to the TV, and punched the power button again. As the screen went dark, she strode down the hallway to her bedroom and shut the door. She lay on her bed and tried to be as angry as she could, but she couldn't manufacture much of anything but sadness, and suddenly she was crying—something she almost never allowed herself to do. She curled up on her side, grasped her pillow, and sobbed for a long time.

Diane didn't know she had gone to sleep, but when she heard a sound in her room, she started and looked up. Jenny was standing at the foot of her bed. Diane could see the change. "I'm sorry for the way I've been acting," she said.

Diane was on her feet immediately. She grasped Jenny and pulled her close. "I need you, Jenny," she said, and the tears came again.

She could feel Jenny's warm forehead against her neck, nestled there the way it had been so many times when she was little. She could feel Jenny's tears seeping into her shirt. "But Mom, we've never been *anywhere*. I just want to see something. I just wanted to see London."

"I know, honey. I'm sorry I haven't been able to take you places.

But we will, okay? We'll figure out a way to get to Europe. I can borrow to do that. I should have done that before."

Jenny stepped back. "We can't afford it, Mom. We don't even—"

"We will. We have to."

"I'll take *you* before long, Mom." And now she looked resolved again. "I'm going to have my own airplane. I'm going to go anywhere I want to. And I'll take you with me."

"Oh, honey, that's not so important."

"It is to me. I'm not always going to live like this."

But that stung Diane deeper than anything Jenny had said all day. Diane had done her best with what she had had. It was so obvious to her that her own mistakes in life had become Jenny's burden, too—and there was not one thing she could do about that now.

Chapter 3

Diane and Jenny got along a little better for the next few weeks, but Diane didn't feel much closeness, and that bothered her. They were going to spend Thanksgiving Day with Richard and Bobbi. When Jenny had been a little girl, Diane had always taken her to Grandma Bea's house, where the whole Thomas family had gathered for a big feast, but years ago Grandma had given up trying to get everyone into her house. All the families had become too big, so they each got together for their own celebrations now. Still, a lot of Diane's uncles and aunts and cousins showed up at Grandma's each year, later in the day, and Grandma Bea always baked enough pies to feed the masses.

But the experience was complicated for Diane. She liked seeing certain of her cousins, but she didn't always feel comfortable with the whole group. She knew that Jenny felt much the same way. Jenny had almost sixty second cousins now, Aunt Beverly's six children having produced almost half that number. Jenny envied those Salt Lake cousins. She considered them very cool, but she also complained to Diane that she wasn't part of them. She couldn't dress as well, couldn't talk about skiing, boating, family trips, and all the other things they were able to do.

Diane, for her part, felt self-conscious about being the only single person among her cousins. Kurt, Alex's son, had married and divorced, then married again, and was still not a very stable guy—even though he'd long since overcome his drug problems—but he was the only cousin other than Diane who had ever divorced. All her relatives loved Diane, accepted her—she knew that—but they always wanted to know whether she had "met anyone," or whether she was going out. She had never admitted that she was, even when she had been dating a little. It was just easier to claim that she was happy the way she was.

But this year Diane had decided not to go to Grandma's. Greg was going to pick up Jenny late in the afternoon and take her with him to Salt Lake for the long weekend. Jenny had not said much lately about going off to live with Greg, but Diane knew how much she liked to spend time with him. He took her to the nicest restaurants in town, and often she would come home showing off what she'd bought on a shopping spree. Greg loved to pick out clothes for her, and took her to expensive women's stores. He had been claiming more than usual lately that he was in financial difficulty, but he would invariably have an explanation for Diane: "I'm sorry I didn't send anything this month, but I don't have a dime in my checkbook. I'm going to lose my house if I can't get some cash flow going. But I couldn't resist charging a few things for Jenny, so she won't feel like a little ragamuffin going to school. Maybe that helps you some, if I can do that once in a while. I'll try to catch up on the child support just as soon as things straighten out with my business."

Diane hated to see Jenny gone so long, but she actually needed a quiet weekend so she could get caught up on her studies. The end of the term was coming up, and she had a major paper due. She figured she could finish her reading on Thanksgiving evening, draft the paper on Friday, and still have time to polish it on Saturday. Jenny would be coming back on Sunday evening. Greg did have weekend visiting rights, established by the judge. There had been years in the past when he hadn't bothered to see her very often, but lately Jenny had been going to his fancy house in Salt Lake about once a month.

Diane knew she had to let Jenny be with Greg that often, and she was trying harder to be careful what she said about him. Jenny clearly wanted her own space, wanted to make her own decisions, and Diane recognized that it was natural for her to feel that way. But Diane had never experienced this kind of tension with Jenny. She hated the feeling that she had to be careful all the time.

Diane and Jenny drove the three blocks to Richard and Bobbi's house early. Diane had offered to bring part of the dinner, but Bobbi had said, "I have everything. And I'll start the turkey early. But if you two would come in time to help me with the cooking, and set the table, that would help the most."

"Are Maggie and Jim coming?" Diane had asked.

"Yes. But I told Maggie to sleep in and only come over in time for dinner. She thinks I'm giving her the day off, but the truth is, if she brings David and Benjamin over early, they'll cancel out any help Maggie could possibly give us. Those boys are like a pair of tornadoes."

Diane's sister Maggie hadn't married until she was twenty-seven, but now, five years later, she had two little boys and was pregnant again. She had married an elder she had met while she was serving a mission in Texas—a fellow named Jim Stokes—but only after he had pursued her for several years. He was a good man, a couple of years younger than Maggie, essentially solid, but still taking night classes to finish up college while he worked for a finance company. Diane always had the feeling that Maggie was the strength of that family, and she was bringing Jim along as best she could.

Ricky, Diane's younger brother, would also be there. He was home from his mission, twenty-two years old and living at home, going to Weber State. Diane was sure that he was going to grow up someday—just not anytime soon. Skiing was very high on his list of priorities, and he could hardly wait for the resorts to open. So far, there hadn't been nearly enough snow, as far as he was concerned. Still, he was a decent student, and Diane supposed he would get around to taking life more seriously at some point.

The day sounded peaceful to Diane, something she had been looking forward to. There would only be the nine of them together, and even though David and Benjamin, who were four and two, could create plenty of havoc, Grandpa liked to play with them—which kept them occupied—and Diane always loved to chat with her mom and her sister.

When Diane tapped at her mother's door and stepped in, she smelled the turkey—and hot rolls. The nice smells took her back to Grandma Bea's immediately, and she suddenly wondered whether she didn't want to drive to Salt Lake later in the day, after all. "Mom, we're here."

"I know. Come in." Mom appeared at the kitchen door, a white baker's apron on and a paring knife in one hand. "I've got work for you to do." She smiled, and Diane was struck by how much she had come to look like Grandma Bea. She didn't have such deep dimples as Grandma, but she had her smile—the shape of it—and she had her manner. Her neck was bent just a little, her head to one side, and she seemed to be saying with her eyes, "Won't this be fun this morning—us girls working together in the kitchen?"

Diane was glad that Jenny liked to be there too, that she hugged Grandma, knew where to find an apron, asked what she should do first, and then started scrubbing and peeling potatoes. In a moment Richard appeared. "Wow," he said. "I haven't seen this many beautiful women in one room since . . . last week, when you two were over here."

"You only say that because you want my Social Security check," Bobbi said. She looked at Diane. "But I don't give it to him. It's my 'mad money.'"

"That's right," Dad said. He shoved his hands into the pockets of his old khakis. "She's been building up our year's supply, buying wheat and canned goods. She's always been like that. Just *wild* and *crazy* with her money."

"Well, I plan to stock up on food storage—the way we should have done long ago—and *then* I'm going to do something wild and crazy."

"I think President Benson has her scared," Richard said. "He's not as gentle as President Kimball was."

President Spencer W. Kimball had died only about three weeks earlier, and Ezra Taft Benson had become the new Church President. "President Benson hasn't said one word about food storage so far," Bobbi said.

"But he will," Richard said. "You know that. You're just getting ready for him."

"Enough commentary from you, old boy," Bobbi said. "Either put on an apron or stop bothering the kitchen help."

Richard smiled and nodded. "I guess I'll find myself something to do," he said. "You know what too many cooks can do."

Diane was struck once again at how handsome he was for a man almost seventy. His crystalline eyes—her eyes, Jenny's eyes—were keen as ever. He never stopped reading, was always interested in his world, but he never pushed his opinions on anyone. Diane was much more like her mother than her dad, but she knew she wanted to develop more of his quiet confidence—and goodness.

Richard left and Bobbi stepped to the oven and took a peek inside. As she shut the door, she asked, "So, Jenny, who was that boy you went to the Thanksgiving dance with?" Jenny had turned sixteen at the end of October, and she had gone out on her first real date the previous Friday.

"His name's Brian Anderson."

"Anderson? Which Anderson is that?"

"I don't know, Grandma. They live kind of by the high school."

Diane was laughing. "Mom always tries to check out the family heritage before she approves a boy."

"I know." Bobbi laughed at herself. "I get more like my mom every year. It used to drive me crazy when Mother would ask me that—what family a boy came from. But it does tell you plenty. I just don't know Ogden as well as Mom knew Salt Lake." She hesitated, turned around, looked as though she were trying to remember something, then asked, "But did you have fun? Is he a nice boy?"

"He's all right." Jenny laughed. "He's kind of weird, if you want to know the truth. He kept staring at me and telling me how beautiful I looked. I didn't mind the first time, but he just kept it up."

"I'm afraid you're going to get a lot of that," Bobbi said. "Just make sure you don't send the wrong signals to these boys. You're like your mom—so pretty that you're going to attract lots of suitors. But it's important you let them know you're a nice girl."

"How do you know? Maybe I'm not so nice. Maybe I took him up to Beus's Pond and made out with him."

"But you didn't," Diane said. "I know. I was up there with a spotlight, watching for you."

Everyone laughed, but Jenny, who was now peeling sweet potatoes, said, "I can do better than Brian. He acted like he was half afraid of me the whole time. If I ever like a boy, he's going to have to know his way around a lot more than Brian does."

Diane caught just a quick glance from Bobbi, one that hinted at concern, and Diane felt the same way. She even knew where Jenny got such attitudes. She had watched Greg operate, seen how he could fill up a room with his personality, take charge—and surely Jenny saw that as her model for how a man should handle himself. Diane wished Jenny would take a closer look at her grandpa, and forget Greg. Diane worried, too, that Jenny didn't sound like a sixteen-year-old. There was something just a little too sophisticated, maybe even hard, about a young girl who was so sure she knew what she wanted from boys, from life, from everything. But, of course, Diane knew better than to say such things to Jenny.

Dinner turned out to be wonderful—lots of good food and good talk. Jenny loved Ricky, and after dinner the two of them had great fun talking about Ogden High, and about movies and music. Jenny liked Duran Duran, Prince, and Sting. She thought it was funny that Ricky liked Huey Lewis and the News and Bruce Springsteen. "You're getting old, Ricky," she told him. "I can't believe how old-fashioned you are. Next you'll tell me you like Michael Jackson."

Ricky jumped up and made an attempt at the "moonwalk," doing it badly all the way across the family room. Then he said, "Sure, I like Michael. But my *favorites* are Donny and Marie."

Jenny moaned and laughed, and Bobbi, seeming a little confused, said, "Well, you *do* like Donny and Marie, don't you?" which everyone found funny—except Bobbi. "But they're so cute." And that got a bigger laugh.

But the fun didn't last long. About an hour after dinner, Jenny told Diane that she needed to get home to pack some things before Greg came for her, so she and Diane left. Diane got out her books and started to study—even felt good about her plan—until Greg actually showed up and Jenny came for a quick kiss and then headed for the door.

"Could we have just a short prayer together before you go, honey?" Diane asked.

"Mom, he's out there waiting."

"He can wait."

"I'll say my prayers, Mom. Don't worry." And she was gone.

Diane wasn't happy about that. She walked to the front window of the apartment and watched Greg hug Jenny, put her suitcase in the trunk of his silver Lincoln, and drive away. She instantly wished she had said no. She didn't want Jenny to go away for the whole Thanksgiving weekend. But saying no would have created new tension, and Diane knew she couldn't have done it.

It was still Thanksgiving Day, and she was suddenly alone. She almost decided to go back to her parents' place. She had been chatting with Maggie when Jenny had insisted they leave, and she would have liked to talk longer. She thought maybe she would. But she had promised herself she would work on her paper. So she sat down with her books, told herself maybe she would run back later for some pie, the way Bobbi had suggested, but knew she had eaten way too much already. And she really did have to study.

Friday morning was worse. Diane got up, knowing she didn't have to go to work, that she had a long day alone, and suddenly she wished she could get outside and do something. The leaves were down. It was too late for a pretty drive up Ogden Canyon, but she wanted to do something other than work on her paper.

But Diane had learned some discipline over the years. She would write the first draft by hand, correct it, and then type the final version. A few of the students in her class had computers now. They told her how quick that made things. They could type a draft into their word processor and then correct everything right on the screen. That sounded wonderful, but she couldn't afford a computer, and she probably wouldn't know how to make the thing work anyway. So she sat at the kitchen table and scribbled down a list of things she intended to include, then figured out an order. It wasn't much of an outline, but it got her started, and she began jotting down a first paragraph. She still hadn't finished a page when the phone rang. She thought it would be Bobbi, but it was a friend of hers from her ward—a single woman named Gloria. "Diane, are you going to the singles dinner tonight?" she asked.

"No. You know I don't go to those things."

"I know. But it's a multi-stake social this time, so there might be a chance to meet some new people, and with Jenny gone for the weekend, I was thinking—"

"Mom called you, didn't she?"

"Actually, no. But I saw her down at the grocery store the other day, and she told me Jenny was going to be with her dad this weekend."

"I can tell you exactly what Mom told you." Diane tried to imitate her mother's voice as she said, "'Gloria, why don't you call Diane? I read about that singles dinner in the ward bulletin. She needs to get out to things like that. She never wants to go to anything, but if you called her, maybe she would.'"

Gloria was laughing. "You know your mom, don't you?"

"That was about it, wasn't it?"

"Well, not word for word, but pretty close. Still, you ought to go. I think I'll stay home if you don't go, but I'd kind of like to get out of the house. Why don't we at least go long enough to see whether it's any fun?"

"You mean, whether Prince Charming happens to be there?"

"Oh, Diane, I've given up on Prince Charming long since. And anyway, if I actually thought he was going to be there, I wouldn't invite you. He'd trample right over the top of me to reach you."

Gloria was at least ten years older than Diane, and both her kids were married now. She'd been divorced for almost twenty years. Her husband hadn't abused her; he'd ignored her. And then he had come home one day and said he didn't like being married.

Diane wanted to say no, had the words ready, but she knew Gloria wanted to go—and wouldn't go if Diane didn't. And maybe, in the back of her mind, was the thought that someone interesting really might show up. "Well, okay," she finally said. "I can tell my mom I went out on a hard search for a husband."

Gloria was laughing again, a high but rough sound that was something of a trademark. She really wasn't the sort to attract a lot of male attention, but maybe that was just as well, judging from the men Diane had met at these things.

Diane actually felt a little better after she hung up the phone. She wouldn't be home alone the entire weekend. She was going to do *something*. So she worked on her paper with a little more enthusiasm and had a draft finished by three in the afternoon. She did run over to her parents' house after that, gave her mom a bad time about what she'd said to Gloria, ate a little of the pie she'd passed up the day before, joked with her brother and dad, and then she went home and actually spent some time getting ready. She had once been a master at the use of makeup, but had lost most of her knack for that over the years. Still, she put in some effort tonight, and she chose a pretty dress she hadn't worn for quite some time—even though it was a little tighter than she wanted it to be. But it was brown and classy, and looked like fall when she added a gold scarf.

When she was ready—a little earlier than she needed to be—she took a long look at herself in the mirror. These colors didn't bring out her eyes, but the touch of blue eye shadow helped, and she could see that she still did look nice. It wasn't like the days when she could walk through the Wilkinson Center at BYU and actually cause guys to stop in their tracks—but she had to admit that she looked better than most women her age. And a thought was playing in and out of her thoughts. Maybe she was "supposed to go" tonight. Maybe there *was* someone to meet.

She waited longer than she needed to, having decided to pick up Gloria a little late. She didn't want to get to the party early and be forced into a lot of small talk. Or, if she'd been honest with herself, she might have admitted that she liked the idea of walking in and seeing a head turn. Maybe, too, she could control where she sat and whom she met.

But Gloria was ready and waiting, and they actually got to the party only about ten minutes late, which turned out to be a little early.

People were still standing around talking. At least this was a dinner, not a dance, so Diane didn't have to worry about the feeding frenzy she had set off a couple of times over the years when she'd gone to dances. Only a quick glance around to see lots of bald heads and gray hair reminded her that if Prince Charming was in the neighborhood, he'd apparently found something better to do. She felt a twinge of disappointment, but she pushed it aside and decided to look about for women she knew. If she could sit by a few friends, mostly older women from her ward, eat a little turkey—and leave early—she might find an old movie worth watching on TV that night.

Gloria was checking the place out too. "There's Camille and Lena," she said.

"Good. Let's go sit with them," Diane said, and the two started across the hall.

Then Diane heard a thin, male voice behind her. "Excuse me."

Diane cringed, but she stopped, and so did Gloria. When Diane turned around, she was surprised. A fairly young man—she thought maybe only a few years older than herself—was smiling at her. "This is the first time I've come to one of these," he said, "and I really don't know anyone. You look to me like the kind of person who might do her Christian duty and make a stranger feel welcome."

"Oh, brother," Gloria said. "You mean she's the best-looking woman in the room, and you thought you better make your move before someone else does."

"Do I look like that sort of guy?"

"Yes."

He laughed. "Frank is my name. Frank Graham—like the cracker. What's yours?" He was looking at Diane again.

"Diane."

"Oh . . . like the goddess?"

"I believe you have me confused with Diana."

"Or maybe Lady Diana. It's an easy mistake to make, either way."

The guy really was a bit much, but he was fairly good-looking, sort of clean-cut, and he did seem to know how lame his own lines were. He was wearing a tan cardigan, maybe a golf sweater—which seemed old-fashioned and rather inappropriate—but at least he didn't have a big belly hanging over his belt. His smile wasn't bad either—sort of ironic, even fun.

"You can join our group of ladies," Diane said. "We women talk mostly about our grandkids and our favorite recipes, but maybe you won't mind that."

"And just how many grandchildren do you have, Diane?"

"I can't even count them all."

"I'm sure you can't." His hair was receding just a bit—maybe he was a little older than she had first thought. But he wasn't scared of Diane. That was always something she liked.

"Come with us and I'll introduce you to our friends," Gloria said. "We need to hurry before I forget your name. At my age, things slip away from me pretty fast." Gloria poked a stubby finger at her head and rolled her eyes. Diane knew she had learned, over the years, to make fun of herself, but Diane also knew this sort of thing was hard for her—that men always looked right past her to the younger women.

When the threesome reached the other women, Gloria said, "Lena, Camille, this is a new friend. His name is Frank, and he certainly is frank. And Graham, like the cracker."

Lena and Camille were both well over seventy. Both of them dyed their hair—Lena, a dark brown, and Camille, a red that was downright brassy. They had both had their hair "set" today. That was easy to see.

"Charmed, my ladies," Frank said. "I *am* like the cracker—*perfect* with chocolate and marshmallow. Do you want s'more?" He made an exaggerated bow. The women all laughed.

That was not a good sign. Maybe *all* his lines were lame. Diane had hoped there for a moment that he really was clever. Still, when they all sat down at a round table, he seemed to know that it was time to back off a little and change his tone. Diane had actually tried to sit between Gloria and Camille, but Frank had stepped rather quickly to her side, and Gloria had given way easily. Now he was next to Diane and he was saying, "Tell me about yourself, Diane."

"There's not much to tell. I'm a Special Education teacher at an elementary school." For now, she didn't want to give him much more information than that. "What do you do?"

"I'm in marketing. I slap a lot of backs, as you can probably tell. But I'm really a shy guy." He grinned. "That other stuff is all an act."

"I don't think I believe that."

"I know you don't. But I read in a magazine that women like shy men, so I threw it out, just to see if you would buy it."

Diane rolled her eyes, but she was still smiling. "So what do you market?"

"Myself. That's what every sales job is, really. But I've worked in several industries, and I've done well at everything I've done. I'm either lucky or good—I'm not sure which. I guess it doesn't matter."

Diane was quickly giving up hope, but she clung to those few moments, at first, when she'd thought maybe he really was someone she wanted to meet.

"I'm sorry. I know how I come across sometimes. It's all the chatter I used to throw around when I'd go out and call on customers. I do it when I'm nervous. But these days I spend most of my life in an office, and when the most beautiful woman I've ever seen isn't looking straight into my eyes, I can actually calm down."

"Who's that? Your secretary?"

Diane knew her line was as dumb as any of his, but she was a little nervous herself at the moment. She hadn't had anyone come on this strong in a long time.

Frank laughed. "No. Not my secretary. She weighs about two-fifty." He leaned over with one elbow on the table and spoke softly. "How in the world have you managed to stay single, Diane?"

Diane gave up.

Now she only wanted to get away—whether she got anything to eat or not.

But a tall man with a bow tie was blowing into a microphone by then. He welcomed everyone and introduced a little fellow who said the opening prayer and blessing on the food. Then he asked everyone to form a line at the buffet table.

There was a bit of a rush to the food, so the women at Diane's table—and Frank—decided to wait for the line to shorten. When they finally did reach the buffet, Diane picked up a paper plate just as a man on the other side was picking up his. He was an imposing man—nice looking, if not exactly handsome—but dressed in a dark suit that seemed cut especially for him. He looked around forty or so, with dark hair, turning gray at the temples. He was wearing a white shirt and a yellow power tie—as though he belonged on Wall Street, not at a dinner like this.

And he was looking at her.

He smiled just a little, and she decided he actually *was* quite handsome. But she'd never seen him before. The thought crossed her mind that he was a visiting General Authority, or . . .

"Are you Diane Lyman?" he asked.

Maybe this *was* Prince Charming. He had a gentle voice, but it was deep and confident. "Yes," Diane said, and the word came out sounding like a question, meaning, "How do you know me?"

But Frank was behind Diane, and he suddenly dropped a hand on her shoulder. "Diane, you didn't get a napkin," he said. "I'll get one for you."

Frank was claiming his rights. *I saw her first,* he was clearly announcing to the other man.

Diane stepped forward enough to pull away from Frank's hand, and she looked back to the man across the buffet table. "Yes, I'm Diane," she said.

But the man was looking at Frank, as though he weren't sure what the rules of this game were. "I'm Spencer Holmes. I—"

"Nice to meet you, Spence," Frank said. "Can you believe how warm it is this late in the fall?"

The man glanced at Frank, then back to Diane, but he didn't finish his sentence. "It has been warm," he said instead.

"I like good weather," Frank was saying, "but we need to put some snow in the mountains. I worry when we get off to a slow start like this. And then, I'm a skier, too. Diane, we'll have to hit the slopes together this winter."

"I don't ski anymore," Diane said, weakly. She daubed some potatoes on her plate. She wanted this man to know she wasn't *with* Frank, but he was staying very close, as though they were a couple.

Spencer Holmes. Why did she know that name? How could she get him to her table, or . . . but it was suddenly too late. They'd reached the end of the table. Spencer nodded and walked away. Frank hardly let him get out of earshot before he said, "The guy shows up in 'semi-formal attire' at an event clearly designated as 'casual.' I'll never understand that."

"I'm sure you won't," Diane mumbled. She walked quickly to stay well ahead of him as they returned to their table.

Diane sat down and looked at what she'd put on her plate: turkey, gluey-looking potatoes, thin gravy, a cranberry Jell-O salad, and green beans that had surely come from a can. Her mind was working hard to find an excuse for leaving as soon as possible. She wanted to meet Spencer Holmes, whoever he was, and it was too late to make a "new" first impression. But how had he known her name?

Frank continued to make jokes, and he ate with dispatch and seeming enthusiasm. "This is better than what I cooked for myself yesterday. TV dinners are a great invention, but they leave something to be desired for Thanksgiving." He looked at Diane. "Have you ever been married?" he asked.

"Yes. I have a sixteen-year-old daughter." She thought that might be something he wouldn't want to hear.

"I have four kids, two in their twenties and two teenagers. My youngest is fourteen. The last thing I ever thought would happen was that I'd get a divorce."

Diane nodded and then tried to turn to say something to Camille.

"I gave my wife everything she wanted—more than she ever could have dreamed of. I built her a house big enough for *a dozen* kids. She had nice cars. I took her to Hawaii, the Bahamas, all over. She dressed like a queen. Then one day this last spring she says to me, 'Get out, and by the way, I want *everything*—the kids, the house, and everything that's in it. You can keep the dog if you want him.' Now she wants every penny I make while I live in a crummy apartment. And why was this divorce so important—even though we were married in the temple? Because, she says, she doesn't *love* me anymore. She told the judge we're not *compatible*. Twenty-six years of marriage and it turns out we're not compatible."

Diane had no idea what to say.

"I don't mean to tell you all my troubles, but my head is still kind of spinning. You know what I mean?"

Diane nodded again.

"I went inactive in the Church for a while. I couldn't figure out how something like that could happen to me. It's like God didn't give two hoots for me. But I'm getting over that. I'm moving on."

Diane was looking across the room. She could see Spencer Holmes sitting at a table with some other people, but not talking to anyone. Then he got up, walked to a trash can, and dropped in his paper plate. He left.

"What about you, Diane? How long have you been divorced?"

"A long time."

"It just didn't work out from the beginning?"

"I guess you could say that."

"I'll bet you're not bleeding this guy for everything he's got. I get the idea from what you've said that you're working, making your own way."

"Look, I don't—"

"I'm sorry. I'm getting too personal right off. Like I told you, you make me nervous." He glanced around at the other women, who were talking among themselves. Diane knew they were embarrassed by the things Frank was saying.

But he didn't back off. "Do you think you'll ever get married again, Diane?"

She stared at him for a few seconds, and then she said, "I doubt it. But if I do, I want someone who's not so self-centered that he can only see his own side of things. And I want someone who thinks before he talks."

"Is that how your first husband was—all full of himself?"

Diane just stared at the guy.

"I know just what you're talking about. My ex was the same way. But she was empty-headed, too. She thought a newspaper was for putting in the bottom of a birdcage. But you seem really smart. I'll bet you are, too."

Diane looked past Frank and said to Gloria, "Remember what I said earlier—that I couldn't stay long?"

"Oh, yes, I do remember that. I can get a ride with Lena and Camille, I'm sure."

"Okay. Good."

Gloria put her hand on Frank's arm. "See. She really *is* smart," she said. "You've got her pegged, all right."

Frank glanced at Gloria and then back to Diane.

But Gloria was saying, "Frank, since you're trying to get acquainted with people, let me tell you a little about me."

Diane slid her chair back, making a scraping noise. A lot of people looked up at her, including Frank, whose eyes were suddenly wide open. She walked across the hall and on out the door. Then she drove home.

When she got there, she tried to find something she could watch on TV, but there was nothing. She watched anyway—watched *Dallas* this time, hardly aware of what was really going on, then the local news and part of Johnny Carson before she switched over to an old Bob Hope movie from World War II days. All the while, she kept wondering about Spencer Holmes. She told herself he was probably another one like Frank, not so bad until you got to know him. But she couldn't fight off the sense that she had missed a chance.

She stayed up very late—for no reason at all—and then, once in bed, lay awake for a long time. It was hard not to wonder why nothing seemed to work out the way she hoped, why life had always taken the wrong turns for her. But she had made a vow a long time ago that she wasn't going to spend her life feeling sorry for herself. She had made all her own decisions; now she had to live with them.

Late in the night, when she couldn't sleep, she finally did cry. She didn't let herself dwell on her troubles; she merely allowed herself a little self-indulgence. But once she started to cry, she couldn't stop herself for a long time.

CHAPTER 4

Diane went to church on Sunday morning. She taught her Primary class of six-year-olds, and she enjoyed the kids, but sometimes she wished she could go to Gospel Doctrine class in Sunday School, and to Relief Society. She did chat with a few friends between meetings, but when she came home that day, she felt as though she hadn't experienced very much of what she always longed for in church: more connections to other sisters, other families. It was nice in a way to have her meetings finished in the morning, but she remembered earlier years when the women in Relief Society had been such a support to her. She sometimes felt as though the Church had given up too much by stacking all the meetings together in a three-hour block. Getting Jenny ready to go back for sacrament meeting later in the day hadn't been easy, but it *had* made the day feel more like a Sabbath.

She changed her clothes after church and then fixed herself a grilled cheese sandwich. Then, on a sudden impulse, she decided to get out of her apartment for a while. She took a drive up Ogden Canyon, even though she knew it was no longer very pretty, and she put a Byrds tape in her cassette player and then a Fifth Dimension album. It was music from her single days, her years at BYU, and maybe not the most spiritual for a Sunday, but she liked to remember that time. "Up, up and away," she sang, "in my beautiful, my beautiful balloon," and she remembered how life had looked to her then—when everything was ahead of her and it only seemed natural that things would work out perfectly.

She felt good when she got home, but when she sat down in her apartment again the loneliness was there, whether she dwelled on it or not. So she got out her books and decided to study for a little while—so she wouldn't think. She had just settled down at the kitchen table when the phone rang, and she got back up to answer it. She expected every call to be from Bobbi, but a man said, "Diane?"

"Yes."

"It's Gene."

"Oh, Gene, it's good to hear your voice. I haven't talked to you for such a long time." Gene was her cousin, one of the ones she had been closest to when she was growing up.

"You didn't show up at Grandma's for Thanksgiving. Where were you?" Gene asked.

"We just didn't make it down this year." Diane sat at the table again and switched hands with the receiver so that the cord wouldn't wind around her neck. "Jenny was spending the weekend with her dad, and I had a paper I had to finish for the class I'm taking."

"Is Jenny still with her dad?"

"Yes. She's coming back tonight."

"Diane, have you read a newspaper today?"

"No. Why?"

"I just got home a few minutes ago, and I was glancing through the Trib. There's a story about Greg. Has he told you he was having legal problems?"

"Legal problems? What do you mean? He keeps saying his business is on the rocks."

"He's been indicted for fraud, Diane. And a couple of other charges."

"Fraud?"

"I know the reporter who wrote the story. I could maybe call him and see what else I can find out, but apparently Greg and his partner have been promising big returns to clients who invested with them, and then they've spent the money. The article claims that some prominent people in Salt Lake lost their entire investments."

Diane wasn't really surprised, but she was scared about what all this could mean. She stared at the grain in her little pine table and tried to think what she should do. Should she head for Salt Lake and bring Jenny home? "Was Greg arrested?" she asked.

"He was apparently charged and released."

"When did this happen, do you know?"

"Before Thanksgiving. Tuesday or Wednesday, I think."

"That means he knew about this, and he still had Jenny stay the weekend with him. I never will understand how that man operates. Most people would be flattened by something like that."

"There was a quote from him in the paper. He said something about it all being a misunderstanding and he was sure it could be straightened out."

"Words. Greg just makes up words. I think he missed Sunday School on the day they explained about 'right and wrong.'"

Gene laughed quietly, then said, "Well, I had a feeling you might not know. I thought I'd better call."

"Thanks, Gene. Really. I'm just going to tell Jenny she can't go down there anymore."

"That might be a good idea. Are you doing okay, Diane?"

She let out a sigh, half a laugh. The lighting in her kitchen had never been adequate. It was a dark little space. She looked out the kitchen door and on through her cramped living room. What crossed her mind, as it often did, was how small her world was, how confined. She knew so little of what Greg was actually up to—except for his version of things. "I don't know how I'm doing, Gene. Jenny is sixteen and starting to think I'm not quite what she had in mind for a mother.

Greg hasn't helped us for quite a while, and now I'm sure he never will. So you know, it's a bit of a struggle. But we'll get by."

"How long before you finish grad school?"

"I'm hoping to have my administrative certificate by next year. That'll make things a little better." She shifted in her chair and raised her bare feet off the linoleum floor, placing them on the chair across from her. "How are you and Emily doing, Gene?"

"Fine. Being bishop is about ten times more work than I ever realized, but it's been good for me, and my ward puts up with my complete absence of administrative skills."

Diane needed to think what this whole thing with Greg was going to mean, but for now, she really liked hearing Gene's voice. "I'll bet you're a *perfect* bishop."

"Diane, I'm not a perfect anything. Ask Emily."

"She thinks you're wonderful. She tells me so every time I see her." And then Diane remembered something. "Hey, you turned forty, didn't you?"

"Afraid so."

"I was going to call you—or send you a smart-aleck card or something—and I forgot to do it."

"That's good. I got plenty of that from everyone else."

"Forty! Can you believe it?" But the truth was, Gene had looked forty for years now—and seemed even older. He had been badly wounded in Vietnam. His health wasn't too bad now, but he had paid a price both physically and emotionally. It had softened him, deepened him, and he was as kind and sensitive as any man she knew, but the war had also taken away some of the intensity and enthusiasm she always associated with the young cousin she had once known.

"Hey, you're coming up on forty yourself. You're not *that* much younger than I am."

"I know how to deal with it, though. I'm going to start lying about my age."

Gene chuckled, didn't say anything for a time, and then said quietly, "It's not been quite like we expected, has it?"

"No. I'm afraid not." She remembered all the times she and Gene and Kathy, another cousin, had sat on Grandma Bea's porch and talked about their dreams. "But you've done well. How are your books doing?"

"I think they're in good health. They get a lot of rest—just sitting on store shelves collecting dust."

Diane knew that Gene was modest about that. He wrote a political column for the *Salt Lake Tribune* that was nationally syndicated now, and he had published two books, one on the lessons of Vietnam, and another that analyzed what he called the "politics of reprisal," an account of Richard Nixon's tragic fall. Neither book was a bestseller, but both were highly respected. Gene's name was well-known across the country.

"Do you think you'll ever run for office, Gene?"

"No. Dad still talks to me about running for his seat in the Senate when he finally gives it up, but I'd rather write about political issues—not have to choose between two or three bad options, the way he's always had to do."

Diane's Uncle Alex—Gene's dad—had been talking about getting out of politics for as long as Diane could remember, but after many years in Congress, he had run for the Senate and now was serving his second term. "But you'd be a wise senator. You wouldn't play games."

"You have to play some of them or you don't get elected."

Diane was sure that was true, and it occurred to her that Gene would analyze too much, probably confuse voters with all the information he had at his fingertips. She also doubted he could handle the pressure and the lifestyle. "Gene, do you still have bad dreams?"

This time the silence was longer. Finally Gene said, "Sometimes. I've decided I always will. But I deal with them better than I used to."

"I remember how sure of yourself you were when we were kids.

You were the family star. I guess you still are, with your books and everything—but you're not the same person, are you?"

"Who is, Di? Life changes us. You're about ten feet taller than you used to be."

"I am?" Diane sat up straight, put her feet back on the floor. She could hardly believe he would say such a thing. "If I'm so tall, how come I feel so beaten down?"

"You've been swimming upstream for a long time. That takes a lot of strength."

"That's an interesting image. I'm a tall fish, swimming upstream."

"Yeah, like a big salmon." Gene laughed harder this time. "Okay, so I mixed my metaphors. I do better when I can write my thoughts, then fix up the sentences later on. But my point is, you've had to deal with some hard things—and you've grown because of it."

"Yeah. I guess." She leaned forward, put her elbow on the table, and rested her forehead in her hand. "But you've been swimming upstream too, and you've done better than I have."

"No. That's not true." She heard him take a breath. "I never feel like I'm quite whole. Those bullets ripped up my insides—and the doctors put them back together—but I still feel like there's a hollow place in there. Emily knows that better than anyone."

"But I keep hearing what a good bishop you are."

"It *has* been good for me. I've let more emotion back into my life than I ever thought I could. Just not as much as I still need to." He paused and then added, "But don't tell anyone I said that. The family thinks it's all over."

"Your dad knows better. And so does my dad, and Uncle Wally. I watch the way you guys cling to each other whenever the family gets together."

"Yeah, that's true. We never talk about our wars now, but we do have a connection."

"Does your dad get mad at you when he reads your column? I read what you said about Ronald Reagan last week."

"He's the Teflon president, Diane. He claims to be the great conservative while he runs up the deficit beyond any president, ever."

"Hey, that's what I've been saying. So when are you going to announce that you're actually a Democrat?"

"Don't tell me things would have been better with Mondale. I'm not a party man. I'm just trying to hold all their feet to the fire."

"And what does Uncle Alex think about that?"

"He's amazing, Di. He cheers me on. I wrote one column taking him to task for voting with Reagan against clean-air legislation. He called me up and said I was right. He'd voted the way he knew his constituency wanted him to, but he wished he hadn't."

"Well, the truth is, I don't really know as much about politics as I pretend I do. Mostly, I quote my dad—and try not to sound as intense as my mom."

"I guess I spend too much time reading," Gene said. "After a while, nothing looks simple. Not even Vietnam—and I had some really strong feelings about that at one time, as you know so well. But I do know something about the cost of war, and I get tired of politicians who just long for excuses to send our boys into battle."

"If I'm ever in charge of a planet, I'm going to make a rule against war. And I've got a couple of other rules in mind. One is that every girl gets a do-over. If she chooses the wrong man to marry the first time around, she can just go back a little in time and erase the whole thing."

"I don't think I like that one. Emily probably would have invoked that one on me by now."

"No. Never." But Diane knew it had come pretty close to that at times. Gene had gone through some terrible years after he'd been wounded in Vietnam, and Emily had had to stick with him through all that.

"Well . . . I know you've been through a lot, Di. I wish I could make things better for you somehow."

"Don't worry about me, Gene. I'm fine."

"Yeah. Me too."

They both laughed softly. "Well, thanks for calling," Diane said. "I won't miss any more Thanksgivings."

Jenny got back early in the evening. Diane was sitting in the living room by then, finally looking at the Sunday *Standard-Examiner*, but she hadn't been able to find the story that had appeared in the *Tribune*. When Greg's car pulled up in front, Diane watched Greg get out with Jenny, get her suitcase for her, and then walk with her to the door. Jenny was wearing a new dress, burgundy in color, and matching shoes. Greg had obviously taken her shopping again.

Diane hoped he was only carrying Jenny's bag for her, that he didn't want to come in. But he did step inside with Jenny, set the bag down, and then nod to Diane. "Did you enjoy the quiet around here?" he asked, sounding unusually humble.

"Not really." Diane walked to Jenny and hugged her, but felt very little response. "It was lonely, actually." She was looking at Jenny, not at Greg.

"Diane, did you see the story about me in the newspaper?"

"No. But I heard about it."

"You need to know, the reporter got a lot of things wrong. My partner was doing things I didn't know anything about. I was as shocked as anyone. I've agreed to testify about the things I know, and no question, the charges against me are going to be dropped."

"It's true, Mom," Jenny said, as though she thought she knew all about it. "The paper made it sound like he would be going to jail and everything, but this detective guy talked to Dad while I was there. He said he understood how Dad got drawn into everything without knowing what was going on. It just makes me sick that they would publish a story like that and try to ruin Dad's reputation."

Jenny picked up her suitcase and headed for her room, as though she wanted to make that one statement and then not have to talk to Diane about it again.

"That's the hard part," Greg said, with some emotion in his voice. "I'm the innocent bystander in this whole thing, but I get my name dragged through the mud. This probably means the death of our business, and I'm not sure what I'm going to do to save myself financially."

"I'm sure you can go back to your dad's firm." Diane knew she sounded less than sympathetic, but she *felt* less than sympathetic, and she wanted him to know that.

"It's not that easy." Greg glanced at a chair, as though he were expecting Diane to invite him to sit down. She didn't. He slipped his hands into his pockets and looked down, this time, no doubt, thinking that he looked humble. But he was wearing expensive suit pants, dark with a pinstripe, leather braces, and a classy striped tie that he'd loosened. He looked entirely too prosperous to plead such hard times. "Dad's sort of semi-retired now, and he doesn't pull as much weight around the firm as he used to. He told me a while back, before I went through this last mess, that he wasn't sure he could bring me back. Some of the attorneys who are now full partners seem to have it in for me."

"Life just isn't fair, is it?" Diane didn't try to hide her sarcasm this time.

Greg gave her a long, hard look. "You like this, don't you? I'll bet you've been downright giddy ever since you heard that I was indicted."

"No, Greg. I haven't."

"Well, no. You wouldn't. What you've really been thinking is, 'There won't be another drop of blood I can squeeze out of *that* turnip.' And I think you're right about that. Go check with the judge this time and see what he says. He might ask you to give *me* a little support for a while. But let's see, you never have been very good about standing up for me, have you?"

"Greg, I think you better leave. And don't ask to take Jenny again. You never should have taken her down there when you knew what was going on in your life right now."

"What's going on? I was falsely accused, that's all."

"I'm sorry, but I don't believe that."

Greg was shaking his head back and forth, smiling, but he was seething, and Diane could see it. His hands had come out of his pockets, and his fists were gripping, rising. "You always assume the worst about me, Diane, and I know how you've tried to poison my own daughter against me, but she's a little too smart for you. Jenny thinks for herself, and she knows me now. You can't keep turning her against me."

"I'm telling you, stay away from her. I haven't told her a tenth of the things I could tell her, but I will if I have to. Maybe she deserves to know."

"I've told her what you'll say. She knows how you've exaggerated everything in your mind over the years—and the kinds of things you'll accuse me of. But it's not going to work."

Diane took a step toward him, almost wishing that he'd strike out at her. "Greg, you think you can wrap enough slick words around the truth and change reality. You're the one using Jenny as a weapon—trying to pull her away from me. I could have been telling her things all her life, and I've never done that because I thought she ought to think the best she could about her own father."

"You've implied plenty. She knows what you think of me. But if you'd *ever* been a real wife to me, we would have been fine together. How could I have guessed that you're only a pretty picture, about as deep as the paper you're printed on? I want Jenny to be real flesh and blood, and that scares you to death."

"Listen to me, Greg. I mean this. I don't want you to come anywhere near Jenny again. I'll get a court order if I have to."

"You can't get a court order. What have I done?"

"You're a crook. Everyone's going to know that now."

"No. Those charges are going to be dropped. You just watch. And don't try anything cute with the judge. I just might be able to talk the man into letting Jenny make her own choice, and you know what—I don't think you'd like the way that might turn out."

"Just leave. Right now." Diane could feel her voice shaking, and she didn't want to cry, didn't want him to win one more time. He played these games better than she did. He always had.

"Good-bye, Jenny," Greg called. "I'll talk to you soon."

Jenny came down the hall. Tears were on her face. "I didn't want all this to happen," she said.

"I know," Greg said. "I tried to explain things, but you probably heard how your mother responded. It's the same old thing. By now I ought to be used to it, but I guess I never will be."

Diane took one more step toward Greg. "Get out of here, I said."

"All right. All right." He looked at Jenny. "I love you, sweetheart. And I *will* see you soon. Just make the best of things for now. Do what your mom tells you, but we'll see what we can work out."

"Greg! Stop that!" Diane was shouting now, and Greg was ducking, pretending that she was pounding him over the head. He stepped to the door, looked back at Jenny and shrugged, and then went on out.

Diane was shaking and crying by then, but she turned back to look at Jenny.

"Mom! What's wrong with you? Why did you do that?"

"Me? What are you talking about? Didn't you hear the way he was threatening me?"

"Threatening? He didn't threaten you. No wonder he says you make things up."

"Jenny, he was daring me to take him on. He thinks he can go to the judge and get you away from me."

"That's not what he said, Mom, and you know it. All he said was that the judge might let me have my own choice. And what's wrong with that? I'm old enough to make up my own mind now."

"Can't you see how he twists things? Everyone else is always at fault. How could he run a business with a partner and not know what was going on?"

"He told me all about that. This guy was keeping separate books and everything. He was drawing money out for his own fancy lifestyle, and then promising his customers that they were going to get rich. He spent up all the money and cheated everyone else—including Dad."

"And Greg wasn't doing the same thing? Look at his lifestyle! Where did he get the money to buy you that dress?"

"He said it didn't matter. He'll probably have to take out bankruptcy. He just wanted to buy me one thing before he lost his house and everything else."

"And you believed that?"

Jenny wiped the tears from her cheeks. "Mom, when he told me what had happened, about the police taking him down to the police station, he broke right down and cried. He said that for him, the worst part was that I might believe all those stories about him and not love him anymore. You should have seen him. His heart was *broken*. And he told me something he's never said before. He told me he still, to this day, loves you, and wishes more than anything that you'd never left him. He was just sobbing when he said it, Mom. It was true. He meant every word of it."

"Jenny, there's something you *have to* understand about Greg. He doesn't *know* what's true. He says whatever he thinks will get him what he wants at the moment, but you *can't* trust him."

"You talk so much worse about him than he ever does about you, Mom. And that's the honest truth."

Diane felt the air going out of her. There was no way to beat the guy. "So if the judge gave you your choice, where *would* you live? With him or with me?"

"Right now, he couldn't take me. Things are too messed up."

"But where would you rather live?"

Jenny drew herself up straighter. She liked to win too. "I don't know, Mom. But I wish you wouldn't treat him the way you just did after all he's been going through lately."

Diane thought of so many things she could say, but she said none of them. Jenny walked back to her bedroom and shut the door.

CHAPTER 5

A few days before Christmas Jenny talked to Greg on the phone and afterward said, "Dad and Marilyn are going to Palm Springs for Christmas. They're leaving in the morning."

Diane had been putting dishes in the dishwasher after the two had eaten. She looked up. "Palm Springs? I thought he was broke."

"I think things are pretty bad for him right now. But he said they just really needed to get away after all they've been through with this legal stuff."

"Is it all over, then?"

"Pretty much, I think. The charges against him are dropped. He just has to appear as a witness in court. I guess his partner is trying to throw all the blame back on Dad."

Diane decided to keep her mouth shut, but imagined the real truth was that two crooks were caught in the act—and each was pointing at the other. Greg was just better at passing blame, and he had probably been quicker to do it. What Diane did say was, "You and I have had a tough autumn ourselves. Maybe Greg ought to pay *our* way for a nice vacation."

Jenny had been wiping off the table with a dishcloth, but she stopped and looked up now. "Mom, don't start."

"I'm not starting anything. It's just interesting that he's always talking about bankruptcy, but he can pay for a nice hotel in Palm Springs."

"I think there are ways he can use that as a business expense. He told me he's meeting with some people down there." She began wiping the table again, now avoiding Diane's eyes.

"What business? I thought his business went broke."

"He's trying to get something started again. He's got some backers in California. He feels like it's going to be a long haul, but a year or two from now he should be in better shape than ever."

"Yeah, well, that's not what he'll tell the judge."

"Okay, Mom. I don't know why I even try to talk to you about anything like this." Jenny walked over and tossed the dishcloth in the sink. "You never try to see things from his side. Can you imagine how he must have felt when the police arrested him? His reputation is hurt forever. He's got that and all his money problems to worry about every day of his life."

Diane thought of a whole lot of things she could have said to that, but she said none of them. Still, Jenny marched away and went back to her bedroom, where she spent the entire evening.

That was how things had been lately. Diane and Jenny had seemed to work out a kind of truce—without ever saying so. They didn't quarrel, but Diane felt an almost constant uneasiness. She was careful what she said to Jenny, and Jenny usually kept her distance. Jenny was spending more time than ever with friends, and when she was home she usually said she had homework to do. There was no doubt that she did have plenty of work, with her advanced classes and heavy schedule, but there had been a time when she would do her homework at the kitchen table, or even in the living room. Now, although she would still talk to Diane when and *if* they ate together, they usually avoided the topics that both knew were awkward.

Diane had feared that Jenny would try to negotiate some time with Greg during the Christmas holidays—even though Diane had ordered Greg out of her life. The fact was, though, Greg hadn't pushed the matter. He had talked to Jenny several times on the phone, but Diane could tell from hearing one side of the conversation that he was telling her to submit to her mother's conditions and not create problems. Of course, Diane always imagined him telling her to stick with her mom—*for now*—and things could maybe change later.

On Christmas morning Jenny didn't get up until after eight o'clock. That was great for Diane, in a way, but she missed those years when Jenny had been the excited little girl knocking on her door, asking if it was time yet.

Diane and Jenny had spent Christmas Eve with Diane's family. They hadn't been there terribly late, but Diane had noticed Jenny's bedroom light on for quite some time afterward. It hurt Diane to see Jenny shutting herself up in her room that way, but she tried to remember herself at the same age, getting really tired of her own mother injecting herself too much into her life.

Diane had showered and dressed before Jenny finally came wandering out in her pajamas and faded yellow robe. "Did Santa come?" she asked, smiling a little, but looking tired, her hair in a tangle.

"I was afraid he was going to stop by to repossess this stuff," Diane said. "It's about time you got out of bed."

"It felt good to sleep a little longer. We get up too early most of the time."

There was something soft in Jenny's voice, and Diane liked it. She watched her as she sat down in the big living-room chair and surveyed what was by the tree. Diane had set out some socks and underwear, a couple of books and a pretty red sweater, all for Jenny. But she knew that Jenny's eyes were searching for something else.

"Wow, Mom, this sweater's beautiful." She finally crouched by the tree and picked up the sweater, holding it against her.

The red was striking against her dark hair, messy as it was. "*You're*

62

beautiful," Diane said. "How would it be to look that great, straight out of bed?"

"Thank you," Jenny said, looking up, seeming pleased but curious. "You *never* tell me I'm pretty, Mom."

"Well, you are."

"Grandma said that everyone always told you how beautiful you were, and it got so that's all you thought about—and you didn't want that to happen to me."

"That's one way to say it. I guess I'd say that I got so I thought that being pretty was *enough,* and I don't want you to feel that way. But that turns out not to be a problem for you. You're not ashamed to be smart."

"Why should I be?" But she wasn't really asking. She was looking at the presents again. "This is what I got for you, Mom," she said, and she picked up a box.

"You haven't opened all of Santa's presents yet," Diane said. "Open that big box."

Jenny's eyes swung quickly back toward Diane, and Diane could see that she knew what it was, that she was excited. She pulled the silver paper off a large, square package and looked at the outside of the box, which had a picture of an IBM personal computer on it. "Oh, Mom, I can't believe it! You really got me one!"

Very few high school students had their own computers, but some of Jenny's friends had gotten them in the last year, and Jenny had spent time at their houses, learning to use them. She had been talking for months about wanting to get one "someday." Diane had wanted one just as much, mostly for the word processor and the thesis she would have to write for her degree. "There's a printer in the other box," Diane said. "I hope you can figure out how to set it up so it works. Those things scare me."

"Oh, I can do that. Don't worry." She was grinning now.

"You have to let me use it sometimes," Diane said.

"Hey, it's half yours. That's only fair. But how did you come up with the money to buy it?"

"Well, IBM is giving teachers a good deal on them, so that helped, and then, I just thought it was something I could go into a little debt for. We both need one."

"Just about all college students are getting them now," Jenny said.

"I've been thinking about that. If you take this one with you, I'll be spoiled. I'll have to think about another one."

"By then, I'm sure Dad can get one for me." But that wasn't the best thing to say. Jenny looked away, and so did Diane. Actually, Diane had hoped that Greg would help with this one, but she had decided not to ask. "Jenny, your dad didn't send anything. I'm sure he—"

"He talked to me about that. He said, when he gets back from California, he'll take me shopping during the after-Christmas sales."

"That's good."

Jenny was looking back at Diane now. "But Mom, I know this was a big sacrifice for you. I do appreciate all you do for me. I don't think you realize that." Jenny came to Diane, reaching. Diane stood, and Jenny embraced her. Diane felt as though she could breathe again—after holding back for a long time.

Jenny spent the rest of the morning setting up the computer. "You got a good one, Mom," she would say. "Wow—256K of memory. That'll be plenty."

Diane had no idea what she was talking about, but she loved hearing Jenny's enthusiasm, and it carried over when they drove over to have dinner with Grandma Bobbi and Grandpa Richard. Jenny hadn't had much time to baby-sit lately, the way she had the last few years, but she had bought presents for the family. They were simple things, but she had considered each person's tastes, and it was gratifying to Diane to think that Jenny was that considerate, especially with school and cross-country and everything else she'd been doing all fall.

She had bought Diane a perfect blouse, pastel blue like her eyes, and classy. Diane wondered how Jenny had managed to buy it at Castleton's, one of the nicest stores in town. "Dad gave me some money, Mom," Jenny told her. "He didn't have much, but he gave me what he had in his wallet one day so I could buy presents. He told me to buy you something, and I loved this blouse. I wanted to buy you a skirt with it, but I just couldn't afford it."

It was another time when Diane decided not to say too much, but she thanked Jenny and told her how much she loved it.

Later in the day, Diane and Jenny rode with Bobbi and Richard to Salt Lake to see Grandma Bea. Most of the family gathered there in the late afternoon, the same as on Thanksgiving. Grandma had baked enough pies, it appeared, to feed half the people in the state. When the four arrived, the place was already filling up.

Diane met her Uncle Wally and Aunt Lorraine in the little entrance area at the front of the big old house. They were taking their coats off, having also just arrived. Wally didn't look good, hadn't for years. The damage done to his body during his POW days was catching up with him, and he looked terribly old for his age. But he was the same Wally. He grasped Diane tight in his arms, and then hugged Jenny the same way. "It's so good to see you two," he said. "We don't see you nearly enough." He stepped back and looked at Jenny. "Hey, when did you become a woman? My goodness, you're as pretty as your mom, and I didn't think anyone would ever match her."

"Take a look at your wife," Jenny said. "She's the prettiest woman I know."

Lorraine smiled the way she always had, with a kind of quiet grace. She hugged Jenny and then Diane. Diane knew that Lorraine had had a hard year. Their son Douglas, who was just a few years younger than Diane and was "mentally challenged," as people in Special Ed were saying now, had died earlier in the fall. He had always been a little boy—and a dear one to everyone. "Is Kathy coming down from Heber?" Diane asked.

"Yes. In fact, she might be here already." Lorraine laughed. "It's hard to tell, there are so many people here."

Diane looked into the living room and the connected dining room. She saw Gene and Emily talking to Aunt Beverly and her husband, Roger.

"There's Danny and Mike," Jenny said. "I want to talk to those two." They were Salt Lake cousins who were close to Jenny's age.

"Get some pie," Wally said.

Jenny laughed. "Don't worry. As soon as Grandma spots me, she'll be trying to feed me. She thinks I'm too skinny."

Jenny walked away, and Diane told Wally, "Actually, she is too skinny. But she runs on the cross-country team. Really, she eats a lot, but she burns it all up, running all the time."

"That's what I need to do," Wally said, patting his stomach.

Wally did look heavy. But Lorraine said, "The medicine Wally has to take makes him swell up. He really doesn't eat much." Then she pointed into the living room. "Oh, there's Kathy."

"Good," Diane said. "She and I need to catch up."

"You heard she got elected to the city council up in Heber, didn't you?" Wally asked.

"Yes. And it didn't surprise me one bit."

"It didn't surprise anyone. She'll probably be the mayor one of these days. Poor Marshall is lucky if he gets dinner on the table once a week. She's off running the town all the time."

"Well, I better go talk to her. We can exchange some recipes and talk about articles in *Good Housekeeping*. That's what we women like to do, you know."

"Kathy doesn't know how to boil an egg," Wally said. "Marshall cooks more than she does."

Diane laughed and worked her way into the crowd, but Alex spotted her and hugged her, and so did Anna, and then Beverly and Roger. Alex wanted to know, "Where have you been? I don't think we've seen you since last summer. Are you going with . . . oh, let's see . . . I'm not supposed to ask you that. You let me know that in no uncertain terms a few years back."

"The answer is no, Uncle Alex. I still haven't found a husband. No one seems to leave them lying around where I can stumble over them. The best men I know are all my uncles and cousins, and I don't think I'm allowed to marry any of those guys."

Anna touched Diane's arm and smiled. "You can do better than these tired old boys. Alex is almost seventy. I'm going to trade him in when the new models come out next fall."

"No, don't do that. He's still pretty cute." Diane kissed his cheek, and then she worked her way toward Kathy again and found her talking to Jenny, the two of them looking surprisingly alike now that Jenny had grown so tall. Kathy was almost forty, still thin, but her hips had widened after four babies. She never had cared about styles, about clothes in general, and she was wearing a brown dress that looked as though it had put in an extra year or two already. Everyone in the family talked about Marshall doing well in his cabinet business, but Kathy was always finding causes to support financially. Still, Diane had never heard Marshall complain. He never had cared much about "appearances." He and Kathy still lived in the old house they had bought when they first moved to Heber, and they had fixed it up nicely, but it was hardly a showplace.

"Diane," Kathy screeched. She was not as much of a hugger as some of the people in the family, but she hugged Diane. "I was just telling Jenny, you two need to come up and see us."

"I heard you're never home."

"Ah, that's not true. You've been talking to my parents, I'll bet. They think I'm gone every night and don't feed my family. But I do."

"But your dad said you're on the city council."

"Oh, that's no big deal. No one else wants to run." She wrapped her arm around Jenny's shoulder. "Hey, this Jenny girl of yours is *something*. She's been telling me what she wants to do with her life: go to Harvard Business School, start her own business."

Diane had heard Jenny say plenty about owning a business, but she'd never heard a word about Harvard. It hurt a little to think that Jenny would tell Kathy something she hadn't told Diane.

Jenny seemed to pick up on that. She said to Kathy, "I don't know for sure about Harvard. It's just what I've thought lately—you know, if I could get a scholarship."

But now Aunt LaRue was heading their way, wearing a bright red dress and lipstick just as radiant. The woman was halfway through her fifties and looked forty. She and John had adopted a baby girl a few years back, and LaRue never stopped talking about the craziness of trying to be a "young mother" in her "old age."

"What is this? The Democratic caucus?" she asked. "Let's nominate someone to run against Senator Thomas."

"I nominate Jenny," Kathy said. "This girl is on her way, Aunt LaRue. If she doesn't turn out to be Sally Ride, she'll be owning her own skyscrapers in New York—the 'Jenny Tower.' She's top in her class at Ogden High, and—"

"I didn't say that," Jenny protested.

Kathy turned to her, took hold of her arm, and stared into her eyes, "Okay, fess up," she said. "What's your GPA?"

"I don't know exactly."

"Yes, you do. Admit it."

"Well . . . okay. I sort of do. I got a B-plus last year, and I've had one A-minus. So my GPA is 3.9, or something like that."

"And that's not top in your class?"

"I'm not sure. I don't know what other people get."

"Yes, you do. I'll bet you can name every *guy* who might be close to you—and you've made up your mind to beat them all."

"Well, there might be *some* truth to that," Jenny said, and she flashed her wonderful smile.

Kathy glanced back at LaRue. "She wants to go east to school, maybe Harvard. We could write letters for her and get her into Smith—easy—but what do you think? Would Harvard be better for her?"

"What do you want to do, Jenny?"

"I want to work in management for a good company, and then, after a while, start my own business."

"What kind of business?"

"I don't know. I haven't figured that out yet."

LaRue seemed a little more serious than Kathy. "Smith is not a great place for business, but it's a good place to get a liberal education. You could do your undergraduate work at Smith and then go to Harvard for your MBA. But I'd do something more than just a business major as an undergrad. I'd take something that expands your mind before you settle into business classes."

"I've thought about that. But it's like I want to know *everything*. I look at college catalogs and I find myself wanting to take every class they offer."

LaRue glanced at Diane. "This is *your* daughter, Diane?" But she seemed to see that the question stung Diane, and she added quickly, "Jenny, when your mom was a teenager, I thought she was a hopeless case. She didn't care anything about school. But look what she's done. And what impresses me is that you're so pretty but still have a good head on your shoulders. Your mom has made sure of that."

"I know. All my life she's been telling me that a woman needs to develop *all* her strengths. And that's what I want to do."

"Right on, sister," Kathy said. "Your generation has nothing to hold it back."

Diane was growing uncomfortable with the conversation. And maybe LaRue was feeling some of that too, because she went on to say, "But Jenny, don't make the same mistake I did. I was so driven to do big things with my life that I missed my chance to do things that were actually more important."

"Hey, you're a mom, after all," Kathy said, "and you thought you never would be."

"But I started way too late, and never had the chance to have my own baby. I wish I'd had someone like John in my life a whole lot sooner. Don't wait as long as I did. Kathy's the one who figured out how to do it all."

Kathy finally seemed a little more subdued. "No. No one can do it all. I've got the ideal husband, who doesn't mind if I do a lot of things in our community. But sometimes I've let my kids down. I'm trying to be a lot better about that now. I really am."

Jenny nodded, seeming to take all their comments seriously. "I guess I do need to think about that. But right now the last thing I want to think about is getting married. Once I make a few million, then I'll look around for someone who wants to spend it with me."

Jenny smiled, but she had finally said the wrong thing to Kathy and LaRue. Diane knew that. Neither one of them had ever cared about money. "I think it would be exciting to develop a business," LaRue said, "but money can really mess you up."

Jenny laughed. "Maybe so. But *not* having money is the biggest mess of all. Mom and I have tried that, and now I'm willing to take a chance on having too much instead of too little."

All this was difficult for Diane, and she knew that her cousin and aunt understood that. Kathy said, "Life can take strange turns, Jenny. There was a time when I thought your mom would be very rich all of her life."

"That's why I'm going to make the money myself. I'm not going to depend on anyone else."

There was something really arrogant in Jenny's tone and it embarrassed Diane.

Things got quiet in the little group, and the hum of all the other talk and laughter filled up the space. "I understand what you're saying," Kathy said. "But Marshall, after all is said and done, is the most important gift in my life. And my kids, intense and crazy as they are, they're the next best thing."

"Jenny will find that out," LaRue said.

But lots of things were left unsaid—because it was Christmas and a party. And soon Grandma Bea pushed her little self into the group. "What in the world is going on here? Not one of you is eating any of my pie, and I've baked so many I'll never know what to do with all of them."

"I've had two slices already," Kathy said. "Pumpkin and cherry."

"And you're still way too skinny. I'm going to get you some apple, with ice cream. And Jenny, you need a whole pie. You need some flesh on those pretty bones of yours. What kind do you want?"

"You don't need to bring us pie, Grandma," Diane said. "We'll come into the kitchen and get some."

"I don't trust such empty promises. Come right now. All of you."

Grandma's dimples were sinking deep, her eyes alight. Diane thought she was surely the most precious person on earth. But it was Jenny who said, "Oh, Grandma, I love you so much," and pulled Bea's plump little body against her "pretty bones."

Tears came to Diane's eyes. There was something right about this girl, if she could just get past sixteen—and maybe a few more years after that.

CHAPTER 6

It was March 1986, and spring had been making a few claims for itself lately, but today, a Tuesday, snow had fallen all day. Diane and Jenny had gotten along better lately—really, since Christmas—but that was partly because Greg had turned up missing again. He had called Jenny a few times, was still assuring her he would take her on that post-Christmas shopping spree he had promised, but he never followed up on his commitments. Diane knew that his absence hurt Jenny more than she would ever admit, but he was always making new promises: he would call her next week, for certain, and they would go shopping for some nice spring clothes. Then "next week" would turn into "next month," followed by a new promise. Jenny would occasionally say something sarcastic about her dad's lack of concern for her—but he could always call again and be right back in her good graces.

Shortly after Diane arrived home from school, Jenny came in with her friend Tracy. The two ran on the track team together. "What are you doing home so early?" Diane asked.

"We didn't have much of a practice today because of the snow. Coach had us work out inside for a little while, and then he let us go. I don't know how we're ever going to get in shape if we don't get some better weather."

"Don't complain," Tracy said, laughing. "I love getting out of there early."

Tracy was shorter than Diane, with lighter hair, and freckles scattered across her cheeks. She had a sort of delta-shaped upper lip that gave her an impish smile. She was cute and, from what Diane had heard, a good student and a good girl. Diane thought it was important, in these teen years, that Jenny spend her time with girls from good homes. It was true that Tracy's parents seemed a little more relaxed with her than Diane was with Jenny, but Diane had to admit to herself, Tracy's mother was probably the one who ought to worry about her daughter being around Jenny. Jenny had been complaining a lot lately about her seminary and Sunday School teachers. "They're just so simpleminded," she would say, "and they think that any of us who don't think exactly the way they do are on our way to hell."

Jenny had been taking a biology class this year, and a world history class. She often mentioned ideas she'd heard in those classes that didn't seem to square with what she'd read in the Bible. Diane had tried to help, and she'd asked her father to answer some of Jenny's questions—which he had done very well—but his answers were complex and intelligent, and he ended up admitting sometimes that the seminary teacher was providing simple answers that high school kids could handle. The problem was, Jenny, more often than not, marched right back to seminary and challenged her teacher with Grandpa's explanations. Her seminary teacher had even called Richard, to sort some things out, and the two had gotten into a bit of an argument—which was almost impossible with Richard.

What Diane feared was that Jenny was seeing herself as some sort of deep-thinking Mormon who refused to buy into "easy answers" about science and history—and thinking herself superior because of it.

But at the moment she was asking, "Mom, do you need to use the computer?"

"It's your computer. But let me ask this—could I use it for a little while later tonight?"

"Wow, you're like the coolest mother I know," Tracy said. "When

73

I asked my parents for a computer, my dad said, 'What in the world do we need a computer for? We can't afford one of those things.' He doesn't understand about word processing and stuff like that."

"We couldn't afford it either," Jenny said, "but Mom knew how much it meant to me."

Diane was amazed. She had expected Jenny to say, "Mom just wanted one for herself. She uses it more than I do."

"So are you two going to be the stars of the track team this spring?" Diane asked.

"I'm not," Tracy said. "I'm supposed to be a sprinter and hurdler, but there are about ten girls who are juniors and seniors who are faster than I am. I'll never get a letter. But Jenny's good. She's like third or fourth best in the distance races."

"You don't know that," Jenny said. "None of us are in shape yet. I ate like a pig all winter and didn't run half as much as I should have."

But Jenny hadn't gained an ounce, and she had run a good deal, considering how wet and cold it had often been when she'd worked out. Diane knew what she was probably thinking, in reality: "What do you mean, third or fourth? I'll beat those older girls." During cross-country season she had worked her way up to varsity and had finished fourth or fifth among her team's runners most of the time. And she seemed to go at her running the way she did everything else. She was certainly expecting to be the best by the time she was a senior—if not sooner.

"So where's Brittney? I thought you three were inseparable," Diane said.

The girls glanced at one another, and then Jenny looked back at her mom. "We haven't been going around together all that much lately. She thinks we're too *unholy*."

"Why? What brought that on?"

"Oh, Mom, you'd have to know her family. They think Donny and Marie are a little too worldly. Britt's mom actually said that."

74

Tracy said, "Britt's dad, after Christa McAuliffe got killed on the *Challenger,* told Brittney that the woman should have been home with her family where she belonged."

Both girls laughed, and then Jenny said, "We're just not Molly Mormon enough for Brittney. I hope you know you're raising an *evil* daughter."

"Jenny, you've been friends with Brittney since first grade. Don't be so harsh with her. It's okay not to have the same opinions about everything."

"Tell *her* that," Tracy said. "She started in on all this stuff about AIDS being sent from God to punish gay people, and we told her that was a bunch of baloney. So then she says, the prophet told some people that—just like privately or something—and her dad had found out about it."

"President Benson wouldn't say anything like that," Diane said.

"He might. He's really right wing," Jenny said. "But I don't care if he did. I don't believe it."

"Jenny, what a thing to say," Diane said. "If the prophet has something to say to us, he'll speak to *all* of us. And when he does that, of course we should listen."

"Mom, I can't believe you'd say that. Dad told me I had the right to my own opinion and the Church can't take that away from me."

"The Church doesn't *take* opinions away. But our leaders advise us."

"Fine. Advise all they want. I don't have to agree all the time."

Diane knew this was the wrong time to take this conversation any further, especially with Tracy there, so she left the girls to their homework and walked back to her own room, but she could see that the next few years were going to test her in every way possible. She remembered how she'd felt a few years back when the Church had announced its formal opposition to the Equal Rights Amendment. Jenny had been young, but she'd certainly heard Bobbi and Diane discuss the issue—

and admit their struggles with the position Church leaders had taken. She knew she was going to have to watch what she said from now on.

On Saturday morning Diane's visiting teachers came by. For once, Diane hadn't forgotten that Terri and Carla were coming, but she sort of wished she hadn't made the appointment. As usual, she had way too much to do: her studies, her classroom preparation, and the cleaning that needed to be done. At least Jenny had gone out to run, and that meant she wouldn't be there to get annoyed by everything the sisters had to say.

"Diane, I don't know how you do it," Terri said at the door. "You look better in jeans and an old sweatshirt than I do when I wear my best dress to church."

Diane laughed and let the words pass. She'd heard those things all her life, but she knew what she was seeing in the mirror lately—crow's-feet developing at the corners of her eyes, and thickening thighs. "Come in. But do you care if we don't talk too long? I've got another paper due."

That wasn't exactly true. She hadn't started on the paper yet, and she had a test to get through before she did, but it was easier to blame things on a paper than to tell the whole story.

"Don't worry, we have busy days ahead ourselves," Terri said. "Carla's son has a T-ball game, and Jay wants me to drive down to Salt Lake with him to the boat show. I don't have the slightest desire to look at a bunch of boats, but both our sons like to go. Me and Sissy, we'll probably see if they have an ice-cream counter."

Everyone sat down, the way they always did, the sisters on the couch and Diane on the big chair across from them. Carla still hadn't said a word, but Terri said, "Okay, let's get on with it, then. Carla has the lesson this time."

Carla read a short message about trusting the Spirit and using the power of faith. When she was finished, she reached in her purse. "I have a little illustration," she said. "To me it makes the lesson a little more clear." She pulled out a Rubik's Cube. "Have you ever tried to solve one of these?" she asked.

"I've played with them a little, but I can't make heads or tales of them. Jenny can solve the thing in about two minutes."

"Really?" Terri said. "She must be a whiz, that girl. Everyone says how smart she is."

"Well, anyway," Carla said, "when you look at one of these and you don't know how to start, it just seems like there's no way you could ever get it figured out. But someone like Jenny, she understands how to solve it, even though we don't. And that's how God is. He knows everything, and when lots of things look hard or even impossible to us, He can tell us how to solve any problem. We just have to trust Him."

Diane nodded. "Good point," she said, but that wasn't what she was thinking.

"Sometimes we make life hard or complicated, but if we go to the Lord, He'll tell us exactly what we're supposed to do."

Again Diane nodded. She decided she didn't want to raise questions today—the way she usually did—and get a long discussion going.

"No matter what the problem is, an answer always comes, and then we know exactly what we should do."

Suddenly Diane couldn't resist, even though she knew she was opening a can of worms. "I don't know, Carla. Life has thrown some confusing things at me, and I've done a lot of praying. I can't say that I've always gotten answers—at least not quick and easy ones."

"Oh, I didn't mean it was quick and easy, necessarily. That's a good point."

Diane folded her arms and leaned forward. The sun was coming in the window behind her, brightening the room but casting the shadow from her chair, her head, all the way to Carla. Diane stared at that shadow, didn't look into Carla's eyes, when she said, "I had two boyfriends in college. I prayed and prayed for my answer—which one I should marry. I finally felt like I got my answer, and it turns out, I made a terrible choice. The one I married beat me down emotionally, and then started beating me up physically—and by the way, Jenny doesn't know that, so don't say anything . . ."

"Oh, no. We wouldn't say anything."

"Well, God could have warned me and I could have avoided a lot of trouble. Or maybe my faith wasn't great enough, and I didn't listen the way I should. All I know is, sometimes really terrible things happen, even though you try your best to do the right thing. God knows how to solve the Rubik's Cube, and He must have known what Greg was going to do to me, but here I am, eighteen years later, still living out the implications of my choice. I guess you can say it's what I was supposed to experience in life—and Greg did give me Jenny—but it's sure not a life with all the yellows on one side and all the reds on another, and everything just perfect."

Diane finally looked at Carla. She could see the red rising in her neck and cheeks, could see that she had no idea what to say.

"I'm sorry," Diane said. "But do you see what I mean?"

Terri said, "I've seen plenty in my life too, Diane. And I don't know why things have to happen the way they do. The one thing I understand is that you trust the Lord no matter what. You don't curse Him. You don't worry the rest of your life that He wasn't fair with you. You do the best you can and trust that life does make sense in some way. That's what I've watched you do for a long, long time. Look what you've made of yourself—and think what you might have done."

Diane wanted to believe that, and she was sorry she had shocked Carla the way she had, but she really did get tired of easy answers. No wonder Jenny was the kid she was turning out to be.

"Well," Carla said, "all I meant was, God's always there for us to turn to. And sometimes, things that look hard turn out to be blessings."

"I know. I didn't mean to sound so . . . disagreeable."

"You're never disagreeable," Terri said.

"Oh, yeah? Ask Jenny. She thinks I'm a tyrant. And what worries me even more, I'm afraid I've raised her to be too much like me. I've taught her to raise questions, but I'm not sure I've taught her to rely enough on faith. I'm scared to death what that's going to lead to."

"Jenny's fine," Terri said. "She's just like you, and just like Bobbi. She's smart, and she's feisty, but she's a nice girl. She's going to turn out great."

Diane wasn't at all sure of that, but she didn't want to talk anymore. She really did need to get on with her work.

"Diane, remember my cousin? The one I told you about, who lost his wife?"

"Uh-oh. I don't think I want to go back to that topic."

"Well, what you said just made me think. He's so lonely, and he's such a good man. He needs someone like you—so smart and everything. And he could make you forget a lot of the things that have happened to you. You two deserve each other."

"Terri, I told you before, I'm not looking. I can't even start to tell you all the bad experiences I've had when I've tried to date—and the last thing Jenny needs is for me to make our lives more complicated."

"Okay. I understand. But look at it this way: He doesn't want to get married either. Here's what I told him. He likes to go to plays, and he goes down to the Utah Symphony and things like that. I know you like those things too. So I asked him, why couldn't you two go together—and just be friends? And he said that might be all right."

"Really, Terri. Thanks for thinking of me, but I'm just not interested."

"But you do like plays, don't you? And classical music, and all those kinds of fancy things?"

"I guess I do. I actually haven't gone to a lot of things like that."

"He doesn't either, not anymore. He ends up giving his tickets away because he doesn't like to go alone. What if he just called you up and said, 'Let's go to a concert or something'? Wouldn't you enjoy that?"

"Uh . . . no. I don't think so."

"That's what he used to say. But since he saw you, he seems a little more willing to talk about it."

"Saw me? When did he see me?"

"At that singles thing they had last fall. I think it was a Thanksgiving dinner."

For a moment, Diane thought of the man who had sat with her at her table, but then she realized. It was that tall man—the one at the buffet table. She had known his name from somewhere, although she couldn't think of it now. "Tell me his name again," she said.

"Spencer Holmes."

That was the name. The man in the suit—the one she'd actually wanted to meet. But she wasn't going to admit any of that.

"He's smart, Diane, and really nice-looking, and he's forty or so—maybe forty-two or forty-three—but not *too* much older than you. He can talk about anything, and he's nice as can be. Don't think just because I'm uneducated and frumpy that he's the same way. You two would have a wonderful time together—you know, just as friends. He's got more money than he knows what to do with, so he might as well be spending some of it to take you to a few things you can't afford."

Diane didn't answer. She only shrugged a little, but she was wondering now what she should do.

"If I could talk him into calling you, you wouldn't turn him down, would you?"

Diane laughed. "Oh, I don't know, Terri. I don't know what I'd do. But it sounds like he's not going to do that anyway."

"Well, we'll see. I think I've got you just about there, Diane. Maybe I can do the same with him. And I happen to be one of those people who thinks if I pray—and then work very hard—I can probably figure out one of those Rubik's Cubes."

Diane was laughing again. "Yeah, but you're praying for 'happily-ever-after' the whole time you're telling me 'just friends.'"

"I know. That's true. But I have to start somewhere."

"Well, try your sales job on him. And if he calls, I'll see what the Spirit tells *me.*" She glanced at Carla and smiled.

"Okay. That's a deal. He's had all winter to think about you. He's got to be weakening by now."

Diane loved Sister Smoot, but she hoped that her cousin actually didn't call. At least, that was what she told herself. But she kept think-ing about the way he looked, and that soft, deep voice she had liked so much. And even if he *was* rich, she wouldn't hold that against him.

A couple of weeks went by and Diane assumed the guy wasn't going to call. And then one night when she was pulling leftovers out of the refrigerator, trying to put enough together for dinner for herself and Jenny—if Jenny happened to stop by—the phone rang. Diane set a couple of bowls on the cabinet and grabbed the phone. "Hi," she said, assuming that it was Jenny calling.

"Hello. I was trying to reach Diane Lyman."

It was that voice, except that he sounded more formal than she would have expected. "Oh. I'm sorry. This is Diane."

There was a bit of a pause. Had she confused him? Why on earth had she said she was sorry? Finally he said, "I believe you know Terri Smoot, my cousin. She's in your ward, I think, and—"

"She's my visiting teacher."

"Yes. Exactly. I believe she spoke to you about me. My name is Spencer Holmes."

"Well, yes. She mentioned you."

"Okay. Good." Another pause. "Actually, Spence is what most people call me."

Diane had no idea what she was supposed to say, so she said nothing. The guy sounded really uptight. She was suddenly sorry she'd agreed to take his call. Her mind raced as she tried to think of a way out of this.

When Diane didn't respond, Spence waited too, and then they both spoke at the same time. Diane was about to say what a good friend Terri was—a pure silence breaker—and Spence was saying, "I'm not sure exactly . . ."

They both stopped. Diane laughed. Spence didn't. "I'm sorry, go ahead," she said.

"I'm sorry. I'm not good at this sort of thing," Spence said, and Diane was surprised at the change of his tone. He sounded nice, even a little scared. But the formality returned when he said, as though memorized, "I think Terri told you that my wife passed away almost two years ago. I have season tickets to the plays at Weber State and to the Utah Symphony, and I sometimes take one of my kids, but they don't really like to go that much, and I don't like to go alone. I have tickets coming up next week for a play, and Terri suggested that you like theater and music and those sorts of things. She thought we might . . ." But he seemed to run out of material, or hadn't ever considered exactly how he might finish his sentence.

Diane finished it for him. "Go together?"

"Well, yes. To the play."

Diane burst into laughter again. "Well, I didn't mean, you know, 'go together,' with that meaning."

"No. I understand. I certainly didn't mean that."

Diane, almost in desperation—still thinking that she wanted to say no—asked, "What play is it?"

"It's something sort of experimental, they tell me. It's very modern. I've never heard of the playwright."

"That's not much of a sales job."

"Oh. Well. The play is actually supposed to be very good. I guess I'm more of an Arthur Miller or Tennessee Williams sort of guy. But I like to see new plays. My wife always tried to get me to broaden my horizons."

Diane was impressed that he knew a few things about the theater, but there was something sort of pitiful about his mentioning his wife in this circumstance, as though she would be sitting between them at the play. Still, he was gradually sounding a little more spontaneous, and she couldn't stop thinking about her first impression of him. "So what night is this?"

"I have tickets for Friday. I think that's the fourteenth or the . . . just a minute, I have the tickets here somewhere."

"It doesn't matter. It's next Friday?"

"Yes. Actually that's the twelfth. I was thinking of . . . something else, I guess." He had begun to laugh. "I guess you can tell, I'm a nervous wreck."

And it was that, the timid laugh, the admission, that convinced Diane. "Well, okay," she said. "I like to think I can try new things too." But now she was laughing. "What I mean is, the play. I didn't mean . . . you know."

"I was pretty sure you didn't mean me. I'm kind of an old thing."

Diane really wanted to say, "How old, exactly?" but she didn't.

"Actually, we sort of met one night. Last fall, at a singles dinner?"

"Oh, is that right?" Diane said, and was immediately mad at herself. She was reverting to her younger self, playing the game, pretending that she hadn't noticed, hadn't paid attention.

"Well, it was just a . . . I said hello is all. But I'm sure you wouldn't remember. Someone pointed you out to me—after Terri had told me about you—so I just asked you if you were Diane."

"Oh, I remember. At the buffet table. You were wearing a beautiful suit."

"I know. I was really overdressed. I hadn't ever gone to any of those activities. And to tell the truth, I haven't gone again since."

"I haven't been to one since then either."

"Well, anyway, Terri's told me a few things about you." Suddenly that memorized cadence had come back into his voice. "She said you've gotten the big rush from some single Mormon fellows, and you're skeptical about this arrangement she's been trying to set up. I just wanted you to know that I'm not on a campaign to find myself a wife. I can't really picture myself ever marrying again. All I have in mind is the play, and maybe some other time, the symphony. You know, that sort of thing."

"Don't worry. If you think I'm desperate to find a man, I'm not. I won't try to put any moves on you." Diane was teasing again, trying to see whether the guy really could laugh, but at the same time, she was also a little offended that he would proclaim himself out of bounds.

"I didn't mean it that way. I just wanted you to know that I wasn't one of those aggressive men you've apparently had to deal with. Do you know what I'm trying to say?"

"Pretty much. Sure. That'll be fine. Let's see what we think of this experiment—the play, that is."

But now he didn't seem sure whether he was being teased again, or maybe just didn't know how to end the conversation. "Okay, well . . . the play starts at seven-thirty. I have your address. How about if I pick you up at seven? We won't have far to go, but we'll need to get parked and walk to the Browning Center and all that."

"All right. Sounds like a deal." Diane didn't mean to be sarcastic, but all his time calculations sounded a little too planned out for her taste. She was also still a little annoyed. He seemed to think that her most appealing quality was that she didn't want to get married. She had a feeling that she had left herself wide open for another dating disaster.

Chapter 7

Jenny came home from her track workout one afternoon the next week looking happier than she had for a while, and strong, considering that workouts often left her depleted. It was a bright day after a wet winter and spring, and it was warmer than it had been in a long time. Jenny was looking tall and tan. "Mom, I need to ask you something," she said.

"Okay."

"Is that pizza I smell?"

"Yes, it is."

"Good. I'm starving." But then she headed off to her bedroom.

The pizza was a frozen one that Diane was heating up—exactly the kind of dinner that always made her a little ashamed of herself as a mother. But it was simple, and Jenny loved Red Baron pizzas. With all the calories Jenny was burning, she could eat all she wanted, so that wasn't what worried Diane. It was her own weight she was concerned about. Since she had accepted the date with Spence, she had been eating less, trying to drop a few pounds. She knew that she was being silly, since the date didn't mean that much to her, but she had a dress in mind that she hoped she could get herself into.

She peeked in the oven and decided the pizza needed a few more minutes. She was just getting plates from the cupboard when Jenny showed up, looking way too alive for a school-day afternoon. "I've got a problem, Mom. I need to talk to you about it. But keep an open mind, okay?"

Diane wasn't sure what the problem was, but she liked that Jenny was looking more like the girl she had always known—so excited about something that she couldn't hide it. She also liked that Jenny was bringing the problem, whatever it was, home to Diane.

"All right. You talk. I'll listen."

"Well, the good part is, I got asked to the prom." Jenny couldn't hold back a shy smile. Jenny's teeth were perfect. She'd never worn braces, and almost all of her friends still had them. The whiteness of her teeth was a gift as well, and they were flashing now, set off against her tanned skin.

"Really? Who asked you?"

"You're supposed to listen and I'm supposed to talk."

"Okay. But talk about the boy first."

"All right. I can do that." Her smile got bigger. Since Jenny had turned sixteen the previous fall, she had gone out several times, but never with the same boy more than once, and Diane was pretty sure that that had been Jenny's choice. She hadn't seemed very excited about the boys who had taken her to the other school dances, but this was clearly different. "His name is Derek Shaw, and he's on the track team with me. Actually, he's on all the teams. Football, basketball, and he could play baseball if he wanted, but he's so fast that he'd rather run on the track team."

"Be careful of *fast* boys."

"No more talking."

"Okay. But I have a feeling he looks very good in track shorts, from the way your eyes are glowing right now."

"I think he probably looks all right—but then, I'm sure I haven't really paid much attention." Jenny laughed. She walked to the oven and looked in. "This pizza is close enough, I'd say. Let's get it out."

But when Diane walked over and looked, she said, "Another two minutes. I like the crust to be crispier than that." The steamy burst in her face smelled good to her too, though. She was really hungry after having eaten only a tiny salad for lunch.

"I don't care how it's cooked. I just want to swallow the thing whole."

"Allow me one slice, and then do me a favor—eat the whole thing before I take a second one."

"It's a deal."

But now Diane was standing with her back to the oven and Jenny was in front of her. "So you like this guy?"

"He's really nice, Mom. He's kind of a big star around the school."

"How old is he?"

"He's a junior, but he's only about six months older than I am. And he's LDS. I think his dad's in a stake presidency—or something like that."

"That sounds good. So what's the problem?"

"You know what the problem is. I need a dress, and we can't afford it. And lately the only thing Dad talks about is how he might lose his house because he's so far behind on his payments."

"We'll manage, Jenny. We can—"

"Here's the part where you have to wait and I have to talk."

"Okay."

"I know what you're going to say. We can shop for fabric, and you or Grandma Bobbi will sew it for me. But—"

"I wasn't going to say that. You know I can't sew well enough, and I don't think Mom would want to take on anything that fancy."

"Well, all right. But here's what I'm thinking." She pressed her fists together in front of her, looking worried. "I don't want to go to Penney's or Bon Marché and get the cheapest thing they have. Do you know what I mean? This is the prom, and I want something nice. Tracy and I have been looking around and—"

"When did this boy ask you?"

"Today. But I sort of knew he was going to."

"Did he just ask you straight out, like a normal human being, or did he have to do one of these productions all the kids do now?"

"It was sort of halfway in between. Out at practice today, he had the whole team gather around, like they were in a huddle, and I was the only one left out. I finally walked over there to see what was going on and he popped out of the middle with this sign that said, 'Get on track, Jenny. Go with me to the prom.'"

Diane rolled her eyes.

"I know. It was lame. He even said so, but you know . . . it didn't matter."

"Not when he looked so cute in those shorts."

Jenny grinned. "He had his sweats on."

"But anyway, you and Tracy have been looking at dresses already?"

"Yeah. Tracy's been going with a boy. She knew he was going to ask. So we've looked around just a little bit. ZCMI has some pretty dresses, and I saw some at Castleton's that are just *gorgeous*. But here's the thing. They really cost a lot."

"Like how much?"

"Okay. That's what I wanted to talk to you about. I know I don't have a job right now, but Tracy said she could get me on at the Burger King where she works. They need people, and they're willing to hire me even if I only want to work like ten or twelve hours a week. And then this summer I could work more. It wouldn't take me too long to pay you back."

"No, honey. I don't want you to do that."

"I know what you're going to say. But listen for just one more minute."

Diane nodded, folding her arms. She didn't like this.

"Is that pizza ready?" Jenny asked.

Diane decided to take it out, whether it was crusty or not. She grabbed some hot pads from a drawer and pulled the cookie sheet out, then slid the pizza off onto a slide-out cutting board in her cabinet. Jenny was already searching for the pizza cutter in a drawer, but Diane said, "Let it cool just a little before you cut it."

"It'll cut okay now," Jenny said. She had found the cutter, and she began rolling it across the pizza. Diane wished she could hear more crunch, but she didn't worry about it. She could see that the conversation could easily get more intense from this point on.

Jenny dished up four slices on her own plate, and Diane took her allotted one. Diane got a couple of water glasses from the cabinet and filled them at the sink, and they sat down at the kitchen table. Diane said the blessing. She asked "that the Spirit might abide in our home," and then, after they both said "amen," she told Jenny, "I think it would be good for you to work this summer. But I don't want you working now. You're too busy as it is, and a pretty dress isn't worth hurting your grades over."

"But you know me, Mom. I'll get the grades. I'll never slack off in school."

"What you won't do is sleep enough."

"Tracy's working. She's getting by okay."

"I'm not Tracy's mom; I'm yours. We'll get you a dress, but I don't want you working until track season ends."

"Okay. But could we take into account that I'm going to pay at least half? I'll work this summer and pay you back the difference between a really nice dress and the one you'll want to buy."

Diane told herself not to take offense—but it wasn't easy. "Let me propose something else."

"Okay." But Jenny sounded skeptical.

"Sister Morgan, in our ward, makes beautiful wedding dresses. What if you saw something you liked and then found a pattern, and she could make it for you? I'll bet you could save a lot. She's really reasonable."

"Well . . . maybe. But this is prom. Do you know what I mean? I'll be looking at the pictures the rest of my life. I'd just like to have the *per-fect* dress, and I'm not sure Sister Morgan could make something that would look that professional. Don't you remember how you felt about that, when you were in high school?"

"Oh, Jenny, I was Bobbi's daughter. And Richard's. They just couldn't imagine paying a lot of money for a dress I would wear once. And you know what? I don't even know where those pictures are now. At the time, it seemed a much bigger deal than it turned out to be. You'll look great no matter what you wear, and the truth is, that boy is going to be looking at your beautiful face, not your dress."

Jenny smiled. "He better look at my face. I don't have anything else to look at."

"Just legs about a mile long, and skin so perfect it'll stop the poor kid's breath."

"Do you really think I'm *that* pretty, Mom?"

"You know how pretty you are."

"I'll never be as pretty as you. Even my friends talk about how beautiful you are."

Diane hardly knew what to do with this topic. She was eating her slice of pizza slowly, making it last. "Jenny, you know my mantra. You're pretty but you're smarter than I ever was, and that's a lot more important."

"Tell that to the boys."

"You tell it to them. Make sure this Derek guy understands who you are and what you stand for."

"Maybe he's the one who'll have to remember who *he* is. I might be *after* that boy."

Diane didn't even want to hear Jenny joke about such things. "Oh, Jenny," she said, "I've got some interesting years ahead of me. I can see that already."

"I'm just kidding. And he knows I'm smart. He's a good student too." She was talking with her mouth full. She gulped some water and then said, "But Mom, here's the thing. Nice dresses have gotten really expensive. They're *at least* a hundred dollars. Sometimes one-fifty, or even two. That's why I want to pay half."

Diane couldn't believe it. How was she supposed to come up with that kind of money? She had been thinking sixty or seventy dollars. But she didn't say it. She had to handle this right. "Well," she said, "let's go shopping. Maybe we can run down to some of the stores now. Let's see what's available, and I guess we could charge it—and maybe you *can* help pay it off. But let's look for better prices than that—and let's just see whether Sister Morgan couldn't make something just as pretty."

"Well, okay." Diane could see how wary she looked. "I can show you some of the ones I really like—but they're mostly . . . quite expensive."

"Well, let's look." And then Diane let herself smile just a little. "I might look around for myself as well. I actually need a new dress."

"I know. You haven't bought yourself anything for a long time."

"Well, yeah. But what I mean is . . ." And now she was smiling more than she wanted to. "I have a date. Someone asked me out, too."

"Who?"

"Don't act so surprised."

"But I am surprised. You haven't gone out for *ages.*"

"It has been a while. And this will probably be the last date for another long while, but I agreed to go, and the dress I'd like to wear, I probably can't get into."

Jenny was suddenly laughing. "This'll be so cool, Mom. Both of us looking for dresses. But I want to know, who's this guy? Is he a good Church member? Does he come from a good family? And what time is he going to bring you home?"

"He's Terri Smoot's cousin."

"Oh, Mom, you've gotta be kidding. You let your visiting teacher line you up? That's sort of desperate, isn't it?"

"Hey, watch it."

But Jenny was cracking up. "I sure hope he's better looking than Terri's husband. Ol' Brother Smoot is not what I'd call a 'pretty boy.'"

"Actually, I saw this man once. He's nice-looking, dresses nice and everything. He's also supposed to have a lot of money." She winked. "That makes him even better-looking."

Jenny's eyes lit up. "Hey, now, there's a thought. Do you think you could marry him right away, and he could pay for my dress?"

"I don't think I can work that fast."

"It's worth a try." But then Jenny looked serious again. "So who is he?"

"His name's Spencer Holmes. He lives on the east bench in Ogden somewhere."

Jenny looked astounded. "Mom, that's Heather Holmes's dad. His wife died—and not that long ago."

"I think it's been about two years now."

"But Mom, Heather is a creep. She treats everyone rotten—just because she's so rich. And she's really a mess. She comes to school looking like Cyndi Lauper. I've even heard she takes drugs."

"Well, that's interesting. But I wouldn't worry about it. He told me on the phone that he's not looking for a wife. He just needed a date for a play he wanted to see—and Terri told him I liked plays."

"Mom, really. Don't start liking him. Heather's in my class. She doesn't like me at all. I can't even believe what a disaster that would be."

"Relax. We're just going out one time."

But Jenny was still looking concerned.

"Maybe I'll come in late and make you sit up and worry about me," Diane said.

"Don't you even think about letting that guy kiss you. I'll be waiting and watching. If he tries anything, I'll go after him with a broom."

Diane laughed, but she was a little disappointed to hear about Spencer's daughter. Maybe she would just get by with her old dress.

Jenny kept her word and ate almost the whole pizza, except that Diane did eat a second, small slice. Then they drove downtown to Castleton's. And it wasn't long until Diane was worried more about the style of the dresses than the prices—even though the prices were hard to swallow.

She ruled out the strapless dresses entirely, which seemed to embarrass Jenny as much as disappoint her. She was clearly worried what the sales clerk was thinking about all this.

The woman was typical of these places, Diane thought. She surely didn't earn any more than a schoolteacher, but she acted as though she were a high society lady, just working for her own entertainment. The woman remembered Jenny and knew exactly which dresses she had liked. She gathered them from several places, hung them on a rack just outside the dressing rooms, then pulled the first one down and held it up for Diane to see.

"No," Diane said, before Jenny could respond. It was a blue-gray taffeta that shimmered under the fluorescent lights, and it was beautiful but, from Diane's point of view, cut much too low in front.

"Mrs. Lyman, you're going to have to tell me what your likes and dislikes are, then. These are all dresses your daughter looked at earlier this week and liked very much."

Diane was annoyed. Surely a woman in a town as Mormon as Ogden knew what Diane didn't like about the dresses she was showing. Her superior tone was obviously a suggestion that Diane was a prude.

"The girl is sixteen years old," Diane said. "I'm not going to let her out of my house in something cut that low."

"Mom, it's not that bad," Jenny said.

Diane tried to take some of the emotion out of her voice when she said, "Jenny, look at it."

The woman nodded, set the dress aside on a table, and then said carefully, "Jenny is not full in the chest at all. A dress that might show some cleavage on a bigger girl wouldn't show anything at all on her. You might want to let her try some of these on before you reject them out of hand."

The woman was now holding up a beautiful yellow dress, not cut as low, but with spaghetti straps.

"I want her to wear something with sleeves. I just don't think she should be showing that much skin."

"I see. Well . . . that's not easy. Not many prom dresses are designed with sleeves these days."

"It sounds like we'd better look somewhere else, then. I would think your buyers would know that a lot of the girls who shop here are LDS, and they want modest dresses."

"Many of us who work here are LDS, Mrs. Lyman, but you'll find that ideas about what looks pretty on a young woman are not all the same. My own thought is, your daughter has wonderful skin, and a dress ought to show some of that. When I see girls swimming these days—nice Mormon girls—most of them are wearing two-piece suits, and many are wearing bikinis. That's a lot more skin than a dress like this would ever show."

"Yes. And when a girl is swimming, a boy doesn't have his arms wrapped around her."

Jenny was ducking her head, and Diane was embarrassed, because she wasn't at all sure she approved of some of the swimsuits Jenny wore. Maybe she should have taken a stronger stand on that, too. She was having a hard time knowing what a good mother should do. The truth was, it seemed only a short time ago that she'd been fighting with her own mom about what *she* could wear, and making all the arguments this sales clerk was making now.

"I think we'll try ZCMI," Diane said, turning away.

"Mom," Jenny was saying, "couldn't I at least try some of these on? I think, if you see them on, you won't find them so bad."

"Let's go see whether ZCMI has heard of sleeves."

Diane kept walking, and Jenny followed her out through the doors. "Mom, wait just a second. Tell me what was wrong with the yellow one. I know it's expensive, but it's the one I love the most—and it wasn't low or strapless."

"Those spaghetti straps are not that different from strapless, Jenny. Haven't you been listening to what they tell you in your Laurel class—or am I the only person still worried about modesty?"

"A lot of Mormon girls wear dresses without sleeves. What difference does that make?"

But Diane didn't know how to make that argument. She just knew how a modest young woman ought to look, and it was frustrating to think her daughter didn't understand that.

"Tracy's mom doesn't have any trouble with dresses like that. The only thing she said was 'not strapless.'"

"Jenny, I've heard about young women who don't get married in the temple because they've gotten so they like to dress immodestly—and they don't want to give it up."

"Oh, come on, Mom. What kind of argument is that?"

"Let's just see what they have at ZCMI."

But when they got to ZCMI, Diane soon found that the dresses were not as different as she had expected. And Diane was starting to wonder just how old-fashioned she was.

"Mom, just let me try on this one dress," Jenny said. "It's my very favorite of the ones here—and really, I like it almost as much as the yellow one at Castleton's."

Diane actually wanted to look at it first, but she didn't say so. She knew she had to be careful right now.

A woman was approaching—someone who looked a little more wholesome than the society lady at Castleton's. "Could I help you?"

"I tried on that blue prom dress a couple of days ago," Jenny said. "I'd like to try it on again and see what my mom says."

"Oh, yes." The woman looked at Jenny. "She was *stunning* in that dress. You'll love it."

Jenny went off with the saleswoman, and Diane waited. She did take a minute to glance through some of the nice dresses, but she saw nothing that appealed to her, and the truth was, she had lost interest in buying anything for herself.

And then she looked up to see Jenny walking toward her. Tears came to Diane's eyes instantly. *Stunning* was the right word. The pale blue was set off perfectly against Jenny's dark skin, dark hair, and pale blue eyes. Everything worked. It was a slender dress, not puffy, the way some of the prom dresses were these days, and it emphasized Jenny's height, her beautiful lines.

"Oh, honey, you're breathtaking," Diane said. "I hate to know what it costs."

"It's not so bad," the woman said. "One-thirty."

"That's plenty bad enough," Diane said, but she was relieved it wasn't more.

"Mom, the back is a little low," Jenny said, clearly worried, and she turned around.

All Diane could see was her little girl's skin, miles of it. There was hardly any back to the gown at all. It seemed way too sexy to Diane.

Diane glanced at the saleswoman. "She's only sixteen," she said.

"I know. It is a little low in the back, but a lot of the girls wear those. And this one does cover up in front."

"And it has sleeves," Jenny said.

"Isn't there anything else that—"

"This is the one I love, Mom. I liked the yellow one at Castleton's—and this one. And this is the best price."

Diane regarded the saleswoman again. "I hate to say this in front of you, but I'm thinking that we could find some fabric like this, and a woman in our ward could make the same dress—only with a back in it."

Jenny's eyes were filling up with tears. But instead of pleading or breaking into sobs, she said, "Fine, Mom. You had your mind made up before we ever came down here. I don't know why we bothered."

She turned and marched toward the dressing rooms, and if she hadn't had her back turned, Diane might have given in. But she could see all that skin again, and she whispered to herself, "Sixteen. The girl is sixteen."

CHAPTER 8

Spencer Holmes wasn't quite as good-looking as Diane had remembered. He had a clean face, lean and strong, but there was a kind of tiredness in his eyes. He seemed a little older than Diane had pictured him, too. But the slight graying in his hair was dignified—and it was nicely cut, as though he cared about such things. He was built strong, too, with a reasonably flat stomach and wide shoulders. He was wearing a tailored suit again, gray and three-piece, with a red and blue striped tie. He seemed classy, even a little old-fashioned. As she looked around the theater, she noticed that he was the only man there dressed so well. Diane hadn't bought a new dress, but she had starved herself for two weeks and had managed to fit into the dress she had hoped to wear. It was turquoise, with a fitted top and a pleated skirt. She liked the skirt, the way it flowed when she walked, and she liked the color. But the dress was a little fancy for a college play, so she was glad that Spence had dressed up too.

Diane also liked that he wasn't one of those nervous talkers who would try to think of something to say every second. She had feared that might turn out to be the case after their conversation on the phone. But in the car, he found things to say without seeming to work at it. Still, he didn't really seem at ease, either. She sensed some self-consciousness in everything he did, as though he had thought it all through ahead of time and was trying to follow his script.

What Diane didn't like was the play. The actors were all portrayed as not understanding one another, talking at the same time, or responding to their own thoughts. Diane got the idea that it was purposefully confusing, probably to show that people didn't make much sense, but she found herself wishing for a little more of a plot somewhere in all the chaos, and eventually she was annoyed that no hint of one evolved.

When Diane and Spence filed out of the small theater, Diane was afraid to admit how little she had liked the play. Spence was apparently quite knowledgeable about the theater. Even after all these years of educating herself and of teaching, Diane sometimes felt she was still her younger self, the girl who had never been all that well-informed. Greg had made her feel stupid so many times that she was sure she would never entirely trust her own opinions. She sometimes expressed herself the way her mother did—with considerable force—but she had never quite overcome the thought that someone else, with more knowledge, would see right through her displays of confidence.

As the two were leaving the theater, approaching the doors, Spence waited, let some others pass, and then held the door with one hand and lightly touched his other palm to Diane's back. That touch reminded her of Greg, but Spence didn't do it with the same sense of command, and he possessed nothing of Greg's self-importance. "Well, what did you think?" Spence asked as soon as they were outside.

It was the moment Diane had been fearing. "I think the author makes a good point about communication—the way people talk past each other and don't really listen."

"I guess that's true. I hadn't thought of it that way."

Diane suddenly felt sick. She had obviously missed the point. Spence had apparently understood what the dialogue was all about. She decided to keep her mouth shut.

"So, did you like it?" Spence asked.

"Well . . . it was *interesting,* in a way. Did you like it?"

Spence chuckled in that deep voice. "To tell you the truth, I got pretty tired of waiting for something to happen. And listening to every-one talk at the same time—that started to make me nervous. But I think I missed the point. You caught on to it better than I did."

"Not really. I don't need to go to a confusing play to understand that the world is confusing. I kept waiting for a story of some kind."

"So you didn't like it much?"

Diane decided to take a chance. "No. I really didn't. I hope you don't mind my saying that."

"Hey, listen, I didn't have the slightest idea what was going on. After the first fifteen minutes or so, the only thing I was thinking was . . ." He burst into laughter. " . . . when will this thing ever end?"

Diane was laughing too. "Oh, good. I'm glad you said that. I was afraid you really liked it and you'd think I was stupid for not under-standing it."

"I don't think anyone understands something like that. Coming out, I heard that guy in front of us telling his friends how 'provocative' it was. And the other people were all nodding. You know darn well they were thinking, 'Oh, is that what it was?'"

Diane liked that. "Deep down, I'm really a *My Fair Lady* kind of girl," she said.

"Hey, I love *My Fair Lady,* and I've seen *Pygmalion.* I liked that, too, but I sort of missed the songs." He laughed at himself. "Don't tell anyone how lowbrow we are. When I go to the symphony, I'm always trying to pick up on a bit of melody here and there."

It was what Diane had often thought. "That's why I like Gersh-win," she said, "or Aaron Copland."

"Two of my favorites. And both Americans. Maybe that's how Americans are. We like a good story—or a nice melody." He was walk-ing beside her, not touching her now, even though he seemed like a "give her your arm" kind of guy. But he did touch her back again when he spotted his car. He guided her to her door, opened it with his key, and waited as she got in. When he came around and got in on his side, he said, "I was thinking we could run over to Bratton's and get a bite to eat. Would you like that?"

"Did you make a reservation?"

"Oh." He stopped. The key was in the ignition, but he hadn't turned it yet. "I didn't think of that. Maybe this late, it won't be so busy."

"Well . . . maybe."

"Yeah. You're probably right. But let's drive by and see." He started the car and twisted to back out. As he did, he said, "Diane, I've got to admit, I've been sort of a stay-at-home guy for quite a few years. I've lost all my dating skills, if I ever had any."

"I know how you feel," Diane said. She was thinking that she liked this guy who had made a lot of money but wasn't slick. Greg had known the whole game, had always made reservations at fancy restaurants, and had always pulled strings to get the table he wanted.

"Is it considered really low budget these days to go down to the Utah Noodle Parlor?" Spence asked.

"Probably. But I've always liked it."

"Celeste and I always went there—all the way back to our high school days. We like those big fried shrimp—even if they're greasy." He hesitated. "I mean, that's what we did like."

"That's what everyone likes." But Diane felt the awkwardness.

"I didn't mean to . . . you know. Maybe I'm not supposed to talk about my wife."

"Why shouldn't you?"

"I don't know. Like I said, I'm not very good at this kind of thing."

Diane was sorry to hear his embarrassment—and especially his sadness. She thought she understood some things about him.

Spence didn't bother to drive to Bratton's. He drove down 36th Street instead, and then took Washington Boulevard into town. The Utah Noodle Parlor was busy, and it took a little while to get in. They had to stand in the entry and wait for a time.

The two didn't really talk very much while they were waiting. Maybe the comparison was setting in, and Spence was feeling how much he would have preferred to have his wife there. Diane was starting to think that he should have taken her home after the play—after their brief talk about their tastes. But maybe it was just as well to find out quickly that, once again, nothing was going to come of another attempt at dating.

They did finally get a table, and by then Diane had noticed something else about Spence. Lots of people seemed to know him, and he remembered everyone's name. He was friendly, shook hands when people approached him, even introduced Diane when there was no way to avoid it, but she sensed his embarrassment. "My goodness, what a pretty girl you're out with," an older woman told him. "He was my bishop back a few years ago," she told Diane. "Now, what was your name again?"

"Diane Lyman."

"Are you from here?"

"Yes."

"Do I know your family, or . . ."

"You might know my father. Richard Hammond. He's a professor at Weber."

"I know the name," the woman said, but Diane could see in her eyes what was registering: Diane had a different name from her father; she had been married. The woman probably wondered who this divorced woman was, chasing her former bishop.

They moved on to their table, and they didn't have to look at the menu. They both knew they wanted shrimp. "Diane, have you lived in Ogden all your life?" Spence asked.

"Almost. My dad took his job here at Weber State when I was just a little girl. But I went to the Y, and I lived in Seattle a couple of years before I ended up back here." They both knew, of course, that she was talking about her married years.

"I've met your father. He's a smart man. I've heard he's a great teacher, too."

"He's kind of low-key. I think some of the younger students find him boring." Diane laughed. "I've had people tell me that—when they didn't know I was his daughter. But he *is* smart. And he's a really good man."

"Terri said you came back and finished your degree here at Weber." Diane nodded. "Yes, I did."

"So what did you major in?"

It was a sorry attempt at conversation, and Spence seemed to know it immediately, his face reddening a little. "At the Y, I majored in nothing at all," Diane said, "except finding myself a husband. When I started over, I got into Special Ed."

"Terri told me a few things about your marriage—things I guess you've told her. I hope you don't mind that she talked about that."

"No. That's fine."

"She says you've worked hard to make a life for yourself and your little daughter."

"She's not little now. She's taller than I am. She knows your daughter."

"Which one? Heather?"

"I think so. Is she a sophomore?"

"Yes, she is." He leaned back and looked past Diane. "Oh, brother, I can imagine what a 'normal' girl must think of my Heather. She's going through a hard time, I'm afraid."

"That's too bad." Diane certainly wasn't going to reveal what Jenny had said about the girl. What also registered was that their situation, awkward all along, had just taken a turn for the worse. She could see it in his face, the way his eyes were avoiding hers.

"So you teach Special Ed?"

It was another halfhearted attempt at conversation, and Diane wanted what he evidently wanted: to eat the shrimp and leave, or, better yet, skip the shrimp. "I do. But I'm back in school. I want to be a principal."

"Yeah. That's what Terri was telling me."

And then came silence again, this time the noticeable kind. Diane took a sip of her ice water. Spence unfolded his napkin and placed it in his lap. And then Diane realized what she needed to say. "Tell me about your wife."

"Oh . . . I don't think . . ."

"You're really lonely, aren't you?"

"Well, sure."

"You said you used to bring her here in high school. So were you high school sweethearts?" Diane glanced around at the booths, thought of him coming here with his high school friends, or maybe just with Celeste at times, probably laughing a lot, feeling very different from how he felt tonight. She was sure now that it had been a bad idea to come here.

Spence was looking down at the Formica table. "Junior high, actually. But I knew her even in elementary school. She was the only girlfriend I ever had. I went to a few school dances with other girls, but basically I was always in love with her." He looked up at Diane and shrugged a little, as if to apologize.

"That's nice, Spence. I know it's a long wait for her, but it must help to know you'll be with her again."

She saw a glint of moisture in his eyes. He cleared his throat, obviously at a loss for words. He seemed relieved when the waitress approached the table just then. She set their plates before them: shrimp with French fries and coleslaw, and slices of white bread on a plate.

When the waitress walked away, Diane could see that Spence was searching for something to say, so she helped him out. "Have *you* always lived in Ogden?"

"Yeah. Born and raised. My parents were too."

"So what did you major in?"

He grinned, seeming to know that she was teasing him a little. "You claim that you majored in nothing; well, I majored in *everything*. I always knew I'd go into business with my dad someday, so I was in no hurry to get out of school." He picked up one of the shrimp and dipped it in a red sauce that had a dab of hot mustard in the middle. But he didn't bite it yet; he looked at Diane. "Everything was interesting to me. I kept changing my major. Dad was out of sorts with me after a few years, so I—"

"Did you go on a mission in there somewhere, too?"

"Yeah. After my first year. I went to Argentina. But all this I've been talking about happened after I got back. My dad kept telling me to pick *any* major, and just finish up. So I finally did finish out a business major—even though I didn't want to—but mostly because he wanted me to get an MBA and I didn't want to do that either. So I talked him into law school. I told him it would help me with all our business dealings—and he could stop paying his lawyer, which he had always hated doing anyway."

"Where did you go to law school?"

"Salt Lake. The U." He had red sauce in the corner of his mouth, but he sensed it quickly, raised his napkin, and wiped it away.

"Were you married by then?"

"Yeah. I got married only about six months after I got home. Celeste had waited for me, and Dad put me on his payroll even though I didn't work all that much. He paid for my college, too, so I guess I'm kind of a spoiled child."

"What kind of business was it?"

"Construction. But not houses. Big buildings—major projects. And I hated every minute of it. It didn't engage my brain the way my subjects in college had. Everyone else did all the work and I sat in an office and shuffled paper across my desk. And then my dad died, very young, and suddenly it was my business. But I still didn't have any zeal for it, so I kept it awhile and then sold it."

"What do you do now?"

"Well, a little bit of everything—like always. I was just a young guy and suddenly I had a whole lot of money, and I could have lived on it the rest of my life. But that's kind of a scary thing, the idea of retiring in my thirties and just playing around. It seemed immoral—you know what I mean? I may sound like a yuppie, but I'm just not. I hear all this 'greed is good' talk lately, and I think, 'What's our world turning into?'"

"Still, it sounds like you are your father's boy, after all. You took Daddy's money and turned it into *more* money."

Spence smiled—a big sort of grin that came on slowly. He seemed to accept her little insight. "Yeah, I suppose that's what I've done. I've had some other businesses, bought some real estate, been partners on some projects. But it wasn't the money itself that I cared about. It was just making the businesses work. I'm always antsy, though. I think I'll move on to something else."

"Like what?"

Spence took a breath and smiled again. "Well, the plan was to let other people manage my businesses, and Celeste wanted to start traveling. I told you I've been sort of a stay-at-home kind of guy. I haven't seen much of the world. But I'd promised Celeste that we would go look around a little. I'm not sure I cared much to do it—but I knew how much it would mean to her."

"And then she got cancer."

"Yup. And it was a real ordeal, Diane. She had a mastectomy, and then chemo and radiation, and all of it just ate her up, little by little. She lasted more than two years, but she didn't have any quality of life after the first year or so. I finally told her, 'Go ahead and let go, honey. There's nothing left to fight for.' But you know, she was worried about our kids and thought she could still help me with them. Of course, the kids and I were pretty much on our own by then anyway, but I'm not sure I dealt with the situation very well. I can cook if I have to, and I can write checks for what the kids need, but I'm not their mom. I tried back then, and I'm still trying, but I've been a busy man all my life, and I wasn't as close to my kids as I should have been. Now . . . I hardly know what my businesses are doing, and I tell myself I'm being a better dad by staying home more, but it's hard to handle everything alone—especially it's hard *for me.* I'm sure some men would do a lot better."

"You seem like a man who can do it."

"I have fun with my kids. We've got a big ski boat and lots of other toys. But I can't talk to them the way Celeste did. I can't figure out what they need . . . and the truth is, I walk around all day feeling like some sort of machine. I try to care about life and get back to being the guy I was, but I don't know . . . I'm just empty, and the kids know it."

"You're trying your best, Spence. That's all you can do."

Diane had almost forgotten to eat. She picked up a French fry, mostly to prove that she was going to make an effort, but she was feeling no appetite. She liked this man, but there was no way she could compete with the woman he was still in love with.

"I've been thinking about going back to college," Spence said. "I used to think I wanted to finish a degree in anthropology. That was what interested me most in college—before my dad put the pressure on me to get a business degree. I'm young enough that if I could get a Ph.D. before I'm fifty, I'd still have quite a few years where I could teach—if someone would hire me."

"That sounds like a great idea. When I got into school and started thinking about my future, that's when I started coming back to life."

"Yeah." He looked at his food. He wasn't eating much either. He finally took a drink of water instead. "But the kids still need me at home, and half the time, when I try to read, I can't keep my mind on the words. My sister says I'm in a depression, and I tell her I'm not because I would never wallow in grief, month after month. But I don't know. I guess that's what I'm doing."

"We all have these ideas about how life is going to work out, and then other things happen. It throws a person for a loop. I don't think people understand that unless they've been through it. My husband didn't die, but the guy I *thought* I married did."

Spence nodded. His eyes seemed to have sunk even deeper beneath his dark eyebrows. "I'm sorry about this, Diane. I shouldn't have called you. As you can see, I'm just not ready for a . . . friendship. I'm still too much of a mess."

"It's okay. I probably understand better than most people. My friends ask me why I'm not out looking for a husband, but they don't understand what happens. Jenny's been my life, and it's like I don't know how to do anything but make sure she comes out all right."

"You're a good mom."

"Jenny wouldn't say so right now. She thinks I'm way too uptight about a lot of things. I wouldn't let her buy the prom dress she wanted because I thought it was too sexy for a young girl. I talked her into letting a woman in our ward make a dress for her. We went over for a fitting yesterday—and it was beautiful—but on the way home, Jenny admitted that she didn't like it as much as the one in the store. She's still mad at me."

"She'll forget that soon enough."

"Maybe. But we've been so close, and now there's a distance between us. When you talk about feeling empty, I think that's what I've felt for almost fifteen years. When I left Greg, I was just lost. I didn't know who I was or what I wanted to do. And I guess I was embarrassed that I'd *failed*. But I had Jenny to cling to, and once I got myself going a little, I just poured out all my love on her. The trouble is, she's at that age now where she wants her independence from me, and I tend to smother her."

"Is she rebelling?"

"Not the way some kids do. She's got it all together when it comes to school and sports, even boys—she's the model kid in most ways.

And she's *highly* motivated. But she's never had anything, and that's made her crazy to have the things I couldn't give her."

"Doesn't her dad help you financially?"

"That's a long story. But overall, not much. He tries to win Jenny over with fancy gifts, but he doesn't come through with the checks he's supposed to pay me."

"Terri told me who he is. I've met him. It's hard for me to imagine that you two were ever married."

"Why?"

"He's . . . how should I say? . . . not a man I think very highly of."

"He's a crook."

"Yeah. I think so."

"Maybe he always was. But I didn't see it when I was young."

Spence was nodding. "Well, as you say, life does take strange turns."

"I look at my friends who married nice boys, had families, stayed active in the Church, and are struggling along, paying their bills, getting ready to send their kids to college and on missions, and I think, I'd give anything to have that life."

"There's just no way to see into the future and predict things like that."

"But it seems like there ought to be. It seems like God should have told me to stay away from Greg. Or, I don't know—maybe He did and I wouldn't listen."

Spence was nodding again. She could see that he felt sorry for her, and that wasn't exactly what she wanted. But she did like his gentleness. "Well, it's been good for me to talk to you," Spence said.

And then Diane, a little surprised at herself, hoped that he would say, "So why don't we get together and talk again?"

But he didn't. They finished some of their food, left the rest, and he took Diane home. He walked to the door with her, thanked her, apologized again for the state he was in, and then simply said, "Good-night."

For the next couple of weeks she hoped that he would call her again, but he didn't.

CHAPTER 9

On a Friday afternoon in May, as Diane walked into her apartment from school, the phone was ringing. She hurried to the kitchen and picked up on about the fourth ring. "Diane?" she heard. "It's Spence Holmes."

"Hello."

"I'm the one who—"

"I know who you are, Spence."

"Well, yeah."

So why wasn't he talking? "How have you been?" she asked.

"Okay. You know . . . not too bad. After we went to the play that night, I decided it might be better if I didn't call you again . . . so I didn't. But I've worried about it. I didn't want you to think that I didn't enjoy that evening. I felt like I needed to call you and at least say that."

"And that's it?"

"Well . . . I'm not sure. But I've waited a long time, and . . . well, anyway, I did like talking to you that night. I just don't want you to get the wrong idea."

Diane leaned forward and let her forehead thump against her yellowing wallpaper. The phone clunked against the wall too, so she had to straighten up. "What? That you would like to take me out again? Or that you actually sort of liked me? Which wrong idea are we talking about?"

"Oh, brother. I'm in over my head again. I should have thought this out before I called. But Heather will be home soon, and I didn't know what time you would get home—so this seemed like the only time I might be able to talk to you for a minute."

"The thing is, Spence, I've got to run. Jenny has a track meet right now. But I think I get the idea. Heather wasn't happy about you going out with me, was she?"

"Actually, she didn't know who I went out with. She just knew I went out—and she didn't like it."

"I got the same thing from Jenny. And she knew that I went out with 'Heather's dad.'"

"Really? Well, I guess that kind of settles that."

"Yes. Definitely. Heather's your boss, and Jenny's mine. We know our places."

"It's really about like that, isn't it?"

Diane bent her neck a little more this time and thumped her head a little harder. She stayed that way, leaning at a weird angle. Spence was always more exciting in her imagination than he was when she had to deal with him in person—or over the phone. "Listen, Spence, here's what I'm thinking. Let's decide if we're men or mice. Why don't we stand up to those girls?" She waited a couple of seconds, got no response, and added, "Or we could sneak around behind their backs."

Spence laughed. "I think I'd prefer the mouse approach," he finally said. "But it might be hard to find a time when both the cats are away . . . if you get my drift."

"Well, my cat is gone a lot these days. But I'm a busy woman. What do you have in mind?"

"Nothing specific. I didn't exactly . . ."

Diane leaned away from the wall, turned, and pulled out a kitchen chair. As she sat down, she glanced at the "rooster clock" that Jenny had given her for Christmas long ago. It was always about five minutes fast—on purpose—but she subtracted the minutes and knew it was after four. She needed to change clothes and be on her way. Jenny was supposed to run at around four-thirty. "Come on, Spence. You have to be a man if you want to get into the mouse business."

"I guess that's right. I will say this. Heather's going somewhere tomorrow. She said she'd be gone most of the day."

"Okay. This is our big moment. Now tell the truth. Is that sort of what you had in mind the whole time? Is that why you called?"

"You tell me. You seem to know what I'm thinking better than I do."

Diane liked that. He was either a smart aleck under that innocent exterior, or he was learning from her—fast. She told him, "I have an awful lot I have to do tomorrow."

"Oh."

"But Jenny has started to work at the Burger King on Saturdays." That had been Diane's compromise with Jenny, that she could work one day a week until school was out. "So I say, let's do something."

"When you say that, I don't want to give the impression that . . . you know . . ."

"Spence, I know. You aren't going to marry me. Heather wouldn't let you anyway. I promise I won't try to hold your hand or breathe on your neck or anything else that might get you excited."

He was laughing again. "I think you're out of my league, Diane. I'm not used to a woman who keeps me off balance the way you do."

"I'll be nice, okay? What time do you want to sneak out? Jenny has to be at work at noon. I can't be gone too long, but maybe we could have lunch."

"Okay. I'll pick you up at twelve-thirty."

"What if Heather decides not to go anywhere?"

"I'll do what any brave man would do. I'll lie to her."

"All right. I knew you had some backbone. Twelve-thirty tomorrow. Or even right at twelve."

"Sounds good. That'll maximize our time."

"You aren't going to wear a suit, are you?"

"No. I'll wear jeans."

"Designer jeans?"

"No. Levi's—501s. I'm not as fancy as you think I am."

"That's good to know."

Diane really had planned a busy day on Saturday, but by the time Spence showed up, she had put in more time trying to look casual, but pretty, than she'd taken to get ready for the play they'd gone to. She had been tempted all morning to run to town to find some decent pants. She'd tried on both her pairs of jeans and then had twisted to look in the mirror. She was worried that she might have to walk in front of him sometime. So she wore khakis, which were a little looser, but they seemed just slightly dressier than she wanted. So she went with an old oxford cloth shirt with the long sleeves rolled up. It was casual, but it was that shade of blue that worked well with her eyes. And her makeup had to be a work of art—just enough to bring out her eyes without seeming to be there at all.

Whatever she had done, it seemed to work. She watched him as she opened the door, and she saw—heard—that little intake of breath that she always hoped for when a guy came to get her. Her own breath hesitated a little as well. Spence was surprisingly tan, and he was wearing a yellow polo shirt that showed off his shoulders really well. He was smiling, too, looking more relaxed than he had on their first date.

It was in the car that she first realized that he wasn't feeling quite as confident as he looked. "I was thinking," he said, "have you ever been out to Antelope Island?"

"For lunch?"

"No. It occurred to me this morning that I haven't been out there for years. It might make a nice ride. So I put some sandwiches together. There's a place out there where we can sit in the shade and eat."

"That's fine. But how long will it take?"

"No longer than a restaurant would—or not much longer, anyway. And we can see the buffalo and everything. They have more than six hundred American bison on the island."

Diane was checking out his car. She hadn't bothered to think who the maker was when she got in, but now she was noticing the wood paneling and the leather seats. She thought it was a Mercedes or a BMW, and it had to be one of the nicest models. She felt as though she were floating, not bumping along the city streets, the way she did in her old Toyota. But she was also thinking about Antelope Island. What was that all about?

"They have that ranch out there, with picnic tables and everything," Spence said. "It's actually a visitors' center. They take kids out there from the schools all the time. I just thought it might be something a little different."

Clearly, he had given this a lot of thought, Diane realized. He was even sounding scripted again. "I thought you said you hadn't been out there for a long time," she said.

"I haven't."

"Did someone tell you about all this?"

"Actually, I called. It's a state park, and the woman who answered told me about the bison and everything."

"And one thing about it, we're not very likely to run into anyone we know in a place like that."

He offered the slightest of nods, and she saw an even slighter hint of color appear on his neck.

"So you said to yourself, 'Anyplace I take this woman around Ogden, someone might see us—and the word could get back to Heather. So let's go out to the middle of the Great Salt Lake, among the buffalo, and not take any chances."

He glanced at her, smiled with more delight than she expected, and said, "Do you have X-ray vision, too—or do you only know my thoughts?"

Diane touched his arm. "Hey," she said, "I'm thinking it's a good plan. I was wondering all morning where you might take me to eat. I didn't want Jenny to find out."

He looked at her again, but this time something had changed in his eyes. He was smiling, but she had the feeling it was the little touch that was registering with him, or at least that was what she was suddenly aware of—even though she hadn't meant anything by it.

Diane found herself wanting not to joke quite so much, not to be quite so clever with him. They rode quietly for a time, and then she said, "How adamant was Heather? Is she really afraid you'll get married at some point?"

"She would never admit to that. But I think she hates the idea that I would bring some 'evil stepmother' into our house." A light ahead of them turned yellow, and he brought the car to a gentle stop; then he looked over again. "Heather doesn't know what she's mad about. So it's sort of *everything* right now. She claimed she was mad that I would go out—because her mom hasn't been dead that long. But she knows that's ridiculous. And with Heather—at least the way she is now—the weaker her argument, the louder she yells."

"What is it she wants? Does she know?"

"Does anybody at that age?"

"Yeah. I think some people do. Jenny does."

"Well, that's true. I guess most young people have their dreams. Heather never seems to think an hour ahead, let alone a lifetime." He was quiet for a time, and then, after the light changed and the car was accelerating, he said, "I wish she did have some dreams. But the worst thing about wanting something is that sometimes you get it—and then you can't remember why you wanted it. As mixed up as she is, I think that's how it would turn out for her."

116

"Is that what happened to you?" Diane asked.

"What?"

"Did you try to get rich and then find out it didn't matter that much to you?"

"Well, no . . . not exactly. I worked for money, just because that's what a guy in business does. What I wanted in life, I already had. And of course, I didn't fully recognize that until . . . well, you know."

He meant Celeste, of course, and Diane didn't want to get into all that again. This kind of talk had hurt her ego a little the first night, but now she could feel how much it hurt him, and the problem was, she couldn't help him. He'd already told her that.

Spence obviously didn't want to go that direction either. He changed the subject, asked her about Alex Thomas, her senator uncle. He ended up, once the subject of politics had been brought up, having to defend President Reagan. And actually, he did a good job of it. Diane had never bought into the idea of trickle-down economics, but he made a case for a positive business climate opening up more jobs. She liked that he wasn't afraid to argue with her, at least in a friendly way, and she liked that he could accept her position at times. What she liked most, though, was that he sounded smart. Any of the issues she brought up, he had already thought about. He didn't respond with slogans and simplistic generalities. "You know who you remind me of?" she finally said.

"I have no idea."

"My dad."

"Oh, thanks a lot. I'm not *that* much older than you are."

"I'm not talking about the way you look. I'm talking about your intelligence—and your considerate way of presenting your point of view."

"You told me your dad was boring."

"No. I said some of his students think he is. I think he's brilliant. And I think he's about the best man who ever lived." She looked out the window, unsure whether she should say it, but then added, "You seem like a really good person."

That brought on another kind of quiet, and Diane realized she had trodden far too close to "friendship" again.

When they reached the causeway leading out to the island, Spence paid the fee at the gate. "Where are the buffalo today?" he asked the woman in the booth.

"If you turn left and follow the signs to the Fielding Garr Ranch, you'll see one big herd right along the road."

"That's good. That's the direction we're heading anyway."

The road was south, close to the water, and they hadn't gone more than a few miles before Spence said, "Okay, I can see them down there—on both sides of the road."

Diane had spotted them too, but she was feeling a little distant now, with plenty to think about. He continued to drive to a place where a few of the big bulls were grazing close to the road. "I brought my camera," Spence said. "Do you mind if I get out and take a few pictures?"

"Not at all. I want to get out too. They don't attack, do they?"

"Sometimes. But if one does, I'll throw my body in the way and save your life."

"I'll take a chance, then," Diane said, and she got out of the car before he could walk around to her door. He did walk to her side, though, and he snapped off a few pictures without seeming to worry much about lighting or background. He was her kind of photographer. He did turn and say, "Smile," and took a picture of her, close up. She thought about teasing him about that, telling him to hide the picture from Heather, but she didn't want to tease anymore.

They stood and watched the animals for a time. Diane was thinking how mangy they looked up close. She was also aware of the flies they attracted. The air was still and very warm for May, and there were no trees—only sagebrush and rabbitbrush and June grass that was already dying into yellowness.

"It's a beautiful sight, isn't it?" Spence said after a time.

"Well, I guess so. They don't do much, do they?"

Spence smiled. "No, they don't. But this whole scene looks like the Old West to me. Think of the days when there were millions of these big beasts all across the country."

"I don't know, Spence. I was thinking, this is what might be left of the world after the radiation blows in from Russia." At a place called Chernobyl, in the Soviet Union, a nuclear accident had occurred just a couple of weeks earlier. No one knew for sure how serious it would turn out to be, but Diane didn't trust the way Soviet officials were playing it down. Some people still felt that the world was in great danger.

"Really? I love places like this."

Diane had a hard time getting excited about sagebrush, but she thought of her dad again, the way he had always tried to get her to see the beauty in things she paid little attention to. Spence was clearly experiencing more than she was, and she envied him.

They didn't stay long. They got back in the car and drove to the ranch, which was well south on the island. There were barns and animals, and some groups were taking tours, but Spence took Diane in another direction. He pulled a basket out of the trunk and walked to a picnic table. He had a tablecloth in the basket, and some nice deli sandwiches. He had planned this—brought cups and paper plates and a thermos of lemonade. Something about all that touched Diane.

They ate and chatted. Diane was rather too aware of some little flies in the air, and she worried about mosquitoes. Spence seemed oblivious to all that. He asked Diane more about her father, and then her mother and her siblings. Diane found herself telling more family stories than she had in many years.

Eventually, she tried to turn the subject more toward Spence, but he answered briefly and then said, "I know you told me that you want to be a principal. Tell me why? Is that better than teaching?"

"It's a change. And it pays better."

"Yeah. I tend to forget that. Teachers just don't get paid the way they should. There's something sort of out of whack in our country that we don't pay educators what they deserve."

It was another chance to get political, but Diane didn't follow the impulse. Instead, she said, "If I can make a little more money, that'll take some pressure off Jenny and me, but the biggest thing is, I want to have a new challenge."

"What's your life going to be like once Jenny's on her own? That's one of the things I wonder about—being alone in a few years."

Was that what he wanted—to keep her near until their daughters weren't calling the shots? She decided not to needle him about that. "I don't know," Diane said. "But it worries me too."

He had finished his sandwich and the pickle that went with it, and had set his plate back in the basket, but he was holding his plastic cup and leaning forward with his elbows on the table. His hands and his forearms looked powerful. He was an imposing man, but his voice was always surprisingly mellow. What was making her a little self-conscious, however, was that he could never seem to rid himself entirely of a hint of a smile. It kept making her smile when she didn't mean to. "You know what we were talking about earlier?" he said. "About kids having dreams? What was it you wanted before 'real life' got in the way?"

"I just wanted to be a mom, have a nice home. All the basics."

"Oh, come on. You must have fantasized about being a movie star. Didn't people tell you that you could do something like that?"

Diane tried, harder than ever, not to smile. "People did tell me that. But I was in a school play one time, and I was awful. Any idea I had about acting went right out the window. I'm just amazed I can get up in front of kids at school. I have terrible stage fright if I give a talk in church."

"Really? That amazes me."

"So what secret dream did you have?"

He laughed. "Who said I had a dream?"

A breeze had come up, which felt good, though it made it a little cooler under the trees than Diane might have liked. She folded her arms. "If you think I must have had one, then you must be judging me by your own standards."

He leaned away from the table. He was obviously trying not to look her in the eye.

"Come on. Let's hear it."

"Just the usual stuff. In grade school, I wanted to be shortstop in the major leagues. But I wasn't any good. The only team I ever made was the high school football team, and I was just a lineman. I'm fairly strong—or at least I used to be—but I'm not athletic."

"But that's not it. That's not your *secret* dream. You're holding that one back."

"So you think you really do have X-ray vision, don't you?"

"I do. And I can see your heart. It's full of some unfulfilled desire that you've never told anyone."

"No, no. That distorts it. It wasn't anything that serious."

"*What* wasn't that serious?"

Now he really was blushing, his ears turning red. "It's one of those things that if I tell you, you'll always use against me. So I'm not going to tell you. I don't want to be teased."

"You big baby. You *are* a mouse. You don't want me to *tease* you. Next you're going to worry that I might *hurt your feelings.*"

"Okay. You admit your secret and I'll admit mine."

"I didn't say I had one."

"Now who's the big baby?" He used a high falsetto to say, "I just wanted a nice house with a white picket fence and ten pretty little babies."

"Hey, what is this? I'm seeing a whole new side to you."

"Don't change the subject. Put up or shut up."

Diane tried to think. She really did want to hear whatever it was he'd dreamed about. She decided she had to make something up. But that wasn't what came out. She said, "Okay, here it is. But you have to promise not to use this against me either."

"Okay. I promise."

"I wanted to marry a prince—and be a princess."

"That doesn't count. Every little girl wants that."

"Not the way I did. I wanted to be a *real* princess. I read everything I could about Princess Grace. I even made a scrapbook full of pictures and articles about her. I tried to find out all the places in the world that still had princes. You know, like in England. I wanted to marry Prince Charles, and I didn't even think he was good-looking. Mostly, I'd daydream about our wedding. When Diana finally got him a few years ago, I was actually jealous—and I wasn't exactly a little girl anymore. I've never told *anyone* that, ever, not even my mother. *Especially* not my mother."

"Okay. That's pretty good. Kind of superficial, but interesting."

"Hey! That was cruel. I thought you were nice."

That made him laugh hard. "I am. Usually. But with you, I have to fight back."

"Fine. So tell me your dirty little secret."

He let his eyes roll upward, as though he were asking himself whether he could do it. "Well," he finally said, "I wanted to be Superman."

"Hey, come on. That's like what you said about me wanting to be a princess."

"In a way. But you don't know how it *preoccupied* my thinking. I would fantasize about it all the time. I was kind of a big lurp of a kid, and the girls never paid much attention to me. So I'd think about how I could impress them if I could fly to the rescue and beat up a bad guy. Or catch some girl falling from a skyscraper. I would imagine myself setting her down ever so gently. Then she would look at me with love in her eyes and tell me how strong I was—you know, all that stuff."

"Yeah. Like Lois Lane would do—and then not recognize Clark Kent about five minutes later."

"Yeah, well, I didn't think so much about that. I would picture myself jumping over a building, bending steel—the whole thing. When I was really young, I would run around with a towel around my neck. I outgrew that, but I couldn't stop thinking about being Superman—not 'til I was way past the age when I should have given it up."

"Well, it's kind of fun to think about you as a boy, imagining all that. It's not much to tease you about."

"I guess the embarrassing part is, I still have these pictures in my mind of 'coming to save the day.'"

"There's one part of this I don't think I understand."

"What's that?"

"You said that you and Celeste were *always* in love—even when you were kids."

"No. I said I was always in love with her. She's the one I used to picture in most of these little daydreams I had. We were friends for a long time before she ever liked me 'that way.'"

"And when you got tall and handsome, she realized you really were Superman."

"I don't think it went quite like that."

"It's still like really finding a prince. Or becoming Superman. You got your dream."

"Well, yeah. That's what I meant earlier. But you don't know it when it's happening."

The quiet returned.

"Look, I didn't mean to . . ." But he didn't know what to say.

"I'm happy for you that you got what you wanted—at least for a time."

He nodded, just barely, still looking apologetic.

But Diane was noticing something else. "Spence, we have a problem."

He glanced around to see where she was looking.

"Don't look. I'm going to turn around, like I'm gazing out across the island."

"Why? What's going on?"

Diane turned, and she talked to the empty space in front of her. "A woman just got out of a car in the parking lot. Her daughter goes to Ogden High and is a good friend of Jenny's. If the woman sees us, Jenny will know about it within hours."

"Do you think this daughter knows Heather?"

"I'm sure she does."

"What can we do?"

"Just keep looking away. I'm going to get a mirror out of my purse, and I'll try to follow her movements. If she walks down the path to the barn—or the bathrooms—we'll make a break for it."

Diane got out the mirror, but directing it on a target was not nearly so easy as she had hoped. She kept moving it around, catching the woman with some kids—fortunately not Brittney, Jenny's friend—and then losing her again. Finally Diane picked up a fence in the background and figured the woman was heading down a path, not coming toward them. She waited a few more seconds and then looked around. "Okay," she said. "She's hurrying her little girl down to the bathrooms. Grab everything and let's get out of here."

Spence was already shoving things in the basket, and then he was up, saying, "Don't forget your purse. Let's go."

They ran across the lawn, under the trees, and dashed out to the parking lot. Spence got Diane's door open, then shoved the basket in the back. He hurried around, started the car, and drove rather too quickly out of the parking lot. By then they were laughing.

"I kind of like this mouse dating," Spence said. "It's exciting. We'll have to try it again."

But Diane wasn't so sure. She had the feeling they were creating a situation that would only get more awkward each time they were together.

Chapter 10

Spence and Diane went out twice during the month of June. They drove to Maddox, a restaurant in Brigham City, the first time. Spence did see a couple he knew, and he was pretty sure they had noticed him, but they weren't people who would ever talk to Heather. The other time, they simply took a drive to Snowbasin and then hiked a couple of miles up a trail. Diane enjoyed herself both times, but she was increasingly bothered that Spence seemed to want a friend—a *secret* friend—and nothing more. Whenever she thought of the possibility of marrying him, she was well aware that it wouldn't work, but she was feeling an attachment that she suspected would only grow deeper with time. And that would only bring pain. What she wished was that they would both stop being quite so practical and just let their relationship develop naturally. That evidently wasn't going to happen, so she decided she was going to turn him down next time he called.

Diane was out of school for the summer, but she was attending classes at the University of Utah full-time, so she was as busy as ever. It felt good to concentrate on her classes and not to be teaching all day, but life felt out of sync. Jenny hardly seemed part of Diane's life anymore—she was working, putting in all the hours she could, and running several miles every day. She spent the rest of her time with Tracy and her other friends, and she just couldn't believe that Diane still had rules for her about what time she had to come home at night.

According to her, the other kids could stay out as late as they wanted on summer nights. She and Diane had gotten into a major argument when Diane had told Jenny she didn't believe that. Tracy, a few days later, had made a point of telling Diane that her parents trusted her and let her make her own decisions about when she came home. That didn't change Diane's mind, and the tension with Jenny continued.

Even worse was that Jenny, in the last week of June, had flown to San Francisco with Greg and Marilyn. Greg was "working on a deal" in California and had invited Jenny to go along. This time Diane hadn't dared to tell her that she couldn't go. Jenny wouldn't be missing school or cross-country practice, and she wanted so badly to see something new. Diane had promised to take her on a trip somewhere that summer, but school was consuming her time, and tuition was taking her money. She and Jenny had often talked about driving to California, but they would have stayed in cheap motels and eaten out of a cooler along the way. Greg was staying at the St. Francis, where Jenny could order room service or go out with her dad to nice restaurants.

When Greg had first asked Diane whether Jenny could go, Diane had asked him, sarcastically, how he could afford a trip like that. "I gotta tell you," Greg had said. "This is a last desperate attempt. I'm trying to put a deal together to get financing on a project I'm trying to get going. If it falls through, I'm losing my house and cars and everything I have."

"So that's why you're staying at a swanky hotel?" Diane had asked.

"You never have understood things like that, Diane," Greg had said. "You don't try to cut a deal with people like this and give them your phone number at Motel 6. Sometimes you have to spend money to make money."

"Even if you don't have any?"

"Yes. Even if you don't have any."

Ultimately Diane had said yes because she didn't want Jenny to hate her, and now she was home, doing homework, and Jenny had called from the St. Francis to say how wonderful everything was. She and Greg and Marilyn had gone to eat at a French restaurant in another hotel, had sat by the window where they could see all the city lights and the bay in the distance. Greg had ordered for her and had thought of everything. She'd eaten escargots for the first time, and crème brûlée for dessert, which she now considered the most luscious food she'd ever tasted. Apparently eating that kind of meal was "spending money to make money." Diane just wished she could get her hands on the money Greg had spent for that one dinner. She could have bought herself a whole new outfit instead of being embarrassed by how often she wore the same clothes to her classes.

On Friday Diane went to her afternoon class at the U. She liked the professor, but she thought he assigned an awful lot of busywork for a graduate class. When she walked out of the classroom, she was thinking how much she would have to do again this weekend. She had hoped to find something fun to do on Saturday, with Jenny not coming back until Sunday. At the very least, she planned to see a movie. Everyone had been talking about *Crocodile Dundee,* and she still hadn't seen *Pretty in Pink* either, even though Jenny had seen it twice.

As Diane walked down the hallway, she decided she would not study today. Maybe she'd get something to eat and go to the movie that night, and then commit Saturday to her books. Maybe she'd get herself a greasy hamburger. It was better than cooking for herself and then sitting home again.

"Diane."

She heard the voice behind her and stopped, but she knew who it was. She didn't need this.

"What's your hurry? Got a big date tonight?"

"No, I don't, Jerry." Jerry Parks was in her class, and had been in a couple of others in the last year. He was a teacher in Clearfield or Clinton or one of those places along the freeway between Ogden and Salt Lake. He had been a coach and a history teacher, but had gotten out

of coaching and, like Diane, was trying to finish his administrative certificate so he could become a principal. Diane didn't like the guy. He
was married, and yet he paid way too much attention to her, saying
things that hinted at flirtation.

"I'll bet you go out a lot, though, don't you?"

"Don't rub it in. You know I don't." She heard her own voice echo
down the hallway, which was mostly empty this time of afternoon. The
lights were even out at this end of the hall; it was illuminated only by
the afternoon sun filtering through the nearby glass doors.

"I don't know that." He had stopped in front of her after she had
turned around. Now he set his briefcase on the floor and slid his hands
into his pockets, as though he were going to stand and talk for a while.
It was obvious in everything he did that he thought he was quite the
ladies' man. He was fairly good-looking; he wore his hair in an early
Jimmy Carter sort of hairdo, combed over his ears, and there was no
question he worked out with weights. He was wearing a black knit shirt
today that was tight across his chest muscles.

"I've got to run. I—"

"Just talk to me for a sec. You've hardly said a word to me lately.
How's your daughter doing? Is she still running?"

"Sure. You know how distance runners are. She works out year-
round."

"I saw her name in the paper a few times this spring. She's doing
well for a kid her age."

"She did do quite well. She's hoping to do even better in cross-
country this fall." Diane took a little step back, just to signal that she
was about to end the conversation.

"My older son is going to be a big-time athlete. He's good at everything. By the time he hits high school, his biggest problem will be to
decide which sports he wants to emphasize."

"That's great. Well, I—"

"I just hope I end up with partial custody."

"What do you mean?"

"Oh . . . you know. Things between me and Gayle haven't been good for a long time. I'm starting to doubt that we can ever work it out. I've tried, but the woman thinks there's only one point of view in this world—and it's hers."

"Well . . . I hope you can work things out."

"You know, the thing about me, I'm kind of simple. I like to be home at night, play with the kids in the backyard, maybe barbecue some hamburgers on a summer evening. Gayle always wants a fancier life than I seem to be able to give her."

Diane didn't really trust that. She'd picked up on Jerry's attitudes in some things he'd said in class. She suspected that he probably wanted to make all the decisions around the house and couldn't handle it when his wife actually had an opinion. "Take the poor woman out on a date once in a while," Diane said, and she laughed. "You probably want to watch sports on TV every night of your life."

"Now you sound like her." Jerry was smiling. But he quickly looked serious again. "You know what divorce is like, Diane. But at least you have your daughter. If I end up alone, I don't know how I can take it. I need those kids in my life."

"Don't get divorced, then. Work it out."

"I wish it were that easy. You ought to know that as well as anyone."

"Jerry, my husband beat up on me. If we had only had a little trouble seeing eye to eye, I would have stayed with him."

"I know what you're saying. But there comes a time when all the love's gone. And what do you do then?"

"You don't love your wife?"

Jerry looked down toward the tile floor for a time, and when he raised his head, there was gloom in his eyes. "Not for a long time, Diane. And I guess part of it is, she's let herself go—really bad. You haven't met her, so you wouldn't know, but she must have put on fifty pounds since we first—"

"Come on, Jerry. The woman's been having your babies. Is that all you care about—that she's gained some weight?"

"Oh, no. I'm not saying that at all. It's not the weight itself. It's the way she's given up on herself. You know, it's mental as much as physical. She slouches around the house like she doesn't care about anything. And she's *negative*. Nothing I ever do is right with her."

"Yeah. And you run off to the gym and pump iron while she's cooking and cleaning and changing diapers."

"Hey, I do work out at school when I can, but I'm not a gym rat."

"Look, Jerry, I really do have to go. I hope things get better for the two of you."

"I just need to say one thing to you, Diane."

Diane waited, but she knew what was coming. She'd seen this approach before.

"Could we walk down to the student lounge and sit down for just two minutes or so? I just need to explain some things to you."

"No."

"Okay, well, maybe this isn't the right time—but I just feel like I've got to get something off my chest."

Diane took a breath and waited.

"When we were in that first class together last fall, you talked a lot about how you deal with the kids you teach, and . . . I don't know . . . it just really impressed me what a great person you are, and how sad it is that you married such a jerk. I didn't know he beat up on you until you said so just now, but I knew he must have been some kind of idiot to mess up a marriage with someone like you."

Diane was still waiting. But she was staring back at him, stern, trying to show that she didn't want this.

"It just occurred to me, even back then . . . you know . . . that maybe if the two of us had met first . . ." He ducked his head for a time, then looked up with all the sincerity he could paste on his face. "You know . . . maybe both of us would have been a lot happier."

"Jerry, just stop right there. You're married, and we're not going to have this conversation."

"But what if I'm not married one of these days? Could we have a conversation at that point?"

"No. Go home and treat your wife the way you should—and make your marriage work."

"I've tried, Diane. I really have."

"I'd love to hear your wife's side of that story."

"Oh, she'd fill your ear. She pretty much hates me now."

"You know what? I have a feeling that if we spent a little more time together, I could get to the same point—without a lot of effort."

"Wait a minute. I've never said anything out of the way to you."

"Jerry, it's inappropriate for you to bring any of this up with me. Don't do it again."

Diane turned and walked away, but behind her she heard, "Oh, well, don't you think your fanny's made of gold? You could lose a few pounds yourself, you know."

Diane spun around. "I gave you the wrong advice, Jerry. You *should* divorce your wife. There's no question, she'll be better off without you." And then Diane was gone again. He said something else, but she couldn't hear what it was—and was glad she couldn't.

She pushed her way through the glass doors and hurried to her car, got in, started it, and then pounded on the steering wheel. She wanted to do anything to create pain—anything to stop herself from crying. But she didn't succeed. A sob broke from her throat. What she hated most was that he had hurt her on purpose, the way Greg had always done. And even more, that she had let his little stab do the damage he had intended.

Was it her fault? Did she trigger something in men that made them want to injure her? She told herself no, that there were just too many men like Greg and Jerry around. She'd seen plenty of them already. They wanted to possess women, walk them about as trophies, take for themselves what they wanted from them, but subservience was the only attitude that completely satisfied them.

Diane forced herself to stop crying. And then she drove home. But the loneliness was back with a vengeance. She didn't eat a hamburger that night—she ate almost nothing, and hated that Jerry had won that part of the battle. She also decided not to go to a movie. She just didn't want to go sit in a theater all by herself.

Jenny got home on Sunday afternoon. She was all motion and excitement. On the way to her bedroom with her suitcase, she called back, "Oh, Mom, it was all so amazing. I didn't realize what an exciting city San Francisco is."

"I haven't been there since I was a kid," Diane said. "I remember it being really cold, though." She followed Jenny to her room and leaned against the door frame.

"It's *brisk*. I loved that. Summer, and yet, not hot. And it looks so different from Utah. It's like all the pictures you see of Europe."

"Did you ride on the cable cars?"

"Oh—everywhere. Mom, I went all over town. Dad was in meetings, and Marilyn only cared about going out at night. So all day I roamed around the city. I feel like it's 'my town' now."

She had thrown her suitcase on the bed, and now she opened it and started putting things away—typical of her to get everything reorganized immediately—but she couldn't stop talking. She'd spent a whole afternoon in Haight-Ashbury, checking out the bookstores and shops, and she'd walked through all the gardens in Golden Gate Park. She'd strolled from Union Square to Chinatown and North Beach, gone to the top of Nob Hill, and even wandered through the sleazy Tenderloin district, "and wasn't scared at all."

"What about Fisherman's Wharf?" Diane asked.

"Oh, sure. You have to go there. But it's mostly just a tourist trap. Souvenir shops and all that sort of thing. Actually, Ghirardelli Square is nice, and I liked watching the sea lions, but Dad said that every tourist who goes to San Francisco heads straight for the wharf, and it's really the tackiest area in the whole city."

Diane felt properly put in her place. She had been ready to say that she had eaten at a restaurant there with her family, but she was certain that Jenny, on the advice of Greg, had not eaten there.

"Mom, you can't believe the dinners we had." Jenny looked at Diane. "These people who were meeting with Dad kept telling him where we ought to eat, and he'd come back at night and take us places that were so amazing. One night we ate in Chinatown, but not at one of the tourist places. This was *real* Chinese food—Peking duck and stuffed dumplings, none of that 'made in America' chow mein kind of stuff."

Diane liked chow mein. Jenny had always liked the Utah Noodle Parlor. She would be "beyond that" from now on.

"So were these business people paying for all these dinners?"

Jenny was putting some of her clothes in a little hamper she kept in her room. She shut the lid carefully and turned around. "Mom, don't do that, okay? I don't know who paid for what. I don't want to get into all that with you. It was the best week of my entire life, and I don't want to turn it into a big argument over Dad not paying his child support."

"That's fine," Diane said. But it didn't cancel what she'd been thinking—Greg putting on this grand show for Jenny, and Diane trying to decide whether she could afford any new clothes before school started in the fall.

"Here's a promise, Mom. I'm going to make a *lot* of money. And then I'll be able to live the way I did this week *all the time.* I'm going to pay you back, too. I'm going to take you places and buy you a house, and make your life the way it really ought to be."

Diane decided not to respond to that, but it bothered her in more ways than she could ever explain to Jenny. There was so much arrogance in her voice, for one thing—and maybe that bothered Diane most. The idea that Jenny would "provide for" Diane was insulting, if the little girl only knew it, and her desire for everything material made Diane wonder what in the world she had taught her daughter.

Diane didn't want to be silent. She wanted this conversation to turn out all right. She knew, in a certain sense, that she was in competition with Greg right now. He had charmed Jenny for a week, and now Diane had to be careful not to seem like the one to put a damper on Jenny's glorious experience. "Well, honey, I'm glad you had such a great time," she said.

"But Mom, it wasn't all just fun. I saw things I've never experienced before—and I really think it's changed me. I know it has."

"What kinds of things?"

"Hunger. I saw men on the streets who had slept in alleys all night. I kept giving them all the change I had. I've seen guys downtown here in Ogden, maybe panhandling for a little money, but I've never seen people who have to live in the streets. Once you get out of the tourist areas, you see that plenty of people in San Francisco have hard lives."

"That's good, Jenny. That is something we need to remember—how blessed we actually are."

"Sure. But there's more to it than that. I want to do something about it. First, I want to make some big-time money—you know, live my dream—but then I'm going to use a lot of my money to make people's lives better. I never felt so great as I did when I gave those men my change. That's how I want to feel all the time. There's just so much you can do if you have money—and nothing you can do if you don't."

Diane knew exactly where all this was coming from. It was

language right out of Greg's mouth. And it made Diane angry. The truth was, Greg never did anything for anyone, and he had told Diane many times that hungry people were mostly just lazy. But he certainly knew how much it would impress idealistic young Jenny to tell her that he only wanted to make a lot of money so that he could do good in the world.

"I talked to one woman," Jenny said. "She was a waitress in this little diner, and it was afternoon and I was just grabbing a sandwich because I'd never gotten around to eating—and she had time to just chat with me. She started telling me about her life, how she'd been on drugs and everything, and, I don't know—it was like the first real person I'd ever met. Around here, it seems like we all pretend that life is wonderful and all that, but this woman had fought her way up from a bad neighborhood and a father who beat her, and she was raising two little kids, doing her best. Do you know what I mean, Mom? It's like I saw real life for the first time."

Diane thought about pointing out some parallels, but she couldn't do it. Jenny was too excited, and Diane knew she had to listen to her, not say anything else.

"Dad's been talking about some investments he's trying to get into—backing start-up businesses and getting a percentage for growing them into something really big. It's the kind of thing that, if you do it right, you can bring in *huge* returns. I think he's right on the edge of breaking through. He told me he'd be happy to show me the ropes, introduce me to that kind of business. I could go to college at the U and work for him at the same time. I could get a business degree, and maybe a law degree—but you know, really learn business from the real world."

"What's happening with that indictment against your father? Is that really all over with?"

Jenny was putting sweaters back into a drawer. She looked over at Diane, who was still standing in the doorway of the bedroom. Diane saw some defensiveness again, and she heard it in Jenny's voice. "That was dropped a long time ago, Mom. He told the whole truth, and his partner is going to end up in jail. He's out on appeal for now, but he's going to have to do his time. The thing is, though, Dad was as surprised as anyone by what the guy had been doing."

Diane nodded. "That's good," she said, trying to sound positive.

"He really does want to do a lot of good, Mom. I get excited talking to him about it."

"That's great, honey."

But Diane's voice wasn't sounding natural—not even to herself—and surely Jenny could hear it. Jenny walked back to her suitcase and looked into it, then turned back toward Diane again. "Mom, I wasn't going to bring this up—and maybe I shouldn't—but I'm not sure Marilyn is the right sort of woman for Dad."

"Why do you say that?"

"She's just . . . I don't know. I hate to say that she's dumb—but she acts like it. She doesn't keep up on anything or have any interests that she ever talks about. I think Dad gets really disgusted with her."

"I've seen her. She's beautiful."

"She's a *knockout.* But she drives Dad crazy with the stupid things she says."

"Did he say that to you?"

"No. You can just tell by the way he talks to her. I think he runs out of patience with her. Sometimes he gets really sarcastic."

Diane knew she had better not comment on that one.

"I don't mean he's mean to her. I just think he gets tired of listening to the comments she makes about everything."

"Well . . . that's too bad."

"I don't think they're getting along very well. I was in an adjoining room, but I could hear in my room when their voices got loud. A couple of times they got in some pretty serious arguments."

"Could you hear both of their voices?" Diane asked.

Jenny took a long look at Diane. Finally she said, "Dad has a louder voice. But I'm sure they were both arguing."

Diane nodded one more time, and she let the whole thing go. She hoped that Jenny had gotten her eyes opened a little, but it didn't seem so. More likely, she was thinking the way she had since she was a little girl, always hoping that Diane and Greg would somehow end up back together.

CHAPTER 11

Midterms for Diane's summer session were coming up. She was settled in at the kitchen table, reviewing notes and rereading the chapters she had marked in her textbook. When the phone rang, she guessed it was Jenny, who would probably need a ride home. Jenny had been working out with some friends from her cross-country team. She had a driver's license now, but no car of her own, and Diane usually preferred to take her places rather than to be stuck home without a car.

Diane slid her chair back from the table and stepped to the wall phone. "Hello," she said, her mind still on her reading. She had been hoping Jenny wouldn't call quite so soon.

"Diane?"

"Yes."

"It's Spence."

"Oh . . . hi." Diane wished she wouldn't feel so much excitement. She knew she had to turn him down this time.

"I was just wondering . . . I was thinking about taking my boat up to Pineview tomorrow—you know, just to run it around a little. I wondered if you could get away for a couple of hours in the afternoon."

"I'm studying for some tests right now. I just don't have the time."

"We could just run up and back. It wouldn't have to take a long time. You could probably use a little break."

"I don't know, Spence. I'm not sure I know what the point of all this is."

"The point is that it's supposed to be a pretty day tomorrow, and there's nothing quite as fun on a hot day as a boat ride."

"And Heather won't be around."

"Well, yeah. There is that."

"Maybe we've played that game out."

"Diane, you need a break from all your studying. Go for a boat ride with me."

"Well . . . I really . . . couldn't be gone very long."

"That's fine. I was thinking about noon, or one o'clock, somewhere in there."

"Let's say two."

"Okay. I'll come by for you."

"You don't have to come clear over here, pulling that boat. Why don't I just meet you at your house?" What she didn't admit—after making her point about Heather—was that she had no idea when Jenny might be home.

"It's not a problem. I could run over in another car, and then—"

"No. Just give me your address. I'll come over there."

So he gave her his address on the east bench. It was a nice area of Ogden, where the houses were old but elegant. She was curious to see what his house was like. But once she hung up the phone, she was immediately sorry she had said yes. She should have told him she had a date in the evening and really couldn't get away in the afternoon. But when she pulled her chair back under the table, she had trouble concentrating on her books. She told herself this would be their last "date"—or whatever it was they were doing. It hadn't felt right to break things off over the phone, but she would do it on their way home from the boat ride, and that would be one stress in her life that she could get rid of.

Jenny managed to get her own ride home, and she was hardly inside the door before she announced that she was leaving again soon. She and some of her girlfriends were going to a movie, she said. She went off to her bedroom for a few minutes and then reappeared at the kitchen door. Her Burger King job provided her with a little of her own money for movies and such things, but to Diane, she seemed to be on the go all the time. Jenny liked certain boys who were probably involved in some of these evenings out. Derek was still an interest, but so was a new boy named David. When Diane asked about either one, though, Jenny wouldn't say much. Derek was "too stuck on himself," she had complained to Diane one time, and David was "cute but kind of dense, if you want to know the truth."

Diane had never shared a whole lot with her own mom back when she was in high school, but she had always expected a time to come when she and Jenny would talk about "everything," since their lives had been so close for such a long time. It wasn't happening, though, and the worst thing Diane could do was ask Jenny too many questions. Jenny revealed what she chose to tell, and would express her feelings only when she was in the right mood. But it was Diane who was close-mouthed today—not wanting to mention Spence.

The next day, at noon, when she dropped Jenny off at work, Diane told her, "I'm going to be gone for a while this afternoon. I should be back by five or so. How late do you work?"

"It depends on how busy it is. Probably six. Tracy will pick me up, so you don't have to."

"Will you be home for the evening, or—"

"I doubt it. Not on a Friday night. I'm sure Tracy and I will do something. Where are you going?"

"You mean this afternoon?"

"Yeah."

Diane had planned what she would say. "I'm going to meet with someone."

But Jenny asked the wrong question. "You mean, down at the school?"

Diane said, "Yes," before she could think of something else to say, and she felt her face get hot. She hadn't planned to lie, not when she had taught Jenny all her life not to do that. But now she had done it. "Well, not actually *at* school, but . . ."

It was a burning day and Diane could feel the heat pouring into the car. She didn't want to get all sweaty and have to shower again before she met Spence. And she didn't want to answer any more of Jenny's questions.

Jenny seemed to notice Diane's embarrassment, but she just took a second glance and then let it go. "Well, anyway, Tracy and I are going to take a short run after work, and then I'll probably be home for a little while before we take off again." She laughed, as if she knew that her life was a little crazy.

Diane told herself that she had better wear a hat that afternoon, and not get herself sunburned. She even decided that at some point she needed to tell Jenny where she had been—just so she wasn't being dishonest.

Diane hurried home and spent what time she had getting ready, even though she was just planning to wear khakis and a T-shirt. She fussed with her hair much longer than she really needed to, and she found herself doing her nails, although that was something she rarely bothered with. And all the while she was telling herself what nonsense it was to worry about such things. Spence surely didn't care what her fingernails looked like—and this *was* their last date.

And then she left a little sooner than she needed to, just to make sure she could find his house. She found it ten minutes early and drove around until she was five minutes late, just so she wouldn't seem too eager. When she drove back into his long driveway, she was stunned by his house. It wasn't one of the old houses in the neighborhood, but a new place, built on a little prominence in the high foothills. Actually, it seemed overdone. It made Diane think of an antebellum mansion in the South, with pillars and even a portico in the front that the drive-way circled under.

A pickup truck was parked in front of the house, with a huge boat already hooked up to it. Diane didn't see Spence, so she walked around the boat to the front door and rang the doorbell. She heard a whole melody of chimes, which struck her as pretentious. She decided that Spence's wife must have been way too busy spending her husband's money. Diane liked a pretty house, but she didn't think people needed to show off their wealth.

Spence was suddenly at the door, smiling, his white teeth flashing, and seeming more relaxed than he had been on the phone. He was wearing jeans and a Hard Rock Cafe T-shirt—hardly what she had expected. "Hey, we're all set. I've got everything in the boat," he said. "Just step in for a minute. I've got to find a hat."

Diane walked in and stood in a little entryway as Spence disap-peared up a flight of stairs. Diane was more impressed by the house now. There was a big living room off to the left, with a vaulted ceiling and a huge rock fireplace. In the back she could see an expansive kitchen with more cabinet space than she had ever seen in a house. What impressed her most was the tasteful way everything was fur-nished. The house itself was rather dramatic, but the décor was com-fortable, with tan finishes, dark woodwork, earth tones. The big sectional couch in the living room looked soft and cozy around the fireplace, and the room looked lived-in. Diane had once dreamed of having a beautiful house. Although she had changed her mind over the years about the importance of that sort of thing, she found herself lik-ing this, wondering what it would be like to live in such a home.

In less than a minute, Spence was jogging down the stairs, a white baseball cap in his hand. "It's good you're here today," he said, smiling.

"I have a woman come in on Thursdays to clean. I didn't do that for a long time, but I just couldn't handle everything. We still make a mess out of the place at times."

Diane saw no sign of that. "Who cooks?" she asked.

"I do, more than anyone. Christine helps me, when she's home from college in the summer. Steve and Heather are always coming and going. I'm afraid I feed them way too much pizza and fast food. Steve charges in, nukes himself half a dozen frozen burritos, and he's gone again. Celeste was a stickler about everyone eating dinner together, but I'm afraid I've lost control of that."

"I know the feeling. Just lately, that's what's happening to Jenny and me." Diane heard the front door open, and she turned. A teenaged girl with wild hair, dyed a strange shade of dark purple, had stepped in. She was wearing an extremely short denim skirt, red tights, and a crazy shirt, all bronze and orange and green. This had to be Heather.

"Oh . . . uh . . . hi," the girl said. She looked taken aback.

Diane glanced at Spence, who stepped quickly toward her. "Hi, Heather," he said. "Uh . . . what are you doing home?" He sounded like a kid who'd been caught doing something wrong. Diane was embarrassed.

"I don't know. I just blew off a couple of classes. I'm kind of, like, sick."

But Heather was looking at Diane, not her dad, as though waiting for an explanation.

"This is Diane Lyman, Heather. We're going to run up to Pineview and take the boat out for a little run." He hesitated, then added, "Do you want to go with us?"

She laughed. "No, thanks. I'm going to go sleep for a while." She was actually sort of cute when she smiled, her teeth straight and white, like her dad's.

"Okay. Are you really sick, or . . ."

"I must be. That's what I told the nurse." She walked on by Diane, looking her over as she passed.

"Nice to meet you," Diane mumbled.

When Heather reached the stairs, she stopped and looked back. "You're Jenny Lyman's mother, aren't you?"

Diane turned and faced her. "Yes, I am."

Heather nodded a couple of times, smiling knowingly. "You've sort of got the same look." She looked at her dad. "She's too good-looking for you, Dad," she said, nodding again, looking cocky.

"Go get some sleep," Spence said. "I'll be back in a little while."

"You weren't even going to tell me about this, were you?"

"I told you this morning I was going to take the boat out."

"But that's not all you're taking out, now, is it, Father?"

"Heather, that's enough."

"What did I say?" She shrugged, raising both hands, palms up, and then she turned and trudged up the stairs.

"I'm sorry," Spence whispered. "She's supposed to be in summer school to make up for classes she flunked last year, but she cuts more often than she attends." He opened the door and they walked out to the truck. Diane climbed in, but she was wondering whether she shouldn't just get in her car and drive back home.

Spence was clearly embarrassed. As he drove along Harrison Boulevard toward Ogden Canyon, he talked some more about Heather's troubles, his inability to deal with her. Diane wasn't sure what to say. The worst thing was, Spence seemed subdued now—the mouse having been caught in his own trap.

But he soon let the subject go, and asked Diane about school, the weather—anything. He seemed set upon keeping the attention away from his own problems.

When they reached the reservoir, he did seem to know what he was doing with a boat. Diane helped him a little, but he had her get in the boat while he got into the water to release it from the trailer. He parked the truck and then got himself even wetter getting out to where he could climb up.

Diane liked the boat ride. It was a hot afternoon, so she liked the speed, the refreshing air, even the spray at times. Spence stood up most of the time, driving, and by then he was laughing and joking with Diane. He seemed to be in his element here—and apparently convinced he should put the little incident with Heather behind him. "I've needed to do this," he told her at one point, and Diane thought she saw that. She had sensed back at the house how strained his life was, maybe mostly because of Heather, but Diane also wondered about the other kids and what problems they might be having. He had a daughter, Allison, who had gone to Weber State for a couple of years and then had married. Another daughter, Christine, was going to Utah State University. Steve was a senior at Ogden High.

Maybe the others were old enough that they were handling things better than Heather. She had been in her early teens all through the illness and was only fourteen when her mother finally died. It was easy for Diane to understand why she was having troubles; still, looking at her, hearing the "attitude" in her voice, Diane thought she understood better why Spence had decided to stay out of an attachment for the present, and Diane certainly didn't want to get in the middle of his problems. She had been a little upset with him for being so intimidated by his daughter, but now she felt sorry for him. He really was dealing with a problem bigger than Diane had ever had to face.

Spence let Diane drive the boat, and Diane found that to be fun. It was a bigger boat than she'd ever ridden in before, and surprisingly powerful. When he took the wheel back, he drove toward the east end of the reservoir and beached the boat on Cemetery Point, a spit of land that protruded into the water from the Huntsville area. "I brought us some lunch," he said. "I thought it would be fun to build a little fire and roast some hot dogs."

"Okay," Diane said, even though she hadn't expected to stay that long. He didn't seem to be a "hot dog" kind of guy, and she wondered how he would manage to find enough wood for a fire.

As it turned out, he had all that worked out. Clearly, he had been planning again. He had a little bundle of kindling and a burlap bag full of scrap lumber. He had also brought his picnic basket again.

He got all that off the boat, and then he helped Diane down. He took her in his arms and carried her to keep her dry. On shore, he set her down gently, even slowly, onto the sand. She stayed close, looked at him. "Thank you, Superman," she said.

He smiled. "I'm sorry that I'll have to change my suit," he said, "and put my glasses back on."

But they didn't laugh. There was a little too much reality in what he'd said, and they both knew it.

Diane was thinking that the heat would be terrible out on the beach, especially with a fire, but there was a picnic area off the beach, complete with little canopies and fire pits. Diane helped him carry all the stuff, and they hiked up the little hill to a picnic table.

As it turned out, he had brought fancy bratwurst, not the usual grocery store wieners, and some bakery buns. He also had a little cooler full of drinks, a potato salad, a vegetable tray, and plenty of condiments. All this seemed to come from a deli, but he had put some time into it, picking out nice things. It all sort of flew in the face of the idea that he had only planned a quick boat ride. She figured he had taken the whole morning to get ready.

He had even brought metal roasting sticks from home, so he didn't have to go looking for switches to cut—which he wouldn't have found out there anyway. By the time the two had roasted their bratwurst and eaten, Diane was becoming increasingly aware that their time together would soon end. She hated the thought of going home and being alone again on a Friday night.

They talked for a time about this and that, nothing important, avoiding any of the subjects that might be difficult. He told her about the projects his company was working on, and she told him about the classes she'd taken that summer at the university. They also joked about their difficulties trying to keep up with what was happening in the world these days—music changing so drastically, and all the movies they no longer felt comfortable going to. AIDS was spreading, and it was frightening to think what it could do in the world if it weren't controlled soon—or if people didn't change their behaviors. They were both just old enough not to feel quite connected to the culture, the values that were taking over everywhere. And they were comfortable with each other, having grown up in what seemed a different kind of world.

They finished their picnic and packed the leftovers back in the basket, but they continued to sit at the table in the shade. A little breeze was coming up the canyon, making the temperature more bearable. "This world really is messed up," Spence was saying. "That's one of the reasons I worry about Heather. Right now, this whole thing she's doing with her hair and her clothes—it just seems like her way to defy me. I don't think she's doing anything really bad; I don't know whether she would ever take drugs or start sleeping with guys. I've talked to her a lot, but she seems to take pleasure in the idea that she's scaring me. She won't open up to me at all."

"I know what you're talking about. I'm having the same trouble with Jenny."

"I thought she was the super kid, doing everything right."

"She is, in some ways." Diane looked out toward the water. There were a lot of water-skiers out there now, making wakes in the water. "But she wants to have her own life. I've probably been *too* close to her over the years. She does well in school, but I'm hearing negative comments about church and seminary, and she thinks her dad can do nothing wrong."

Spence nodded. She liked that his hair had gotten messy and he wasn't doing anything about it. But the subject had brought a solemnity into his eyes. "Her dad's a slick character. I had some real estate dealings with him one time. I've watched him work on people. She'll see through him sooner or later."

"Maybe. But I don't want her to get too disappointed, either. She has a right to think her own father is an okay guy."

"Not if he's dangerous to her."

"I know. That's the other side of it."

"Do you think I should clamp down on Heather—tell her she can't go around looking the way she does?"

"Isn't it a little late for that?"

Diane hadn't meant the words as a rebuke, but she could see that he had taken them that way. He gave a solid nod and said, "I just haven't known what to do. When Celeste was alive, Heather was our stalwart. She kept telling the rest of us that we had to have faith. We had to keep praying and Mom would be all right. I told her over and over that it might not turn out that way, but that would make her furious. When Celeste finally died, I think she saw it as my fault—that I hadn't prayed as hard as she had. Not that she actually said that. She never tells me what she thinks now—but she won't go to church, and when I try to get her to come to family prayer, she refuses. You just know what she's thinking—that she asked for bread and got a stone. And now she's going to get back at God."

"That's hard."

Diane saw the tears well up in Spence's eyes. He looked away and was silent for a long time before he said: "I keep telling myself she'll grow out of this. She talks a little more to her sisters, and they keep assuring me that Heather's still Heather, underneath all that changed appearance. But she was such a sweet little girl—always a daddy's girl—and now she goes out of her way to get to me, any way she can. I keep thinking that if I give her some room for a while, she'll come back to me sooner or later."

"She could be waiting for you to say, 'Enough is enough.' Maybe that's why she keeps pushing you."

"I know. I've tried that—to some degree—but it sets off an explosion every time. My other daughters keep telling me to back off for now, but I don't know. Every day of my life I feel like I'm handling the situation wrong. I watch Steve, too, sort of reacting the other way. It's like he's decided not to have emotions. He won't talk about his mother, won't respond to anything. All he wants from me is money so he can buy every toy he can think of. He's got a sound system in his room like you wouldn't believe, and he goes in there, cranks his music up, and just stays there. He's got a few friends, but he's not close to them the way he used to be."

"What about your older daughters?"

"Allison does the best. She's got her husband now. She's working while he finishes college, and they're still in that 'newlywed bliss' stage of life. Christine was depressed for a long time, but she's pretty resilient. She's doing well in college, getting good grades and everything, and she takes classes at the institute. She's probably the most religious of the kids." He chuckled. "The scary part is, Heather is probably the smartest. In elementary school, she was a whiz. I never thought I'd have to worry about her."

"Yeah. That's how Jenny was. And still is, I guess. But she has her own demons. This thing of having her dad come into her life, disappear, show up with presents, disappear again—it all takes a toll. She's *driven* to do big things in her life. It's like she thinks she has to make a lot of money and own fancy homes—anything to be important in the world."

"My kids have had too much. I know that now. I set out to build Celeste a dream house. You know how that is, when you're young, and you get these ideas in your head. But the house I built never did fit Celeste's personality. She made it nice—turned it into a house for a family—but it wasn't her dream; it was mine. And she didn't have it very long. Now, I just want to get rid of the thing as soon as I can, except that I don't want to create one more big change right now. I guess I'll wait until Steve and Heather are more on their own—if that ever happens."

"We're all dealing with stuff, aren't we? Everyone is. The problems just take different shapes."

"I guess. But if we all had the chance to pick our problems in the premortal life—the way some people claim—I don't think I picked losing Celeste. I'm not strong enough." He smiled. "I think the Lord got me mixed up with someone else."

There was a long pause while Diane and Spence both looked out at the water. Diane felt miserable. "I want to wade in the water," she said. She got up and headed toward the beach. She didn't know whether he was following, but when she looked back, he was gathering everything up, and then he was heading her way, carrying the picnic basket and the cooler. Diane sat down and pulled off her tennis shoes and socks and rolled up her pants.

When Spence reached her, he said, "Diane, I'm sorry. I didn't have to get into all that again."

She walked into the water. She liked its coolness.

"I do need someone to talk to, but it's not fair to ask you out and then just unload everything on you."

"It's fine. We were both talking about our problems." She stepped deeper into the water, not minding if her pants got wet.

"I don't see how I could marry anyone—not in the foreseeable future. But it's nice to have a friend."

"I have no interest in getting married either, Spence. I already told you that."

"Could we keep getting together once in a while—you know, just to . . . talk. I won't blubber to you about Celeste. I would just—"

"You *should* talk about her, Spence." She had gone in almost up to her waist in the water, knowing all the while that it was a stupid thing to do. She thought about diving in, swimming a little in her clothes, just to feel cool all over. "But what about Heather? Is she going to throw a fit when you get home?"

"Probably."

"So what is it you want me to do? Keep sneaking around behind her back?"

"No. I'm going to be open with her about this. I'll tell her we're just friends. But are you okay with that?"

"I don't know, Spence. I need to think about it. I think it's probably not a very good idea."

He didn't say anything, and she kept easing her way into deeper water. "Be careful," he warned. "There's a drop-off out there, not very far out."

"Okay," she said, and she didn't go out any farther. But she wanted to.

Chapter 12

Spence didn't call during the weekend, and he didn't call on Monday or Tuesday. Diane began to believe that he had seen what she had: that it was pointless to keep getting together. But on Wednesday evening she answered the phone and heard, "Diane?"

"Hi," she said, and felt her breath holding.

"So how's the studying going?" he asked.

"Okay," she said. "I got through my first midterm all right. I have one more this week."

"Oh, come on. I'll bet you're the star student in all your classes."

That was actually sort of true, but Diane didn't say so. She told him, "I get good grades, but I have to study my head off. I can't read something once and have the information cold, the way Jenny can. I hate to admit it, but she got that from her dad."

There was a little hesitation, and Diane wondered. Maybe he was calling to tell her he wouldn't be calling anymore. It was what she had decided was best—but now, with him on the phone, she was afraid he would say it.

"I was wondering, would you and Jenny like to come over on the 24th of July? The kids could swim, and I could barbecue some steaks."

She leaned back against the kitchen cabinet. "I don't know, Spence. Do you think that's a good idea?"

He laughed. "Probably not. But it seems worth a try—you know, just to let our kids get to know each other a little better. I've been thinking, maybe it would be good for Heather to be around someone like Jenny. They're both smart girls, and they might like each other once they get past their obvious differences."

"Or hate each other."

"Yeah. Maybe. But I'd like to see what could happen."

Diane didn't know what he meant by that. Was he thinking he wanted to spend a lot of time with her, and so he wanted to test the waters to see what their kids would think? Or was he hoping that someone could help him with Heather? "We usually go to Salt Lake on the 24th," she finally said. "My mom's family has a big get-together, and Jenny really likes to be with her cousins. I think she'd be mad if I tried to pull her away from that."

"Well . . . what about the day after? The 24th is on a Thursday. I've decided to take that whole weekend off and stay around here. If I tell the kids I have a little party cooked up on Friday, maybe I can get them to stick around. I'll invite my married daughter and her husband, and you can get to know them, too."

"I thought the whole idea was just to get together and talk once in a while—as friends."

"Well . . . yeah. But everyone ought to get acquainted."

Diane wanted to ask him why, but she didn't. She wanted to think, though, that he'd been thinking about her since the day on the boat— the same as she'd been thinking about him. "Well, let me check with Jenny. I don't know whether she has any plans. I guess we could try it."

Two weeks later, Diane and Jenny were standing at Spence's front door and the doorbell was ringing. Diane glanced at Jenny, who was rolling her eyes as the chimes went on and on. Jenny had finally agreed to come, after a long negotiation, but she wasn't happy about it.

Spence answered the door. He was wearing swim trunks with a blue shirt over the top—but it was a nice dress shirt, a pinpoint weave, starched. "Come on through," he said. "Everyone's out in back by the pool. Wow, Jenny, you're a beauty."

Diane glanced to see Jenny blush. "Thank you," she said. Then, when she stepped inside, she said, "Oh, my gosh!" She did a slow 360, taking it all in. "Your house is *wonderful.*"

"Thanks. It's really too big for me, with all the kids leaving. I'll probably put it on the market one of these years."

"Hold on to it a while and I'll buy it from you. That's my goal—to have a nice house in Utah, and one in Switzerland, and one in Bermuda, or somewhere like that."

Jenny had said things like that to Diane at times, but she'd never been quite so specific. Diane was always amazed at Jenny's confidence, how easily she spoke to adults, and especially how much she liked to reveal her extravagant goals. It almost seemed her way of saying that she was not like Diane—not some twenty-thousand-dollar-a-year schoolteacher. In her own mind, she was apparently already rich, with only the matter of acquiring some money left to finish the project.

"That's great," Spence said. "I used to talk about things like that, but somewhere along the way, I lost interest. I told your mom, I'm really kind of a stay-at-home guy. I like to travel once in a while, but I don't think I'd like to be bouncing around from one house to another."

"I'm happiest when I'm on the go," Jenny said, as though she was already living her dream. Diane often wondered what would happen to Jenny if she ended up settling for far, far less.

Spence led the two back through the big kitchen, which Jenny also loved, and out the back door to a covered patio. Diane could see Heather sitting at the far end of the pool. She was under an umbrella, not out in the sun, and she was reading a magazine. A tall boy was in the pool—Steve, Diane assumed. Alongside the pool, on a towel, was another young woman, lying facedown in a two-piece swimsuit. There was a Sprite can close to her head, a container of lotion, and a well-worn paperback book, presently unopened.

"Come here for a minute, Steve, Christine. I want you to meet someone."

Steve pulled himself out of the pool immediately. He was built well, like his father, but thinner. His hair was slicked back, wet and black, and he had dark eyes, too—probably more like his mother's. He grabbed a towel and threw it over his shoulders, then walked toward the patio. He was a nice-looking boy, but there was a swagger in his walk, and as he approached, he seemed almost too easy about his mostly naked body. "Hi," he said.

"Steve, this is Diane Lyman. And this is her daughter, Jenny."

"I've seen you at school," Steve said. "What are you, Heather's age?"

"Yes," Jenny said. She was wearing tan shorts and a pretty purple T-shirt, with her swimsuit underneath. She seemed to grow an inch every month these days, and she was looking very tall and very tan. Diane watched Steve's eyes run over her, as though he were trying to decide whether he was interested.

"Aren't you on the track team?"

"Yeah. You play tennis, don't you? I see you out on the court when we're running sometimes."

Christine was finally approaching. "Sounds like she's been checking you out, Steve," she said.

"No doubt. I *do* look good in tennis shorts."

Christine's complexion was much lighter, but Diane had the feeling she dyed her hair to make it so blonde. She was tall, too, but she looked softer, a little pudgy around the middle and in her thighs. She was wearing black Ray-Ban sunglasses that hid her eyes, so she wasn't easy to get a take on, but Diane heard some malice in her voice when

155

she said, "Right, Steve. If you looked half as good as you think you do, you'd be *perfect.*"

"We'll let Jenny judge," Steve said, smiling. "Would you say I'm perfect—or just *close* to perfect?"

"Actually, you remind me of a movie star," Jenny said. She rubbed her chin. "I'm trying to think which one. Oh, yeah, I know. Pee Wee Herman."

That got a big laugh from Christine, who added, "No. I think he looks more like Richard Simmons. You ought to see his hair when it's not plastered down."

Steve, all this time, was shaking his head. He was trying to smile, but Diane wasn't sure he liked what he was hearing. "Very funny. Very funny," he mumbled, and then he walked back to the pool, dropped his towel, and dove into the water. Diane could hardly believe that Jenny had said such a thing to someone she had barely met. She wondered how Jenny treated people at school.

Christine had clearly enjoyed Jenny's little insult, but just when Diane thought maybe the two were going to hit it off, she said, "Well, I've got to get ten more minutes of sun on my back," and she walked away.

Heather hadn't moved from where she was sitting, and Spence hadn't asked her to. Diane had the feeling that she had told her dad not to push Jenny on her, and Spence was avoiding a scene. But now that the other two had walked away, Jenny was left just standing there.

"I think Allison and her husband will be coming up from Salt Lake sometime this afternoon," Spence said, "but you never know with them. 'On time' is an hour late, and 'late' sometimes becomes 'never.'"

Diane suddenly realized that she had no idea what to do. She actually did have a swimsuit on under her clothes, but she was not sure she wanted to swim. She was too self-conscious about the extra pounds she was carrying. She wasn't sure she wanted Spence to see her.

"Jenny, do you want to swim?" Spence asked. "Diane, maybe you could help me figure out when this chicken has cooked enough. I usually do steaks, but the girls wanted chicken today."

Diane glanced at Jenny, who was looking out toward the pool, clearly unsure what to do. "Go ahead and swim," Diane said, but Jenny didn't answer. She knew Jenny well enough to know what was going through her head. She was well aware that she was pretty, but she also worried that she was too tall and skinny. She was probably asking herself whether she wanted to strip down in front of Steve and dive into the pool with him.

"Go ahead. I'll come in and swim with you in a few minutes."

Jenny must have considered the alternatives. If she didn't swim, where would she sit, whom would she talk to? So as Diane walked away, she slipped her T-shirt over her head. When Diane looked back, she was already jumping into the pool, as though she wanted to cover herself up with water as fast as she could. But she was a good swimmer, and she swam the length of the pool and back, then turned and started another lap.

Near the pool was a big, brick barbecue pit. Several chicken breasts were cooking on the grill. Spence began to paint them with more barbeque sauce, and he said, softly, "This is really sort of awkward. Heather threw a big fit about it. She wasn't even going to come out here. I told her, for once, that I wasn't taking no for an answer, but she settled in down where she is, and she's just daring me to bring Jenny over to her. If I do, I don't know what she'll say."

"Maybe we should just stay a few minutes and then—"

"No. If I let Heather decide for herself, she might do the right thing. She's really unpredictable. The one thing I always know is that the harder I push, the more she pushes back."

"Jenny will probably go say something to her. That's just the way she is."

"I hope she does. Heather likes to be difficult, but sometimes—

without any warning—she can suddenly be halfway human." He laughed. "Or at least a fourth."

Diane looked back and saw that Jenny was still doing laps, still avoiding everyone. "Maybe I should get in the pool," Diane said.

"Go ahead. Take a swim. I can manage this chicken."

"Okay. But don't look."

"What?" He turned toward her, still holding the brush he had been using on the chicken.

"I'm too fat. I don't want you to see me in my swimming suit."

"Fat?"

"Yes. Gravity's gone to work on my body. All my fat cells are slipping downward."

He was still looking amazed. "Diane, I can't believe you'd say that. Every woman who sees you must say, 'If only I looked like that.'"

"*Every* woman wants to look like someone else."

"And who would you like to look like?"

Diane smiled. "I don't know."

"See. You can't think of anyone."

"Demi Moore."

He laughed, and she loved the way he squared himself to her and looked directly into her eyes. "You can't be serious," he said.

"Well, no."

She could see in his eyes that he meant all this, that he really did think she was pretty—and she liked that—but she wondered, too, as she always had, whether that was all that he was seeing. How did she really compare to Celeste?

"Well . . . anyway. You go ahead and swim, and I won't watch . . . much."

Diane smiled, and then she walked back to the covered patio. She took off her clothes and left them with Jenny's, but she was still hearing what he'd just said, and she was feeling the way he had looked at her. As she walked toward the pool, she saw that he did take a glance.

And he smiled. She smiled too, and maybe blushed. This was all too much like being a teenager again.

She hurried and dove in, but she wasn't nearly the swimmer that Jenny was. She paddled into the middle of the pool and waited there for Jenny, who was still doing laps. "Hey, slow down," she said.

Jenny stopped and stood up in the water. "I decided I'd get my workout in," she said. Diane saw her spot Steve, who had pulled himself out of the pool again and was sitting at the deep end with his legs dangling in the water. "Do we have to stay very long?"

"Spence has the chicken about ready. Once we eat, we can just go."

"They're all so *charming.* Heather won't even look in my direction."

"I know. It's awkward. But let's see how it goes."

"Why? What's this all about? Are you and Spence thinking ahead or something—how we'll all be one big happy family?"

"No. Not at all. We're just friends, and Spence wanted his kids to get to know us."

"That doesn't sound like 'just friends' to me."

It didn't to Diane either. She wished she did know what was going on.

It wasn't long until Spence got the lunch ready. He brought a long table out from the house and set it up on the patio, then had Christine help him set it. As it turned out, he—or one of his kids—had prepared a big tossed salad and cut up a lot of fruit. There was also some of that same potato salad he'd taken with them on the picnic—surely purchased at the same place.

Diane was wearing a rather conservative one-piece suit, but she wasn't sure what to do to cover herself once she got out of the water. She hadn't brought any sort of pool wrap. So she got out of the pool and headed straight for her clothes. She slipped her shirt and shorts on, along with her boat shoes, and figured her clothes would dry soon enough in the heat. Jenny did the same thing, but the Holmes kids didn't bother. Christine and Steve came to the table with towels over their shoulders, and Heather, when she finally walked to that end of the pool, didn't have to change. She was wearing black in all this heat—black jeans and an old Def Leppard T-shirt. She sat down at the table, as far from her dad as she could get, and didn't say a word.

Two places were set for Allison and her husband, but they still hadn't come. That left a blank space at one end of the table, with Spence on the opposite end. Diane and Jenny were on one side, Diane facing Christine and Jenny facing Steve. Heather had chosen the spot across from no one.

Spence called no attention to Heather. He looked around, seeming unsure, and then focused on Steve. "Son," he said, "would you say the blessing?"

Steve said a prayer, but it was quick and perfunctory, as though he hadn't wanted to say it, and that added to the tension.

People started passing food, saying nothing, until Spence said, "Jenny, you're quite the swimmer. You looked like you could go on like that forever."

"Hey, she's a distance runner," Steve said. "She's got big lungs."

Christine found that much too funny, and Diane was pretty sure that Steve had made a veiled reference to her flat chest—or at least that Christine had taken it that way.

"Have you been running a lot this summer?" Spence asked, obviously choosing to avoid Steve's comment.

"I run all year. I'm sort of addicted to it, I think. I feel rotten if I go a few days without working out."

"Oh, me too," Christine said. "No pain, no gain. There's nothing quite like the burn I feel when I walk from the house all the way out to my car."

Heather liked that. She bent to look around Steve at Christine, and she nodded a couple of times. "Now, me, I like to go *straight* to the pain," she said. "I just bang my head against a wall."

"Yeah, well, little sister," Steve said, "you've banged your head a few too many times. Can't you see that Jenny's *making something of herself?*"

Steve was laughing, but his sarcasm was obvious. Maybe this was a little revenge for the Pee Wee Herman comment.

But Jenny didn't flinch. "You're right about that," she said. "That's exactly what I'm doing." Diane saw her focus on Steve, then Christine, then Heather, sort of staring them down, as if to say, *You aren't going to get to me.*

Steve and Christine were both smiling, and seemed willing to let the whole matter drop, but Heather said, "I already made something of myself." She lifted her hands and threw her head back. "Ta da! What you see is what you get."

"Yeah. That's what we're afraid of," Steve said.

But Spence was clearly nervous about the way all this was going. "So how's the chicken?" he asked. "Did I overcook it?"

Steve made a comment about it being "not quite cremated," but at least the question had taken the attention off Jenny. For a time the conversation wandered, but the three siblings turned everything into a joke, and usually into little insults directed toward each other. Diane wanted to get away as quickly as she could. Spence had warned her that his kids had problems, but she thought they seemed like spoiled brats more than anything, convinced that they were wonderfully clever. At one point, Steve made fun of Heather for her bad attendance at summer school, and Heather, again, turned that into a sarcastic remark about Jenny, the "good student." She made the term sound like a dirty name.

Christine, almost as though she knew what Diane and Jenny must be thinking, finally said, "Jenny, don't let my siblings bother you.

They're still in their formative years, and slow in the process—sort of *unformed.* I'm sure it's all part of losing their mommy at such an early age."

"Jenny likes my form," Steve said. "She's been checking me out in my tennis shorts."

"I'm formed," Heather said. "*De*-formed. But at least I don't have to go running every day—and feel the pain—just to *make something of myself.*"

"Heather, that's enough," Spence said.

But Steve was already saying, "I don't buy your theory, Christine. Jenny would appear not to have a dad, and she's not messed up like Heather."

"I do have a dad." Jenny's voice was suddenly a little too tight.

Steve didn't back off. "Oh, really? So where is he?"

"He lives in Salt Lake."

Spence raised both his hands. "Steve, let's stop this kind of—"

"Divorced, huh? I think that's supposed to mess a kid up pretty bad, too."

"That's why she needs to make something of herself," Heather said. "She's de-formed like me. She just tries to hide it—like all the other phonies she hangs around with at Ogden High."

"Heather, I'm not going to listen to any more of this," Spence said, his voice louder than before.

But Jenny was already pushing back her chair and standing up. "Look, I didn't ask to come over here. I didn't want to. But at least I know how to act like a human being. I think you three escaped from some zoo."

Jenny tripped a little getting past her chair. In two long steps she reached the back door, swung it open, and was gone.

"Diane, I'm sorry," Spence said.

"Hey, I didn't mean to get anything started," Christine said. "I was just joking around."

"I didn't hear anything that made me laugh," Diane said. "Jenny's had a lot to deal with in her life. And yes, my divorce has been hard on her. But she does the best she can. I think maybe you three ought to do the same thing."

What surprised Diane was that she didn't see defiance coming back from any of them. Heather had been ducking her head during Jenny's departure, but now she glanced up for a moment. There was a surprising sadness in her eyes.

Steve said, "Look, I'm sorry. I was just, you know, giving her a hard time—like she did to me. I didn't mean anything."

"I don't buy that, Steve," Spence said. "You three spend your whole lives insulting each other and making fun of everyone else. You get so you think that's normal—and it isn't. It would break your mom's heart if she heard you. And I don't know what to do about it."

"I better go find Jenny," Diane said. She looked at Spence. "Thanks for . . . asking us." And then she looked at Heather again. "I'm sorry about everything. The way things have gone in your life. I hope you'll all be okay."

She got up and walked on through the house. She realized that Spence was following her, but she didn't turn back until he said, "Diane, I really am sorry. Tell Jenny that, okay?"

Diane opened the front door. "I guess we should have known what would happen."

"Maybe my kids learned a lesson. I'm glad Jenny stood up to them."

"I don't know. But you know what they were saying—whether they even know it or not. They want me to stay away from their dad, and they don't want Jenny moving in with them."

Spence's head dropped down. "Maybe. I don't know."

"Well, anyway, thanks for . . ." She couldn't think how to end her sentence, so she simply nodded and slipped out the door.

Jenny was not in the car, so Diane got in and drove down the hill.

She found Jenny almost two blocks down the street, walking hard. When the car stopped, Jenny seemed to think things over before she opened the door and got in. "I can walk home, Mom," she said. "If I had my running shoes, I could run the whole way. But you could have stayed."

"No. I didn't want to. I was proud of you. You told them what they needed to hear, and it actually seemed to embarrass them." Then, after a moment, she added, "Spence told me to tell you how sorry he was."

"Well, tell the whole bunch of them that I *have* a father—and I'm not looking for a replacement. And I sure don't want any of them for brothers and sisters."

"They know that," Diane said. "We don't have to tell them."

Diane settled back and drove. There was nothing more to say. Some things really were impossible. And once again, Diane had to deal with the realities of her life.

Chapter 13

In October Greg gave Jenny a car for her seventeenth birthday. Nothing about that made sense to Diane. He had supposedly been on the edge of bankruptcy for years now, barely putting bread on his table—and then he had shown up with a pretty red Toyota Corolla, only four years old. He had had an explanation, of course—something about a broke client offering it to him because he couldn't pay his bill. "Why don't you sell it, if you're so strapped for cash?" Diane had asked him.

Standing in the apartment in front of Jenny, Greg had said, "I could, Diane. I thought about that. But let me do this for Jenny. I know I haven't done enough, and I just want her to know how much I love her. It'll be a nice little car for her, all the way through college. It gets great mileage and it . . ."

Diane had quit listening. She had lost another one to Greg. Jenny, of course, was thrilled, and by suggesting that Jenny not have the car, Diane had turned herself into the "bad guy" one more time. Jenny had gone outside with Greg and looked the car over, talked to him for a long time, and then hugged him before he walked back to Marilyn, who had driven their other car. And then Jenny had gotten in her new car and driven away while Diane watched through her living-room window. Diane had cooked Jenny a nice dinner and baked a cake, but Jenny didn't come back for hours, and when she did, she said she'd eaten with some of her friends. This was revenge, of course. Jenny was well aware that Diane had cooked dinner for her, but clearly she was angry that Diane hadn't wanted her to have the car, probably mad that Diane had spoken rather harshly to Greg, and surely happier to be with her friends.

Diane had bought Jenny a pretty outfit, pushing her budget beyond the breaking point to do so, and Jenny had thanked her, only to suggest afterward that she might take it back and look around for something to exchange it for. "I like the skirt, and even the sweater's nice, but I just don't know where I'd ever wear something like that."

It was the way Jenny often reacted these days. There had been a time when the two had been on the same page about almost everything; now it seemed that Jenny started with the assumption that Diane's taste would be wrong.

Or maybe Diane was a little more sensitive than usual lately. Since July, Diane had talked to Spence on the phone a couple of times, but they hadn't seen one another. She had not been willing to talk to him for long, either. She just didn't understand what he hoped to gain by keeping in touch. He was the first to admit that nothing could come of their relationship. Still, she felt a loss of something—even though it was nothing she'd ever actually possessed. She wanted to be happy, and it didn't help to have him call every now and then. She needed to move ahead with her life, concentrate on her goals and work hard in her night classes.

When Christmas came, Diane gave Jenny money to use at the after-Christmas sales, and then felt the pain on Christmas morning when Jenny had only a couple of little packages to open. Greg had sent nothing, but a package came a couple of days after Christmas, sent from Puerto Vallarta, Mexico, where he and his wife had apparently gone for the holidays. He'd sent sandals and a silly Mexican skirt that Jenny would surely never wear, but he'd also sent money, Jenny said. She wouldn't say how much. But when she shopped with it, she brought home much more than she'd bought with the money Diane had given her.

Jenny spent most of her Christmas vacation days with her friends, especially Tracy, but they weren't running these days—or at least not much. That fall Jenny had announced one day that she had quit the cross-country team. She had been leaning toward the bathroom mirror, taking her contact lenses out, when Diane had stopped at the bathroom door to ask how her day had gone. "Terrible," she'd said. "I quit the team, and Coach acted like I'd murdered somebody."

"You quit? Why?"

"My hamstrings have bothered me for weeks—and they're getting worse, not better. They'll never clear up unless I rest my legs for a while. I need to concentrate more on school anyway. I'm taking so many hard classes now."

Diane hadn't cared whether Jenny kept running or not, but it had bothered her that she would quit in the middle of the season. That wasn't like her. "And the coach was mad about it?"

"He's a jerk, Mom. He told me I'd gotten lazy and didn't want to push myself anymore. He doesn't believe me about my hamstrings."

"Why haven't you mentioned that? You didn't say a thing to me."

Jenny had spun back from the mirror. "Thanks, Mom," she'd said with measured hostility. "I'm glad you don't believe me either. I wouldn't expect anything less of you."

Those were the most hostile words Jenny had ever directed at Diane, and Diane was too shocked to respond. She'd simply walked away from the bathroom door. What Diane was sure of was that she had caught Jenny in a lie, and that was what had made Jenny so angry. The truth was, Tracy had turned an ankle earlier in the season and had stopped running. Diane was sure that Jenny had merely wanted to spend more time with her. Diane could see what else would be coming: Jenny would want to go back to work at Burger King, and all of that was so that she'd have more money for clothes.

In fifteen minutes or so, Jenny had come to Diane in the kitchen. "I'm sorry, Mom," she said, and she started to cry. "I shouldn't have talked to you like that. But this has been really hard on me. Coach made me feel like a failure for quitting."

Diane had held her in her arms, hoping for a little breakthrough between them, but Jenny was hard to embrace now, so tall and hard, and not quite willing to bend. Diane couldn't help thinking that Jenny was handling the situation too much the way Greg would have done: always with an excuse, using icy words, and then seeking forgiveness.

All this scared Diane. She didn't know what would happen to Jenny. It seemed time for her to start coming back a little from that fifteen- and sixteen-year-old self-absorption. Jenny had always been so clear about her goals, and winning the state championship in cross-country had been one on her list—something Diane really thought would happen. This was the first time Jenny had backed away from something difficult. Maybe her legs *were* bothering her, but it seemed more likely that there were other girls who were better than she was, and she had given herself a way out of the competition. She was also letting Tracy have much more influence on her than she had ever allowed before, from anyone.

Diane worried, too, when she listened to Jenny talk on the telephone to the many guys who called. She toyed with them, teased them, seemed to know exactly how to keep them interested and hold them at a distance at the same time. Diane was glad that Jenny hadn't ended up dating one boy all the time, and that she seemed to be more likely to hang out with a bunch of kids of both sexes—not go steady the way some of her friends were now doing. At the same time, Diane almost wished that Jenny could demonstrate a capacity to make a connection that would go deeper than manipulation.

But all this was something Diane watched and didn't comment on. Jenny bristled whenever Diane tried to probe a little about the guys she went out with, or questioned any of her choices. Diane would hear

Jenny talking to Tracy either on the phone or sometimes in Jenny's room late at night, and the two seemed to be sharing all their thoughts and feelings. Diane longed for the same experience, to hear Jenny say what she really thought and felt. She told herself that she and Jenny would be closer again someday, but as fall had moved into winter, and 1987 had begun, Diane felt ever more alone.

On a Saturday morning in February, Jenny got up late and wandered into the kitchen in the sweats she liked to sleep in this time of year. Diane had been up for three hours and was a little annoyed that Jenny wouldn't get up and help her clean house—when there was obviously so much to be done—but she didn't say anything. "Sorry I slept so long," Jenny said, as though she knew what Diane was thinking. "I've been really wiped out lately."

"That's fine," Diane said, "but could you clean the bathroom before you take off somewhere? I'll do the rest of the house."

"Oh."

Diane was kneeling in front of the oven, which she had been scrubbing with a Brillo soap pad. She looked up now.

"Could I maybe do that later on today—or maybe on Monday? I promised Tracy I'd help her with her math homework. She's about going under with trigonometry."

"Don't worry about it. I'll get it." Diane heard her own curtness, and she knew she'd said the wrong thing.

"No, Mom. That's fine. I'll clean the bathroom before I go. I know what you'll *think* about me all day if I leave."

Diane, still on her knees, pulled off a rubber glove, brushed some loose hairs away from her face, and took a breath. "It's okay," she said. "Help Tracy. It's good of you to do it. I can manage the cleaning." She was trying, but there was still too much effort in her voice, too much labored control.

"You know what I've realized lately?" Jenny said. She had taken a step closer to Diane and was standing tall in her gray sweats, her arms folded. Diane didn't ask; she waited for what was coming. She could see in Jenny's Greglike stare that she was barely holding back her rage. "You don't even like me. You hate everything about me. Every time I walk in this apartment, it's the first thing I feel. You don't think I should go anywhere. You hate my friends. You want me to be that little girl you could control every minute, the way you always did when I was younger."

Diane turned and sat on the floor, leaning back against the kitchen cabinet. She knew she had to be careful. "I don't mean to make you feel that way," she said. "But I think most of that is in *your* mind. It's not in mine."

"Oh, is that right? And when was the last time you *supported* something I decided to do? You question every decision I ever make, and you drop all your little hints about the way I do things. Last weekend it was that I'm 'running around' too much, and before that it was that you don't like the way I talk to the guys who call me. Just once I'd like to hear you say that you think I do something right. I got all A's again last term and you hardly mentioned it."

Diane was trying to keep her breathing even, and she tried to soften her voice when she said, "That's probably true, Jenny. I think I do get used to you getting good grades, and I probably do take that for granted."

"What do you mean, it's *probably* true? Don't patronize me, Mom. You're doing what you always do. You try to placate me by saying you don't have anything against me, and then you start in nagging me again."

"Jenny, I don't have anything *against* you. I guess I am having a hard time accepting that you're grown up now. I'm sorry about that. But you need to know, I am proud of you."

"You are, huh? Well, I'll tell you the difference. Dad gave me a hundred dollars as a way to congratulate me. You said, 'That's another great report card,' like it didn't mean a thing to you."

"Greg gave you a hundred dollars?"

"Yes. But he told me not to tell you. He knows what you think of *him,* too."

"What I think of him is that for seventeen years, he's done as little as he possibly can to help us—and then he buys you off with token presents."

"Don't start again, Mom. I've heard all this too many times before."

Diane stood up. "Can't you see through him, Jenny? He's never stood by you the way he's been ordered to do, but you turn into putty in his hands every time he puts some money in your hands—just a pittance of what he's supposed to give us."

"Give *us,* huh?"

"Yes. You cost money, whether you realize it or not, and he's supposed to help me with that."

"Well, I'm deeply sorry that I *cost* you so much."

Diane pointed a finger into Jenny's face. "Don't do that. You know what I'm saying, and you're turning it around just to stab back at me. It's *exactly* what Greg always did to me."

"And you *hated* him, didn't you? Just the way you hate me—because you think I'm too much like him."

Diane pulled the other glove off and set it on the counter. She held on for a time, and then she said, "Jenny, I love you. More than anyone in this world. And I loved your dad just as much at one time. You don't know what happened, and it's not anything I want to talk about."

Jenny let her arms drop to her sides, and she said almost matter-of-factly, "I know more than you think I do. I know how *cold* you were.

171

You were the beauty queen—but you didn't know how to love anyone but yourself."

Diane felt the breath go out of her. She couldn't think what to say. Those were Greg's words—Diane had no doubt about that—but she couldn't believe that Jenny would use them. It was her way of striking the most reckless, painful blow she could, and she'd said it with acid in her voice.

"I know about your problem, Mom. I know you couldn't handle the *intimate* part of marriage. Maybe it's not something you can help, but I'm sure that's what destroyed your marriage. I think it's better if you know that I'm aware of that."

Diane was still staring at Jenny. There was so much she needed to say, and she had no idea where to start.

"I'm sure you think Dad shouldn't have told me those things. But he was actually trying to help me understand you better."

"And what did he say about the things he did to me?" she asked.

"He warned me. He told me a long time ago that sooner or later you'd start accusing him of things. He knows he has a temper, and he told me exactly where he crossed the line sometimes. But you took little things and blew them into *huge* things, and then you exaggerated everything when you talked to the judge."

"And you believe that?"

Jenny didn't answer. She stood for a long time, her arms still at her sides, her eyes set. "Here's what I believe," she finally said. "You probably both made mistakes, and you both have your own problems. But at least Dad believes in me. I'm happier when I'm with him. So . . . I think it's time for me to leave. Dad's told me for years that I could come and live with him if things ever got too bad here. I used to think it would hurt you too much, but I've gotten to the point where I don't think you really care. I'm going to go pack now. I think it's the best thing for both of us."

She walked out of the kitchen and off toward her bedroom.

Diane was suddenly more frightened than angry. She couldn't think what to do. She had to stop Jenny, but she needed to handle things perfectly. She tried to think for a time, and then she knelt and prayed. "I need to say the right things," she told the Lord. "Help me."

Diane got up. She tried to calm herself for at least a full minute, and then she walked to Jenny's bedroom. The door was locked, so she knocked. "Jenny, let's talk about this."

But Jenny didn't answer. Diane could hear her moving about, heard a drawer open, knew she was packing.

"Jenny, please. Before you leave, let's talk this out. These problems aren't as big as you think they are."

Still no answer. Diane could hear a rustle of clothing, the sound of hangers sliding as Jenny sorted through her closet. She remembered the little device that she could use to unlock the door from the outside. She felt above the door, on the frame, but couldn't find it. She stepped to the bathroom door and found one there, then used it to open Jenny's door. When the door came open, Jenny turned to look at her. A suitcase was on her bed, already closed. A sports bag was bulging and zipped. Jenny had stacked most everything from her closet on her bed next to the suitcase. "Mom, it's the best thing for us," she said. "Let's not get into a big fight. In a year or so I'll be leaving anyway. It's not so terrible if it happens now."

"What would it hurt to talk things through?" Diane asked.

"I think we've said enough. I wish I hadn't said some of the things I just told you. I was mad and I spoke too harshly. But it's just as well that all of this comes out in the open. Now that it's said, though, I don't see any way I can stay here."

"You told me what your dad said about me. Don't I have a right to give my side of the story?"

"No. Because that's not the point. I just think I get along better with Dad, and I'll do better living with him—and you'll be happier without me bothering you so much all the time."

"Jenny, you're my life. You—"

"That's just the problem, isn't it? I'm your *project*—your life's work. Maybe you can't help it, but the only thing you want is to create me in your own image—and we're just nothing alike. I need to live where I have the freedom to be myself." Jenny had thrown a pair of jeans and a T-shirt over a chair. She picked them up now, and then got underwear that she had set out on the top of her dresser, and she walked toward Diane. "Excuse me. I need to change," she said.

Diane let her go by, and Jenny walked into the bathroom. Diane could only think of the little girl she had dressed so many times—now thinking she needed to be alone to change her clothes.

Diane waited by the door, tried hard to think what she would do— say—this time. It was her last chance.

Jenny stayed in the bathroom a long time, and Diane realized she was packing up her personal things. When she finally came out, she was carrying a little travel bag that she kept under the bathroom sink.

"Honey, listen to me for a second," Diane said. "I think it probably has been good for some of these things to come out. I've been standing here thinking that I haven't treated you the way I should lately. I do question you too much, and I don't express my love nearly as often as I should. I brag about you all the time, but I don't tell *you* how proud I am. That's something I can work on. But we can be okay. You don't have to leave."

Jenny had set out a pair of socks, too. It was so like her to plan what she would wear, even when she had been so upset. She sat on the bed and folded her long body forward, slipping on one sock and then the other, but she didn't speak.

"Could you at least wait an hour before you decide for certain? Could we talk that long?"

"Oh, Mom, please. You know you can't take an hour off today. The house needs cleaning. That's your agenda for today—and you don't like to adjust your plans."

Diane knew that Jenny felt that way about her—that she wasn't spontaneous enough—but what did Jenny understand about working full-time and raising a daughter, all on her own? Time *was* precious to her.

But she couldn't argue. Not now. "Please, Jenny. Give me an hour, and we'll talk."

"I owe you an hour because you've given me your whole life— right? You've *sacrificed* for me every day all these years?"

"Don't do that, Jenny. Just talk to me before you make this decision."

"No. I'm going. I've told you why, and I don't want to go over it all again." She tied her second shoelace and stood up. "I've been thinking about this for a long time. It's not a sudden decision, even though you think it is."

"You don't even know whether Greg is home. They could be out of town again."

"I talked to him yesterday. He told me the same thing he's always said: Anytime I need to move in with him, his door is open. But I told him, 'Oh, no, Dad. I can stick it out until college.' And I thought I could. But I'm tired of sticking it out. I want to be happy."

Suddenly Diane had heard enough. "Oh, Jenny, don't pretend I've been so terrible as all that. You love this *victim's* role you're playing."

"Well . . . maybe I learned that from you."

Diane heard Greg in every word. And suddenly she saw with a new clarity that she couldn't let Greg have Jenny. He would distort her, ruin everything Diane had tried to teach her all these years. "You're not going," she said. "You can't. I have legal custody, and you don't have any choice in this. I want to talk—and I'm sure we can resolve all this—but I'm not going to let you leave."

Jenny turned toward Diane and took a long look at her. And then she walked to her dresser. She opened the bottom drawer, reached under some old sweaters, pulled out a picture frame, and brought it to

Diane. She turned the frame so Diane could see the picture, and just let her look. It was a picture of Jenny with her date to the prom, taken last year. But in the picture Jenny was wearing the yellow dress from Castleton's—the one that Diane hadn't let her buy.

"Dad bought it for me," she said. "He didn't see a thing wrong with it. I hated that dress you had made for me, and I knew right then that we'd never see things the same way. I left here wearing that dress, and changed at Tracy's house. But I made my mind up that I would stay here until I graduated from high school—and then I'd go away and be myself. But I can't wait that long. Dad gives me room. I know some things about him—I don't think he's perfect—but he trusts me, and that's what I need for now."

"He'll ruin your life, Jenny. He's a crook. And he's an abuser. If he hasn't hurt Marilyn so far, he will, and if you cross him, he'll hurt you too."

"Sorry, Mom, but I'm not buying that one."

"You're not leaving. I won't let him have you."

"That's still the contest—played out over my whole life." Jenny grabbed her suitcase and her overnight case, and she walked toward Diane, who set herself in the doorway. "Don't do this, Mom. I'm going to pack my car, and then I'm going."

"No."

"All right, then. I won't pack my car. I'll come back for my stuff. But I'm leaving." She set her luggage down and tried to push past Diane, but Diane grabbed her by the arms and held her back. Jenny stopped for a moment, seemed to think things over, and then suddenly twisted and pushed hard against Diane's grip. One of her arms broke loose, and Jenny lowered her shoulder and drove past Diane. Diane tried to keep hold of her, but the other arm pulled from her grip, and Jenny ran down the hall. Diane ran after her, but when Jenny reached the front door, she spun back and said, "You can't stop me, Mom. Don't try."

Diane was facing her, but she knew she couldn't wrestle with Jenny, that she wouldn't win that one. "Please don't leave. Please," was all she could think to say.

"I'll come back for my things when you've calmed down. It's better this way. Just think about it for a while and you'll agree with me."

And then she was gone, and Diane was curled up on the floor, sobbing. She didn't know whether she could live. She tried to pray, but she was angry with the Lord. She'd needed Him, and He'd done *nothing* to help her.

Diane stayed on the floor for a long time, and then she did the only thing she could think to do: She called her mother. Bobbi came over immediately. The two talked, and Bobbi held Diane. She kept saying, "This is going to work out better than you think. Jenny's too smart to be taken in by Greg. Once she's around him all the time, she'll know what he's really made of."

"He'll let her do what she wants, and that's all Jenny cares about right now."

"But she's a good girl. You've taught her the right things. She'll come back to herself. And she's right about part of it: She *will* be on her own before much longer, and you can't do anything about that. You've already done most of what you can do."

Diane didn't believe that. These were crucial years, and Diane had to keep Jenny away from Greg.

When the phone rang later that day, Diane was not surprised to hear Greg's voice. She had known the call was coming, had even known the tone he would take.

"Listen, Diane, I know you're upset, but Jenny's fine, and we're going to take good care of her. You don't have to see this as a tragedy."

"It *is* a tragedy, Greg. I won't let you mess up her life."

"I guess I knew that's what you'd say. But I think you need to think of Jenny, not yourself. I want to drive up, today if possible, and get her things, and then I'll get her into school on Monday. Who knows?

Maybe she won't like the change, but I think you need to give her some time to try this. I promise you I'll do my very best with her."

"You can't do this legally, Greg. I'll call the judge on Monday—today, if I can find his number. He'll have her out of there. He'll throw you in jail."

There was a pause, and then Greg's other voice was in her ear. "Don't mess with me, Diane. I've already taken pictures of the marks on her arms. When they turn into bruises, I'll take those pictures, too. If you want to fight me in court, I can tell you right now, you'll lose. I'll pull out every stop to show what kind of hateful mother you've been to this poor kid. I should have done it a long time ago, but I didn't want to have this fight."

"You've tried to undermine me every way you could. And you bought her off whenever you thought that would work. You had no right to buy that prom dress for her."

"Let's see. The judge should be very impressed by that argument. You bruised her arms, and I bought her a nice dress for the prom. I think I'd like to have this fight after all. And remember, I don't have to pay for a lawyer and you do. I can run up a bill for you that you won't believe."

Diane was gripping the receiver, wanting to scream. "Greg, you don't scare me anymore," she finally said. "You're an evil man, and in the long run, you're going to pay for who you are. I will *not* let you have my daughter."

She hung up the phone, but not before she heard him laugh.

CHAPTER 14

Diane didn't sleep that night. She finally gave up and got out of bed at about four o'clock. She tried to read her scriptures, which she knew she hadn't done enough of lately. She hoped for something specific that would comfort her, but her mind wasn't on the words, and she didn't read for long. She stood up. She wasn't going to sit there and feel sorry for herself. She would get an attorney and she would fight. Jenny would hate being brought back by force, but she would thank Diane someday. Diane didn't have much money to work with, but maybe she could find a lawyer who would let her pay the bill over time.

She thought of Spence. He had a law degree. Maybe he could advise her. If nothing else, maybe he could help her find an attorney who would be fair with her. She decided she would call him once a reasonable time came for him to be out of bed.

She took a shower, dressed, even paced at times, as she waited for the sun to come up. At one point she picked up her scriptures again and read her favorite words in Mosiah—King Benjamin's teachings about owing everything to God, about showing appreciation, about the things that really mattered in life. She tried to think that way, and she got down on her knees and prayed for guidance and faith. It was Sunday morning and she didn't want to call too early, but at seven-thirty she couldn't stand to wait any longer.

The phone only rang twice before someone picked up. She hoped that meant that Spence hadn't been asleep. "Hello," he said, and she was surprised at the comfort she felt in his voice.

"Spence, it's Diane. Did I wake you up?"

"No. I wake up early—even when I want to sleep in. I must be getting old. Are you okay?"

"Yes . . . well, no." And suddenly she was crying—something she hadn't expected to do.

"What's happened, Diane?"

She swallowed. "I guess I wondered if you could give me some legal advice. Jenny's left me and gone to her father. He has visiting rights, but that's all. He can't keep her, can he? Can't I make the judge send her back?"

Diane didn't like the quiet that followed. She was sitting at the kitchen table with her terry-cloth robe wrapped around her, over her clothes, and she was still shivering.

"Diane, I've never actually practiced law, and this is an area I really know nothing about. Isn't she coming up on eighteen?"

"Not until next fall. And I don't care about that. I know Greg's values. I know what she'll learn from him. I won't let him take her away from me."

"But she chose to go, didn't she?"

"Look, Spence, never mind. I shouldn't have called. I'll figure this out for myself."

Diane was about to put the receiver down when she heard Spence say, "Wait. I'm just trying to give you some idea of what you have to think about. At Jenny's age, I suspect a judge will take her preference into account. Once you get into a legal fight over something like that, it can get very nasty."

"But what can I *do?*"

"Okay, here's what I'd suggest. I have an attorney who does our taxes and that sort of thing. He wouldn't know any more about this kind of law than I do. But he's got a partner who works with domestic matters—divorce and all that. I know him pretty well. I can give him a call, and I'm sure he can guide you in the right direction."

"Would I have to pay him a lot of money up front? I don't have very much saved."

"Don't worry about that. I'll take care of it."

"No. I can't do that. I've made my way through everything all these years. I can manage this, too."

"Diane, money is simply not an issue for me. I'd love to help you."

"No. I don't want that."

The silence lasted longer this time, and Diane was about to thank him and get off the phone, but Spence said, "Explain to me why it's a bad thing for one person to help another. Is there something I missed in my study of the gospel?"

"We should take care of ourselves—if we can."

"Where does it say that?"

Diane had no idea, but she knew it was true. "It's just best."

"Okay, listen. An expenditure like that won't affect my life in the tiniest way. It could make yours tough for a while. Let me at least pay this for now, and we can worry about your paying me back later."

"But I will pay you back."

"That's fine."

Again she heard the mellowness of his voice, the comfort. She was not sure she had even called him for his legal knowledge. He had continued to call her every now and then all through the fall and winter. They had talked about Jenny, and about Heather, and they had understood each other. He hadn't asked Diane out again, and she knew he wouldn't—couldn't—but she did like to talk things out with him sometimes.

"Would it help any if I came over today—and we could, you know, talk about all this?"

"Well . . . sure. But you have church . . . and . . ."

"I'm out by noon. What about you?"

"Yeah, I am too. I don't feel like going, but I guess I will."

"Did you sleep?"

"No." And now she was fighting not to cry again.

"This is going to be okay, Di. It will. Jenny doesn't have the problems my kids have. She'll be all right. What if I come over about one?"

"Okay. That would be fine."

"All right. I'll make something simple for the kids to eat after church, and then I'll drive over."

"If you need more time, it doesn't matter. Two is just as good."

He laughed. "One will be fine. The kids would rather eat sandwiches than one of my pot roasts, any day."

He said good-bye, and Diane hung up the phone. But she was thinking of his gentle voice, his assurance that Jenny would be all right, and she was touched by the name he'd called her: "Di." People she'd gotten close to, all her life, had always called her "Di."

Church was difficult for Diane. Jodi Jackson, a girl just younger than Jenny, was the youth speaker, and she talked about being thankful for her parents and all they had taught her. In Sunday School, the teacher, Brother Dobbs, reminded everyone of David O. McKay's statement that no success in life compensated for failure in the home. It was a quote she had heard many times, but today Brother Dobbs seemed to be speaking to her, accusing, and she found herself wondering what exactly President McKay had meant. Hadn't she done her best? Had she really failed? What had President McKay thought of all the people who had devoted themselves to teaching their kids what was right—and then had watched them choose another path all the same?

As Diane was leaving Relief Society, Sister Markson asked her where Jenny was. "Is she sick?"

"No," Diane told her, and tried to say something that was essentially true. "She's spending the weekend with her father."

"Listen, I've been going to ask you something." Diane could guess what was coming. "My husband's brother is a little older than you, but he's a good man. I've been wondering whether you wouldn't want to go out with him sometime."

"No, thanks. I don't think so."

"He's a little over fifty, and he's certainly no Mel Gibson, but he's a nice man, and he has a pretty good job. He'd think he'd died and gone to heaven if you went to dinner with him sometime."

"No. I really don't want to date right now. Things are just too . . . complicated."

"It's kind of the same for him. His wife walked out on him and accused him of all sorts of things that just aren't true. And she's got his kids saying things about him now. He's such a nice man, and he's so lonely. If you could just—"

"I'm sorry. I just can't." She knew she probably ought to offer some reason, but she was about to break down, so she merely turned and walked on out the door.

But she had seen that look that was so familiar to Diane—that hint in people's voices, in the understanding way they nodded their heads—that said that they felt sorry for her. She was the divorced woman—a sad story to everyone. Sometimes people said to her, "I can't imagine that someone as beautiful as you are can't find another husband." Maybe they meant well, but Diane could almost hear them saying to themselves, "I'm not as pretty as you are, but at least I got myself a man—and kept him."

After church Diane heated up some soup she had made earlier in the week and made herself a tuna sandwich. She didn't change her clothes, and didn't admit to herself that she thought she looked good in the blue dress she was wearing—one that Spence had never seen.

As Diane ate, she kept thinking about Jenny. What was she thinking by now? Was she feeling any regrets about the things she'd said? Was she wondering whether she really wanted to live with Greg and Marilyn? Did she worry about Diane being lonely?

Spence showed up exactly at one—as though he had been careful to time his prompt arrival. It was the way he seemed to do things. Diane saw him coming up her walk, looking powerful in his dark suit and red tie. He had a way of walking, as though he always took the shortest distance between two points and wasted no time in getting there.

She let him knock before she went to the door, and then she felt sort of silly when she reached out and shook his hand. He laughed a little at that too, but then he took a careful look at her face and said, "You've had a hard day, haven't you?"

Diane nodded. "People asked me where she was. I guess I'm going to start hearing a lot of that."

Diane was motioning for him to sit down in her upholstered chair, but he stood in front of the chair and waited. "Let me tell you something," he said. "The worst thing you can do to yourself is to worry too much what people think. The way Heather looks, I get stares from people all the time, and when I do talk her into going to church with me, I'm always a little embarrassed. But it's more important to worry about her than about the impression we're making. It's taken me a while to figure that out."

"I know. You're right. The truth is, what bothers me more than anything is that Jenny would choose Greg over me. She told me she's happier when she's around him."

"After all you've done for her?"

Diane heard the irony in his voice. "What?"

"Isn't that what you find yourself thinking? You've done everything for her, and she doesn't appreciate it?"

Diane nodded. "Sure. I guess I do think that."

"It's what every parent thinks. And it's what no teenager ever can understand. But they get it when they get a little older."

Diane sat down, and then Spence did. Diane realized that it had been his politeness that had kept him standing. Did men like that still exist?

"But you *have* worked hard for her," he went on. "I don't think people understand what it's like to handle everything alone, the way you and I have had to do."

"Actually, I've probably had more help than you've had. Mom took care of Jenny when I was going to college, and Dad's this really tender man who loves Jenny and me and looks after us in all kinds of ways."

Diane couldn't help but notice the way Spence was watching her. All winter she had longed to see him look at her in that way. She thought again of the time he had picked her up and carried her, set her down so lovingly. Superman.

"Well, that's good of your parents," he said, rather absently, as though he had other things on his mind himself. "They're not rich people, and they could be running around now, spending all their money on themselves."

"They'd rather live simple lives—that's just what makes them happy. They give to more causes than most people who have ten times as much money."

Spence nodded, as though the statement had caught his attention. "It's interesting you say that. I've decided I need to give more of my money away. I've been thinking a lot about that lately."

Diane was feeling preoccupied, and wasn't sure she wanted to talk about that at the moment, but she asked, "Who would you give it to?"

Spence stretched his legs out, almost reaching Diane. "I don't know," he said. "But I've told you before, money has never meant much to me."

"That's because you've always had so much."

"Actually, that's probably true. But you know me; I would have rather been a teacher."

"If you'd done that, you'd now be wishing you had gone into business with your dad."

He laughed, flashing those nice teeth. "Maybe. But I don't think so. As it's turned out, I think money's been a curse to my kids."

Diane was still thinking about Jenny. "In Gospel Doctrine today, our teacher quoted President McKay. 'No success can compensate—'"

"Don't even say it. I think about it every day."

"Is it our fault?"

"No. Not entirely. But what eats at me is that I *have* made mistakes. And now I can't go back and undo them."

Diane knew the feeling. She and Spence took a long look at each other, and she felt the closeness between them. She liked him, but what they shared—what they were going through at the same time—added something extra. She also saw the irony: They needed one another, but the very kids they were so worried about were the main reason they couldn't be together.

Maybe Spence was thinking the same things. She could see the sadness in his eyes. She could also see the way he was looking at her, as though he wanted to say something. Maybe he was thinking what she was: *I wish this could be different.*

What he finally did say was, "I haven't given up the fight. Heather's angry, but she's still that little girl who used to love me more than anyone—you know, way back there somewhere, long ago. I just keep waiting for that child to reappear, the pretty little girl who liked to sit on my lap and hug me."

"All night I kept getting a picture like that in my head," Diane said, and the tears obstructed her vision again.

"Jenny just wants to test her wings a little, and maybe she's been taken in by all her dad's machinations, but at least she's not hating everyone and everything—like Heather."

Diane thought about that for a time. "I think Jenny is sort of angry, though. She's mad for a different reason—because we've never had anything."

"She's young. She has you and your parents and your senator uncle, and all those Thomases to look to. She'll know who she is one of these days."

"So will Heather. She can't live with someone as good as you are and not know what's right."

"Do you think I'm good?"

"I don't just *think* so. I feel it every time I'm around you. What I always think is that if I'd met someone like you, instead of Greg, my whole life would have been different."

But it was the wrong thing to say—much too forward—and Diane knew it. She wished he would say something, say that he liked her, that he thought she was good, too, but he didn't. He sat silent for a long time, and then he said, "I called Ken Douglas just before I came over here. He's the lawyer I mentioned. We didn't talk much, but he did say it was important to handle a case like yours delicately. If you force Jenny home, she might react against you, and that could make things worse."

"I know. I thought about that all night. But I'd rather deal with that than to let Greg destroy her."

"Be careful it's not your ego speaking. You could beat Greg and lose Jenny."

"No. I don't mean that. I know that man, and his sick values are getting into her already. I can't let her stay with him."

"Well, talk to Ken. He says there are things you can do."

"How much do you think it will cost?"

"When you start paying attorneys, dollars go fast. But don't worry about it. Let me do this for you. I told you, I want to start doing more good with my money."

"And I told you I'd pay you back."

He nodded, but he didn't seem to take the idea very seriously. "What could I do with my money, Diane? I really do want to start giving it away."

"What do you care about?" Diane's mind was not entirely on the question. She could still feel him watching her. He wouldn't say anything to indicate how he felt about her, but she could *see* that he did like her. As a young woman she had learned little tricks—ways to smile, hints to drop, playful little teases—but she didn't want to be like that with Spence. She wanted him to pay attention to the person she had become.

"What do you mean, care about?"

"There are so many suffering people in this world. Are there some that get to your heart more than others?"

"I'm like everyone else. I see children starving in Afghanistan, or other places in the world, and it makes me sick to think that I have so much and they have so little. But there are organizations out there trying to feed them. What I wonder is how I could change something somewhere. I don't have enough to make a big difference, but I wonder how I could make things better for *some* people."

"I don't know, Spence. I've never had to think what I'd do, since I just struggle to get by." Then she thought better of what she'd said. "Of course, our idea of struggling is to have a nice home, plenty of food, and a car to drive around in."

"I'm sure if those folks in Afghanistan looked at you, they'd think they were seeing a queen—all dressed in royal blue, and so beautiful that you would take their breaths away." He waited a moment, and then he added, "The way you do mine."

It was not often that Diane was caught off guard. She felt the heat in her face as she said, rather lamely, "It's the only nice dress I have."

He nodded, didn't follow up, and his own cheeks were pink. "Well, anyway, here's what I've been thinking lately. What if I picked a place, a village somewhere, maybe in South America where I served my mission, and tried to do something to help a few people—maybe help them get clean water, medical care, better farming methods, things like that?"

"If you want to help them in the long run, maybe you should teach them skills. Reading, for instance."

"You're kind of an expert on that, aren't you?"

"You mean teaching people to read?"

"Yeah."

"Sort of. But there's no great trick to it. The problem would be figuring out how to teach people in another language. I guess I could teach someone, through a translator, how to teach reading. If it were Spanish, you could help me. Or I could learn the language if I had time to work on it."

"Would you like to do that?"

"What do you mean?"

"What if we worked together? We'd have to plan things out, figure out what we wanted to do exactly, but with your educational background and my business background, maybe we could get poor people set up in little businesses, and then teach their kids to read, so they could get better educated. I'm just thinking out loud, but to me it sounds exciting. I need a new challenge, and this time I don't want it to be all about me, about money. I'm even thinking it would be good for my kids if I could get them involved in working with me on this."

"I'd love that. I'm tired of what I've been doing. I'd like to try something else."

"I thought you wanted to be a principal."

"I do. But I'm like you. I'd like to reach beyond my own little world."

"Maybe we could set up schools in places that don't have them. You're learning everything about that, aren't you?"

She laughed. But she felt surprisingly excited. "Not really. But things would be pretty basic in places that have *nothing*."

"Let's think about it, okay?"

"Sure."

Then he sat up straighter, and she saw a change. "It's not something I can do right now," he said. "I've got to get my kids through a few more years first. And you've got Jenny to worry about."

She knew what he was saying: *Diane, don't jump to any conclusions here. I'm not proposing. I'm only talking about a partnership—and the pretty blue dress is not the point.*

They talked for a long time after that, and it was all pleasant, but he seemed to be breathing just fine, no matter what he had said before. And when he left, the living room was just as empty as it had been that morning.

CHAPTER 15

Diane was on her way to Salt Lake, driving too fast. She had just gotten off the phone with Ken Douglas, the attorney Spence had put her in touch with. Diane had talked to him several times in the last two weeks, but the man wasn't much help. She wanted him to fight for Jenny. Instead, he kept repeating the same warnings Spence had given her: Judges often let children decide for themselves when they were as old as Jenny. "He's a criminal, for crying out loud," Diane had told him, with little control left in her voice. "Doesn't that matter to anyone?"

"I looked into that, Diane. There's no record against him. All charges were dropped. And you told me yourself, if you start getting into that sort of thing, he's taken those pictures of Jenny's bruises, and—"

"I did not bruise that girl. I grabbed her arms and she pulled away, but Jenny would never let a judge believe that I had abused her."

There had been a pause, and then Mr. Douglas had said, "You don't know that, Diane. I've seen cases where people will say whatever they think they have to say to get what they want."

That had been too much for Diane. She could just imagine Greg instructing Jenny, teaching her the lies she had to tell. She *couldn't* let Jenny stay in his grasp. She had thanked Mr. Douglas, hung up the phone, and headed for her car. She had made that call on a Friday afternoon right after she'd come home from school. Now she was driving the mountain highway and was almost to Farmington. She had Greg's address, but she had no specific plan; she only knew she was going to his home and she was going to tell Jenny that she had to come home—and somehow she would convince her.

All the way to Salt Lake Diane thought of things she could say. She would try to be calm. She'd tell Jenny how much she loved her, and she'd tell her that she knew, as a mother, that Jenny was making a mistake. Somehow she'd find the right words, and she'd take her little girl in her arms and hold her, and she'd bring her home. By now, surely Jenny was realizing that she'd made a mistake.

When Diane found Greg's address on the east bench, in Holladay, just south of Salt Lake, she was taken by surprise at how stately the house was, with tall white columns across the front in a Greek-revival style. There was a gate, which was open, and a long driveway, but she parked out on the street and walked to the front door. She stopped long enough to say one more little prayer, and then she rang the doorbell. She was beginning to think no one was home when she finally heard footsteps. The last thing she had expected was for Greg to answer the door, but when the door opened, there he was. She stood looking at him, hardly knowing what to say. She'd thought she might have to deal with Marilyn, or that maybe Jenny would come to the door herself, but she hadn't considered having to face Greg.

"Hello, Diane. What can I do for you?" He was wearing jeans and an old plaid shirt with the shirttails hanging out, as though he hadn't been to work that day.

Diane tried to sound calm. "I'd like to talk to Jenny."

"Sure. You can do that—if Jenny wants to talk to you—but Diane, I'm going to be in the room with you."

"Just let me have a few minutes with her alone."

"No." He gave Diane a little smile. "I know what you did to her the day she left. I can't stand by and let that happen again."

"I didn't *do* anything to her."

"You're forgetting that I have the pictures."

Diane wanted to scream at Greg, but she held her composure. "Please, just let me talk to her."

Greg stepped back and motioned for Diane to come in. "She's in her room. I'll see what she says."

Diane stepped inside. "Don't tell her not to talk to me, Greg."

"You don't have to worry about that. I don't operate the way you do." He walked away.

It was all Diane could do not to tell Greg what she thought of him. But she knew better. That was what he wanted, to get to her, have her blow up in front of Jenny and set everything back again. So she stood in a tiled entryway and tried to calm herself. Before her was a huge living room with a curved stairway to a second floor. There were big bay windows in the back, looking out toward the mountains. She could see a huge stretch of lawn that was covered with snow. She had suspected something of this sort, just not this scale of opulence. She thought of all the times Greg had stood before the judge and told him he had no money.

Greg made her wait for a long time, and she knew very well what was happening. He was "preparing the witness," telling Jenny exactly what she needed to say.

But when the two finally walked into the living room, from off a side hallway, Jenny was smiling. "Hi, Mom."

And Greg was saying, "Oh, I'm sorry. Did I leave you standing there all that time? Please, Diane, sit down."

Jenny came to Diane, hugged her rather stiffly, and motioned for her to sit on a white, U-shaped sectional couch. The two sat down together. For two weeks Jenny hadn't called, hadn't made any contact, but now she was acting as though nothing had happened.

Diane turned toward Jenny on the couch. She tried to forget that

Greg had taken a seat in a leather recliner across the big room. "Honey, I can't tell you how much I've missed you," she said.

Diane tried to pull Jenny into her arms again, but this time Jenny held back a little more. "I've missed you too, Mom. But I'm doing fine. Everything's going great. You don't need to worry about me."

"But I do worry about you. You haven't even called."

"I know. I should have. But I thought I ought to give everything a little time. And I—"

"That's what Greg told you to do, didn't he?"

"Come on, Mom. Let's not argue. This is working out fine. I'm in school now, at Olympus High, and I really like it. All the kids have been great to me, and I like my teachers. I'm feeling like this was the perfect thing for me. I'm up against some great students here. I think this will help me get ready for college."

This was all a little too practiced, Diane thought, but Jenny did seem comfortable, even happy. It was frustrating to see her so "together," so confident in her decision. "Honey, listen to me for a minute. No one in this world could possibly love you as much as I do. I'm glad you like the school, but you need to be with me. I want you to come home."

Diane saw Jenny glance toward Greg, but he didn't say anything, and Diane didn't look at him. "Mom, I know what you mean. You do love me, and you've looked out for me all my life. These last two weeks I almost packed up and came home about ten times—because I have missed you. But I'll be leaving for college next year anyway. This is just a little earlier separation than we expected."

"Jenny, it's so much more than that, and you know it."

"I don't. Really. You think I'm choosing Dad over you, and I'm not. I just think it's better for me right now, and probably for you, too. You need to start thinking about the things you want to do with your own life, without me as your main focus."

Diane heard Greg again, the things the two of them had talked about as they had diagnosed Diane's "problems." "You'll always be my focus, Jenny. You need to understand that."

Jenny gave a condescending nod, as if to say, *Good point.* "Well, sure. A mother is always a mother. But children grow up, and they have goals, and they move on. Dad and I have talked and talked about the kind of life I want to have. What I'm thinking now is that I'll get a law degree after college. If I can't get a scholarship to a major university, Dad said I could stay here and go to the U. He'll help me. And here's what we're talking about. Certain prospects are finally opening up for him. It's stuff that could really break big—land development and that sort of thing. He'll need help, and he and I could go partners. I think this might be my answer for how I can meet the goals I've always talked about. Dad can get me started, and then I'll take the business over so he can retire early . . ." She glanced at Greg and smiled. " . . . but I'll always look after you, too. You deserve so much more, and I want to make sure you get it."

"Those are not the things that matter to me, Jenny."

"I know. And in the long run, getting rich is really not the most important thing to me either, but—"

"Have you been going to church?"

"Well . . . yeah."

"What does that mean?"

"I just mean we haven't gone yet, but yes, I'm planning to go."

"The Church means nothing to your dad, Jenny. He'll tell you it does, but it doesn't. And one of my greatest worries is that you'll go the same direction."

"Mom, that's just not true. Dad and I have talked *so much*. We've had some of the best religious conversations I've had in my whole life."

From across the room, Greg said, "Diane, don't try to tell Jenny who I am. She's learned more about me since she's been here than she's ever known before—after what you've been telling her all her life."

Diane knew she was losing. Her hands were shaking, and she could feel that she was about to break down. She couldn't let that happen. "Jenny, look at me." Jenny did look into her eyes. "Honey, I've actually *never* told you all I should have told you about your dad. He's as deeply dishonest as any man I've ever known. He'll say whatever he thinks he has to say to get what he wants. If you go into business with him, you could end up in jail—and even if you don't, he'll destroy all your values, everything you've learned. He's a manipulator and a thief—and he's an abuser. One way or another, he'll hurt you more than anyone has ever hurt you."

Diane turned and took one long look at Greg, who smiled at her. Then he looked at Jenny. "I told you exactly what she'd say, didn't I?"

Jenny nodded, but she wasn't looking as pleased as Greg was. "Mom," she said, "that's the wrong approach to take with me. Dad wants the very best for me, and he's opening doors so I can get where I want to go."

"And all you're thinking about is making money—and maybe going to church once in a while, if you happen to feel an urge."

"That's not true at all. Dad and I have talked for *hours* about things we could do, once we've made some money. We want to help people who don't have a chance in this world."

"Jenny, Greg has never helped anyone but himself in his whole life. You can't be silly enough to believe him when he talks about things like that."

"Okay, Diane, that's enough," Greg said. He stood up. "You've had your say, and Jenny's given you her answer."

Diane stood too. "I'm going back to the judge, Greg. I have a lawyer. Maybe police will have to come and get Jenny, but somehow I'm getting her away from you."

"And that's how you think, isn't it? She *yours*. You own her. You'll make her into whatever you choose—and she won't be allowed to decide for herself. I think what Jenny likes about me is that I'm not trying to *mold* her. I'm trying to give her wings so she can fly."

Diane gripped her shaking hands together. "I'm going to court, Greg," she said. "I'm bringing her home." But the sobs were breaking from her, and she knew she sounded weak and scared, not powerful, the way she wanted to.

"I can't wait to see you in court, Diane," Greg said. "I'd like nothing better than to finally tell the judge my side of the story. I've listened to enough of your lies about me."

Jenny stepped closer to Diane and put a hand on her shoulder. "Mom, let's not go through all that. If you love me, you'll do what's best for me."

Diane looked into her eyes. "You've got to trust me, Jenny. This is a case where I do know what's best."

"Mom, I'll always love you. And we'll always stay close. But just let *me* decide. It's my life."

Greg had approached, was standing close. He gestured toward the door. "May I see you out?" he asked with exaggerated politeness.

Diane turned toward him. "This is just one more way to knock me down, isn't it? You couldn't control me with your fists, so you're taking the one thing that you know matters most to me. But I won't let you do it, Greg. I won't."

"Please. It's time for you to leave." He smiled just a little, as though he wanted Jenny to see his restraint and pleasantness. But Diane knew what he was actually feeling—the elation of victory.

Diane drove west to State Street, but she realized that she didn't want to go back to Ogden and her empty apartment. So she turned east again on 21st South and drove to Sugar House. She parked in front of Grandma Bea's house, and then walked up those familiar wood steps onto her big porch. She never came there without thinking of her childhood, of all the wonderful times she had spent with her grandparents, her cousins—the easy joy that always seemed natural to her in those days.

She knocked on the front door, then tried the door and found it unlocked, as always. "Grandma," she called, "it's Diane."

She heard a faint voice, probably from the kitchen, and then she heard it better as she stepped inside. "Come in, honey. Come in," Grandma was saying.

By then Grandma had pushed through the door from the kitchen. Diane met her in the living room. But she wasn't prepared for what broke loose inside her. She wrapped Grandma Bea in her arms and was crying hard before she could get a word out.

"Oh dear, what is it?" Grandma asked.

Diane couldn't speak. She tried to get her breath, gain control, but she continued to cling to her soft little grandmother. Finally she managed to say, "Greg's taken Jenny from me, Grandma."

"I know a little about that," Grandma said. "Bobbi told me about it." She gripped Diane a little tighter and let her cry.

After a time Diane was able to say, "I'm sorry. I don't want to burden you with my worries, but I just needed to talk to you."

"It's all right. That's my job—worrying about all my grandkids. It's almost my only source of entertainment." She laughed a little and Diane let go of her, smiling herself. "But I don't understand how that man could steal your daughter away."

"She wanted to be with him, Grandma. That's what hurts so much." Diane had to fight not to cry again.

"Well," Grandma said, "I think I can figure that one out. I know that smooth-talking rascal of an ex-husband of yours. And I know how teenagers think. I've raised a few of them. But don't you worry about Jenny. She'll figure that man out in no time."

"That's what Mom keeps telling me. But I don't see any sign of it so far."

"Come into the kitchen with me. I've got cookies in the oven."

So Diane followed Grandma back to the bright kitchen. Wally had hired someone to rebuild it a couple of years back. It had new oak cabinets and nicer appliances, but the old table was still there, in the corner, and the smell was the same. "Here I am baking cookies like a typical old grandma. I hate to be so predictable, but you know how it is when the kids come. They expect their cookies. And they usually start showing up on the weekend."

"You'll never be predictable, Grandma. You're one of a kind."

"I'm getting to be the oldest—of *any* kind. I can hear my bones rattle when I walk around in this big old place—like I'm a skeleton, haunting my own house." She pulled out a chair for Diane and motioned for her to sit down. Grandma moved more slowly now, took smaller steps, had to ease herself into a chair. She had lost weight lately. She wasn't quite as plump as Diane usually thought of her, and she had lost color in her face. All the same, her face hadn't changed much—her pretty smile with the deep dimples and far fewer wrinkles than most people her age had. Her hair was entirely white now, but she kept it short and simple, actually looking rather perky.

"Don't I get any cookies?" Diane asked.

"Well, sure. But I only have one batch out of the oven, and they're just starting to cool."

"That's how I like them."

"Well, don't expect me to get back up, after all the work it took me to sit down. And while you're getting us some cookies, get some milk from the fridge."

Diane was already up. "They're oatmeal, aren't they? With raisins."

"Some things don't change, honey. Maybe I bake them for the kids, but I choose the ones I like. They all want chocolate chips, but I like raisins better."

Diane got out a carton of milk and was looking for glasses in the cupboard when Bea said, "Now tell me what brought this on. What got Jenny thinking she wanted to move in with Greg?"

Diane poured the milk and brought it to the table, and then she placed some cookies on a plate and brought that over. As she did, she explained what had been happening: about Jenny's growing independence, and Greg's influence on her. When Grandma asked, she explained the legal situation and her attorney's hesitancy to push the matter. While Diane was talking, she checked the oven to see how the next batch of cookies was doing. On the counter Grandma had set out two more sheets covered with daubs of cookie dough, and there was a big bowl of dough waiting. It had to be a double batch, or more.

Grandma listened and asked more questions. Finally, she said, "I don't think I'd push the legal side of this too hard. If Jenny's as stubborn as most of the kids in this family, she'll just dig her heels in when you try to bring her back home."

"That's what everyone tells me, Grandma, but it drives me crazy. I know Greg, and I know how he twists things. He'll take control of her, and he'll have her hating me. You can't believe the things he's told her already. According to him, he didn't ever do a thing to me. The problem was all with me—that I didn't . . . you know . . . *satisfy him* the way a wife should."

Bea glanced up, and Diane saw the flash in her eyes. "I think I'll see if the boys left any baseball bats around this place. I'd like to find that man and beat him over the head with one—just to see how much he likes it. They should've put that coward in jail where he belongs."

Diane smiled at the thought of Grandma beating up on Greg. "I just feel like I need to get Jenny home where I can keep her in the Church."

But Bea didn't respond to that, and Diane wondered what she was thinking. Diane sat down at the table and took a bite of one of the cookies.

"Jenny has to see this for herself, Diane—see what that man's all about. And she will. She's a smart girl."

"You sound like my mom."

"Well, that's not an accident. Bobbi thinks she's the smartest woman on the planet, but you need to know, she got her brains from me, not from your grandpa." Grandma gave Diane a sly look and burst into laughter.

"Well, you're both smarter than I am, but—"

"Oh, no. Don't try to tell me that. I've seen what you've done with your life since you had to leave that wife-beating husband of yours. You may be the smartest one of all of us."

Grandma had said things like that to Diane before, but the words touched her this time, and she felt the tears come back to her eyes again. She wanted so much to believe in herself right now. "She's so young, Grandma. And Greg is such a liar. Am I just supposed to sit and wait while he pulls her away from me?"

"Yes. I think you have to wait. I've done a lot of that in my life. And I'm not a patient person. But sometimes we don't have a choice."

Diane thought maybe she did have choices, but she didn't say that to Grandma. She was thinking that coming here was nice, but it didn't change anything. She still had an empty apartment to go back to when she finally left.

"You know who my first big worry was over—I mean, with my kids?" Grandma asked.

"Aunt LaRue, I guess."

Grandma laughed. "Well, you're right in one way. She worried me plenty. Most people wouldn't imagine it now, but Wally was the one who put me through as much as anything back when he was Jenny's age. He always thought he was in Alex's shadow, and he didn't seem to have an ounce of determination in him. He just piddled around, didn't try his best in school or in anything else. And then he came in wanting to join the army. We let him do it, but it was one of the hardest things I ever did in my life. That was all long before he was taken prisoner in the war."

"But look what he did, when he had to do it."

"I know. And that's just my point. For a long time we didn't know if he was dead or alive. We worried that he didn't have enough grit to get through an experience like that. But look what he did. I guess we'd taught him right, and Al had always made such a big thing about the Thomases—that the kids had to be like the pioneers, keep going no matter what, and all that. As it turned out, I think he had plenty of the Snow side of the family in him, too—and we have a little grit ourselves." She laughed again. "He was gone from this house almost five years, and I worried about him every single day—and night—he was gone. That's just how raising kids is most of the time. You teach them, and then you trust that they've learned something."

"Still, though, if you could have pulled him out of that mess, you would have."

"Sure. But maybe that would have been a mistake. Look at the man he is now. A lot of that came from him doing what he had to do—and doing it on his own. Jenny thinks she knows everything right now. She thinks you're only her mom—who doesn't know half as much. But you're going to get a lot smarter to her in the next little while. She'll come back to you."

"I hope so, Grandma. But what if it takes her *years* to get her bearings? Or what if she never does? Greg's going to take her away from the Church, and he's going to have her pulling shady deals with people, the same as he does."

"Nope. I know my Jenny. She reminds me of you and Bobbi. She won't cheat anybody. She knows right from wrong."

Diane wished she were that sure herself.

"LaRue was the one in our family who thought her parents weren't very smart. And Wally had his worries about Kathy. But look at those two women now. They're doing just what they ought to be doing. Those two worried about ten years off my life, I'm sure, and it took them a long time to get things straightened out in their heads—but they came back to what they'd been taught in their homes."

"What about Kurt? He's still struggling."

"I think Kurt's going to be all right in the long run too. I love that boy as much as any of you kids. And he loves me. Any boy who loves his grandma that much is basically all right."

"You believe in *everyone,* Grandma. But some people get messed up and stay messed up."

Grandma stared straight back at Diane and didn't say anything for a time, but Diane saw the steel in her eyes. "That's what it takes, Diane. If we believe in them, love them and trust them, they see who they are through our eyes. That's just how it is, and it's how it will be for Jenny. You stick with her. But give her a little room for now. She needs it."

Diane thought Grandma's logic was anything but airtight, but she believed in the look of those eyes, and she felt a little surge of hope.

"Here's some advice for you, Diane," Grandma said.

"Good. I need it."

"You've given too much of your life to Jenny, and you haven't looked out for yourself. Jenny knows your determination; she needs to see more joy in your eyes. She worries about money because you've always had to, but she needs to see that you *are* happy, whether you've got a lot of money or not."

"My money situation is gradually getting better. Once I get my administrative certificate, I can start making a better living."

"You're missing my point, Di. You need to be happy. You can't tell me that you couldn't have found a husband by now if you'd really wanted one. I think you need someone besides Jenny in your life."

"It's harder than you think, Grandma. The pickings are pretty slim out there."

"What about this widower fellow Bobbi told me about?"

Diane wasn't surprised that Bobbi had talked to Grandma about Spence, but it wasn't anything she really wanted to go into right now. "He's got too many problems with his own family. He's not interested in getting married."

"People can figure those things out if they're really in love."

"Tell him that. He's the one saying he can't think about marriage for now."

"Well . . . don't waste your time on him, then. I'm just saying that it's time for you to stop sacrificing, entirely, and decide what will make you happy."

"I am happy. If I could get Jenny—"

"No, Diane. I don't think you're happy. You've got to get that spark back—the one you had when you were a little girl. I haven't seen that excitement in your eyes for a long, long time."

Diane knew that, but she had come to think that that was how life would always have to be for her. She wasn't sure what she could do to change it.

"I loved your grandfather with all my heart. For a long time, I thought my only purpose in life was to raise a family and love your grandpa. Nothing wrong with that. But I found out I needed to find something for myself, too. I needed to know what I could do, what brought me a little private pleasure, just for me. Life goes by way too fast, but you know what? You're just starting. You're not even halfway through, and once Jenny's on her own, you'll still need something inside you that tells you why you want to get up in the morning. It's time you figured that out for yourself."

Diane nodded. She knew that was true. She really did need to decide who she was going to be once Jenny was gone. But the thought scared her. For a long time, she had been figuring out life one day at a time, just surviving. She needed to assess what it was all going to add up to.

CHAPTER 16

On a Sunday evening, after wondering all day whether Jenny had gone to church, Diane picked up the phone to call her, but then put the receiver down again. She didn't want the same kind of conversation to repeat itself, and she was afraid she would only beg Jenny again. So she looked up the number for her cousin Gene instead.

It was Danny who answered the phone. "This is your aunt Diane," she told him.

"Oh, hi. Did you want to talk to my dad?"

"Actually, I wanted to talk to you. I was wondering, have you seen Jenny at Olympus High?"

He laughed. "Hey, *everyone* has seen Jenny at Olympus High. All the guys are talking about how gorgeous she is. I see her out running after school, so I talk to her once in a while. I don't want anyone to know she's my cousin, though. I figure it'll improve my reputation to be seen with her."

"Is she just working out, or is she on the track team?"

"She's on the team. I hear she's good, too. And she's already more popular than I am, even though she's only been around these last few weeks."

"What has she told you, Danny—I mean, about why she's there?"

"Not much. Mostly she just says that it's been a good decision for her. She was telling me how she wants to go to law school and all this stuff—and how she's going to be partners with her dad."

"So it sounds like she's happy?"

"Oh, yeah. She's having a great time."

"Well, that's good. Are they good kids she's going around with?"

"Pretty much. Most of them have a lot of money, and they think they're pretty hot, if you know what I mean. I know a few of them that do some drinking, but I'm sure Jenny wouldn't do that."

"I hope not. Hey, don't tell her I called, okay? She'd hate it if she knew I was checking up on her."

"Okay, I won't say anything. But doesn't she call you or anything?"

"Actually, no. It's kind of a long story, Danny, but I guess, mostly, she wants some independence right now."

Danny hesitated, as though he wasn't sure what to say. Finally he said, "Well, look, I'll keep track of her a little, if I can. I'm not on the track team, but some of us football players go out and run in the spring—to stay in shape. So when I see her, I'll do the family thing." He laughed. "I'll remind her that she's a Thomas and has to be an example to the entire world—you know, walk across the plains with a smile on her face and all that stuff."

"You do that, Danny." Diane laughed too. Every teenager in the family had always made fun of the same thing, but Diane knew it did make a difference—the sense they had of who they were.

"So did you want to talk to my dad?"

"You mean the bishop is actually home?"

"Yup. I'll get him. And don't worry. Jenny will be okay. I'll tell her which guys to avoid."

"Do that, Danny. Seriously."

Diane had been leaning against the kitchen cabinet, but now she sat down at the table. When Gene answered, she said, "Danny already told me what I wanted to know, but I thought I ought to say hi. For one thing, I wanted to tell you what a great article you wrote about the Iran/Contra thing that Reagan's gotten himself into."

He laughed. "You're loving it, aren't you? Seeing Ronald Reagan in a mess?"

"No. He'll get out of it. He always does. But your article helped me understand what the heck is going on. That's probably the last thing you want to talk about, though—at the end of a long Sunday."

"Actually, I've been planning to call you and haven't gotten around to it. Danny told me a while back that Jenny was down here now. I wondered whether you were all right with that."

"No. Of course not. But at her age, it's hard to tell her what to do."

"Did the judge let her go to Greg, or—"

"No. She just went. And everyone tells me not to fight it. So far, that's what I'm doing." Diane still wasn't sure she believed that was the right choice. Just saying it seemed like defeat. She bent forward, grasped her forehead, and let her elbow rest on the table. Thinking about Jenny running track again, meeting guys, going on with a new life—and Diane not being part of it—was hard for her to accept.

"Danny says she seems to be all right," Gene said. "She's a top student, he tells me."

"Yes, she is. I just worry what kind of influence Greg will be."

"Yeah. That's what I was thinking." He hesitated. His voice was always so soft now, so considered. "You're lonely, aren't you?"

"Yeah, I am."

"I'll tell you something, Di. To me, it seems like maybe you've had more than your share to deal with."

"I guess we both have."

"But things have come around all right for me. It seems like it ought to be your turn."

"I know. I think that way sometimes, too. But Grandma tells me that I have to find happiness inside myself. Do you think that's possible—just to make up your mind, and suddenly feel good about life?"

"It's interesting you would bring that up. Grandma told me pretty much the same thing a long time ago, and in a lot of ways it turned my life around."

"Really? You've never told me that."

"It was not long after Grandpa died. I was trying to get back into life after Vietnam and my surgeries—and all the crazy stuff that was going on in my head. I was still having a lot of ups and downs. We were at Grandma's house one Sunday afternoon, and I said something to Emily that Grandma didn't like. I can't think what I said, but it must have been something pretty mean."

"I can't imagine that."

"Well, then, your memory is not very good. I was pretty rough on people for a while—especially on Emily. But Grandma heard me, and she grabbed me by the arm and dragged me into the kitchen. She pointed her stubby little finger at me and said, 'All right, Mister. Enough is enough.'" Gene laughed.

"Are you serious?" Diane leaned back in her chair. "I can't imagine her doing that."

"Well, she did. And then she dressed me down. I don't remember all of it, but one thing I remember word for word. She said, 'You've felt sorry for yourself long enough. It's time to buck up.' Those were her words: 'buck up.' And then she said, 'You start treating that girl the way she deserves to be treated. And you start right now. Either that or you're going to lose her.'"

"And that helped you?"

"It did. I knew she was right. I knew it was finally time I made a choice. I was angry about the war, and angry I got wounded, and I was taking it out on anyone I could. Grandma was right: I was going to ruin my life—and Emily's—if I didn't make a change. After all the counseling I'd had, and talking to your dad and Alex and Wally, it was finally Grandma telling me I had to 'buck up'"—he laughed again at the thought—"that got me thinking right."

"I've been telling myself that I need to choose happiness. I can't find all my meaning in Jenny. I know that. But I get up every morning feeling so empty that it's all I can do to get myself ready and down to the school. And then I come home to this apartment and . . ." She didn't finish her sentence. She couldn't.

"Well, remember, Di, I couldn't make a choice like that until I'd managed to survive for a couple of years. Give yourself a little time to figure things out. Grandma took a while herself. Do you remember when Grandpa died, how Grandma was telling everyone she was going to travel and go to the symphony and make the best of the life she had left?"

"Yes. And she did it, too."

"I know. She did travel some, and she did do things with some of her friends, but she told me the last time I was over at her house that she missed the days when we were all at home. She said that the best part of life was loving and being loved—having a husband and a family."

"Oh, thanks. That's just what I needed to hear."

"I didn't mean it that way. I just mean that she's *not* happy every minute of every day. She makes the best of things and chooses not to feel sorry for herself—but she still misses Grandpa."

"So what do I do, Gene? Give me some good bishop's advice."

"I don't believe much in handing out advice, Diane. People usually know already what they need to do. I would say, though, that you probably ought to decide what you want to do with your life. You'll be a great principal, if you go at it 'full speed ahead'—and you'll make a lot of difference in some kids' lives."

"That's true. I've got to get focused on that again." She did feel a hint of joy at the thought of dedicating herself to kids, to doing a good job. "But what about loving someone and being loved?"

"That would be good too, Diane. If it happens, I would be overjoyed for you. But I don't think you can wait till then to be happy. I suspect you need to find your own happiness—and then share it with someone when the time comes. If you're not happy, you'll have nothing to give."

"I know. That's what I've been telling myself. So maybe it's time to 'buck up.'"

They both laughed, but Gene did add, "Just don't be too hard on yourself. This is almost like a mourning time right now, getting used to Jenny being gone."

"Yeah, I guess it is. But I do need to start thinking right."

Diane thanked Gene and wished him well, and she said good-bye. After she hung up the phone, she got up and walked into the living room. She sat on the couch and stared at the streetlight outside. The world seemed awfully dark, and the light out there didn't shine very far. She was tempted to cry again, to wonder about Jenny, but she made a choice. She got up, walked to her bedroom, and got her scriptures off her shelf. She had wanted to start *studying* the New Testament—not just read it, but really study. She had even bought a couple of resource books to help her—and then hadn't gotten around to them. She decided she would start right then.

Another couple of weeks passed and Jenny still didn't call. And then one night Spence telephoned. Diane had wanted to talk to him, but she had resisted, knowing that he too needed to figure out how to make the step.

"I was just wondering how you're doing," he said. "Was Ken any help to you?"

"I guess so. He talked me out of going to the judge, and I've decided that's the best advice."

Spence laughed quietly. "Well, he's a wise fellow. Always has been. Some lawyers rush in and make a mess, but he thinks things through."

"Jenny seems perfectly happy with Greg. Her cousin sees her at school, and he says she's doing well."

"Does that bother you?"

It was the right question. Diane had been fighting that impulse—telling herself not to wish for Jenny's misery. "I'm trying to be patient, Spence. I'm trying to be happy. It's what I need to do."

"That's interesting. I've been having the same discussion with myself."

"Are you getting anywhere?"

"I don't know. Sometimes. What about you?"

Diane was leaning back against the kitchen wall. She hadn't turned the light on and now she was feeling the dark. She walked forward, stretching the cord, and flipped the light switch. "I've studied more lately, so I've done better in school. And I've used some of my time to study the gospel. I've enjoyed that. A teacher even told me yesterday that I seem to be almost my old self again. The truth is, I'm faking it most of the time, but I figure if I *act* happy, that's a start."

Diane heard Spence chuckle in that deep voice of his. "That's about where I am. But it's hard to get over all the worries."

"I know. Because worrying accomplishes so much. It's hard not to get hooked on all that success."

He laughed again. "Yeah. Good point." Before she could say anything, he added, "The reason I called, I was just thinking—do you wanna go for a ride?"

"A ride?"

"Yeah. Just take a little drive—up the canyon or somewhere?"

"I don't know, Spence. We shouldn't really drive cars around, just to be driving them."

"Hey, I thought the energy crisis was over."

"It won't be for long if we don't all conserve a lot more than we do."
But she was teasing, and she hoped he could hear it in her voice.

"Is that your only excuse?"

"It's not an excuse, Spence."

"Well, then, is that your only well-founded reason for not wanting
to spend a little time with me?"

"Spence, you're the one who told me . . . you know . . . that this
can't go anywhere."

"That's why I just want to drive around. That's not going anywhere." He sort of chuckled, as though he thought he'd gotten off a
good one. "I just need to talk to you. I want to tell you what's been happening over here. Maybe you can advise me a little."

Diane did want to see him, but she didn't want to feel anything for
him. So she decided to say no—and then she didn't. "Well, all right.
When are you coming?"

"Twenty minutes?"

"Thirty."

"Okay."

Diane had gone for a run that afternoon after school—another
one of her attempts to feel better about herself—and she was still in her
sweats and hadn't showered yet. She dashed into the shower now, thinking that she never could have managed all this in thirty minutes back
in her younger days. She washed her hair quickly but didn't dry it, then
slipped on some jeans and an old purple Weber State sweatshirt. She
thought about putting on a little eye shadow and lipstick, but decided
no, she didn't need to look good for him. But she did take a look at herself, and then grabbed her curling iron and her hair dryer and did what
she could in five minutes.

She was ready in twenty-five minutes. That gave her a few minutes
to sit down and relax, to seem as though she hadn't been rushing. What
surprised her when she walked outside was that the car he'd driven over
was a little Datsun two-door. "I brought the car that Steve drives most

of the time," he said. He turned and grinned at her. "It gets good mileage. We can drive for a while and not deplete the world's oil supply all that much."

"That's how you rich guys think. You don't care about oil shortages as long as you've got gas in your car."

He stopped. "Ooh. That hit home." She stopped too, and she could tell that it really had. "Would you rather just stay here, and—"

"No. I want to get out of the house. I just wanted to put the blame on you for what I want to do." She was half serious, half not. But she smiled, and he took a big breath, faking as though he was fighting for air. She knew what he was joking about: that she had taken his breath away again.

So they got in the car and they drove. They headed north along Harrison Boulevard toward Ogden Canyon. They chatted about this and that for a time, but as they were reaching the mouth of the canyon, Spence asked, "How long has Jenny been gone now?"

"Almost seven weeks."

He nodded, kept looking ahead. "Is it getting any easier?"

"A little, I guess. At least I don't think about her every minute of every day."

"That's good, in a way," Spence said. "Heather doesn't let me think about much of anything but her. She does anything she can to fight the system—mine or the school's."

"Maybe you need to let her fail."

"She is failing—failing everything, every day."

"But there aren't any consequences. She's got everything she needs—from you—and what she seems to be doing is throwing a prolonged tantrum, just to keep your attention."

"I know that. We've worked our way into a cycle that I don't know how to break out of."

"Well . . . I'm not one to be telling you what to do, but I'm trying to get my own head straight about some things." She leaned against the door, looked more toward Spence.

He gave her a little glance and said, "Like what?"

"I've been running every day after school, and eating better—just because I like the way that makes me feel. I bought some tapes so I can start learning a little Spanish while I drive in my car. I need that at school, but it's also something I could use if I ever try to do some sort of humanitarian work—the way we talked about. I made up my mind, if Jenny gets a scholarship for college, and I have a little more money when I become a principal, I'm going to take a look at the world a little bit—maybe figure out where I could accomplish something."

"I thought we were going to be partners in that work."

Diane wasn't sure how to answer him, but she decided to tell him the truth. "Spence, I can't wait for you. I need to be happy, and I'm figuring out what that's going to take. You're not ready to move ahead; I have to be. It's that or choose to be miserable, and I'm not going to do that."

They were passing the Gray Cliff Lodge, a place Diane loved. She had eaten there once long ago, with Greg—back when she'd thought her life was leading toward an easy ride. It was strange to think of it now, strange how accustomed she was to thinking of life as a hard pull. But she really liked thinking that she had some things to look forward to. Spence needed to know that she wasn't waiting for *him* to make her happy.

"I guess you're right, Diane. But I don't think of myself as choosing not to move ahead. I just feel as though I'm in the middle of this huge mess, and I don't know what to do about it. But I want Heather to know, no matter what, how much I love her. I think of the day we brought her home from the hospital, and how completely I loved that little thing—and now I see her with her hair green one day and fire-engine red the next, and I just try to remember she's still the same kid."

"The trouble is, when you try to show her you love her, you do things for her, or buy things for her—and that just leads back into all the same problems you've been talking about."

"No question about it. And I know it. But I don't know how to break out of it."

"Maybe she wants you to say no to her."

"I've been told that—by professionals in the business. And I've tried. But you've never seen anything like the rage she goes into. I guess I'm supposed to be consistent, but I let her beat me at that game— over and over."

Diane decided not to harp on the issue, although she did feel a little impatient with him, that he wouldn't take some of the steps he knew very well he had to take.

Spence continued to drive, silent for a time, and they came to Pineview Dam. Diane thought of the day they had spent on Spence's boat, of their picnic. It struck her that Spence was playing a game with her, too—coming near from time to time, then always retreating. Diane thought of Grandma Bea. "Let me tell you something my grand-mother told me," she said. "It's what I started to tell you on the phone."

"Okay."

"She said that I have to find a way to be happy myself, so Jenny will know what happiness looks like."

"That makes sense to me, Diane. It really does. Heather has said as much to me—that she's sick of me walking around looking like I lost *everything* when I lost Celeste."

"Well . . . it's worth thinking about."

"The thing is, she may want to see me happy, but I don't think she understands what it might take. One thing she can't stand is for me to . . . you know . . . pay attention to anyone."

They both knew what that meant, and Diane was a little embar-rassed. "I'm not saying that, Spence. I don't think that two unhappy people become happy by joining forces."

He looked at her longer than a driver ought to, and he smiled rather mischievously. "It *might* help."

But that sort of flirting was annoying. He was the one always pulling back. "No. I don't think so. I think Grandma is right. I'm fighting everything I've been feeling, and I'm trying to move ahead with my life."

"Hey, it's not as though I don't know you're right. I've got to make the same commitment to myself." Diane could see the little peninsula where she and Spence had picnicked. Spence was looking that direction too. He said, "That was a nice day, Di. The best day I've had since . . . everything happened."

"But?"

"No buts."

"I heard it in your voice. There was a *but* at the end."

He glanced at her and smiled. "Well, you know what I told you that day. I don't think anything has changed."

Diane let her breath blow out and hoped he heard it. She wanted him to know that she was disgusted with his keeping in touch, asking to see her, and then always ending with the same parting words.

But he didn't turn the car around. When the highway turned left toward Huntsville, she thought he might continue around the reservoir, or simply turn back, but instead, he turned right—east—toward South Fork Canyon. He had no way of knowing that she had spent a day there with Wade once, back when she had thought he was the boy she would marry.

He drove on to the picnic area, and when it seemed like maybe he was finally going to turn back, Diane said, "Let's get out of the car. There's something I want to show you."

So they got out. They still didn't talk, but Diane led him down the hill to a little log bridge that crossed the creek. "Okay," she said, "there's something you have to experience. Stand right here." She took hold of the thin log that formed the railing of the bridge. "Lean out like this and stare straight down at the water."

The water was running swiftly today, the spring runoff still heavy. The air was thick with the smell of mud and life, and the trees were budding out around the bridge. There was a lushness coming on that was hard to resist.

"Do you feel it yet?" Diane asked, and she was seeing, feeling, the old sensation she remembered.

"Feel what?"

"Stare at the water—just past the edge of the bridge. Just focus right on it."

"Oh," he said in a kind of gasp.

"Are you flying?"

"Wow. Yes. It's an optical illusion. It's like the water is standing still and we're soaring over it, backwards."

"Shut up, okay? Don't explain it, just feel it."

He laughed. "Woooooo," he said. "It's wild. It feels like we're going a hundred miles an hour."

"I told you, shut up."

"Okay. Okay."

And they flew. Diane had forgotten what it did to her stomach. She had to look up every few seconds, just to keep herself from getting sick. Finally, she stepped back. Spence did too. And he looked at her. "That was something," he said, beaming. "I offered to take you for a ride, and you took me for one."

"We didn't burn any oil, either."

"Nope."

But he wasn't smiling as much. He was looking into her face, and then Diane took a chance. She stepped forward, slid her arms around his waist, and said, "Don't talk. Don't think." She reached her face toward his. She wasn't sure whether she had kissed him or he had kissed her, but their lips met.

217

And he kept holding her, even after she thought it was a long enough kiss for a first time.

She was the one who finally pulled away. Then she stood looking up at him. "Okay, it's time for you to tell me that we have to think of our kids, and not try to make each other happy," she said. But she saw the *but*. She saw that he was scared, or worried, or unsure. And she acknowledged the truth of what Grandma had told her: She couldn't wait for Spence. If she wanted to be happy, she would have to find her own path to get there. No prince was in her future. No Superman to save her.

CHAPTER 17

Spence didn't call again. Diane was glad that she felt some anger toward him. It was good to find out that he didn't have the courage to move ahead with his life. She might have let him play her along for a long time, only to be disappointed. This way, she could forget about him, and she made up her mind to do just that.

She had been telling herself for all these years that there were more important things for her than to marry again. Life wasn't a fairy tale. Spence had a lot going for him, but he was turning out not to be a prince at all. Princes, at least in fairy tales, didn't waffle, didn't show up and then disappear again. She had managed all right for all these years, and she could continue to manage. And that determination—mixed with a little anger—was what she knew she needed now. It was time for her to think about her own future and to stop thinking of herself as victimized and lonely.

Diane worked hard on her final papers for the term at the university and on her preparation for her final exams. She tried not to think so much about Jenny. She knew she had to trust that Jenny would get her own head straight one of these days; Diane could no longer take responsibility for her decisions. Or at least that was how Diane thought on her good days. Jenny was now calling once in a while, but her calls were always short and not very informative. Diane still struggled when she didn't hear from her for a week, but she was fighting against discouragement, and she tried to fill her days with hard work.

Some of the teachers at her school knew about Jenny, knew what Diane was going through, and they commented that they were happy to see her return to her old enthusiasm. She and one teacher, a woman her own age named Tara, who had never married, vowed that they were going to take a trip to Africa next year—whether they could afford it or not. They talked about it almost every day, about the projects they might be able to get involved in there, and it really did inspire Diane.

One morning, when Diane arrived at school, she saw Betty Zimmer, her principal, in the hallway. "Diane," Betty said, "do you have a minute?"

"Sure," Diane told her, and they walked into her office.

Betty was a tall, strong woman. She was forthright, even a little commanding in her tone at times, but she could also be wonderfully tender with kids. She knew all their names and went out of her way to show them individual attention. In most ways, she was the kind of principal Diane hoped to be.

Betty motioned for Diane to sit on the little couch in her office, then sat on a chair nearby, not behind her desk. "Diane, when are you going to have your administrative certificate finished?" she asked.

"This summer, if everything goes as planned."

"Is there any reason that wouldn't happen?"

"No. Not now."

Betty laughed. "What does that mean?"

"Well . . ." Diane leaned back on the couch and folded her arms. "You know how worried I've been about Jenny. But I'm moving ahead now. I can't spend my life preoccupied and always fussing about her. She's at an age where she has to start figuring some things out for herself."

"That's right. It's what I told you, isn't it?"

Diane smiled. It was what everyone had told her.

"You know how much I want to see you get a good job when you finish your certificate. There still aren't many women principals in our district, but I was talking to the superintendent the other day, and he came right out and said that he thought some of his best administrators *are* women." She laughed loudly, the way she always did. "Of course, he *did* say, 'at our elementary schools,' like women just couldn't handle a junior high or high school."

"That's because we can be 'motherly' in an elementary school."

Betty laughed. "Yeah, I'm *motherly,* all right. My only kid is Frank, my dog."

Diane knew the story. Betty had named her dog Frank after a man she'd been engaged to years ago—a man who had backed out just a few weeks before the wedding was scheduled. She always joked that she went home every night and gave Frank a good kick—but the truth was, she treated the dog as though he owned the place.

"Well, I didn't get into all that—although I felt like saying maybe we'd be better off with women at all levels, including superintendent." She laughed again. "But what I did say was that you would make a first-rate principal, and I thought you'd be ready by fall."

"Oh, Betty, thanks."

"Well, I hate to lose you here, but I think it's what you need now— a new challenge. And there's no doubt in my mind that you'll do a great job."

"I'd like to try. I've learned a lot in my classes, but I've learned a lot more from you."

"Well, anyway, you're on his radar screen now, so finish up that certificate, but long before that, you need to apply for those openings. He's starting to look right now. One principal is retiring this year, and one—a man, of course—is probably moving to a junior high. So there'll be two openings for sure. If I were you, I'd drop by the district office right away—this afternoon, maybe—and pick up some application forms."

"I will," Diane said. She got up. "That'll give me something to focus on. Betty, thanks for saying something to him."

"I wouldn't do it if I didn't know how sharp you are. You're good with kids, but you also keep track of the details, work well with people—all those things. Be sure to have me write a letter for you."

Diane left the office uplifted, feeling stronger, and she did go by later that day and pick up an application. Afterward, she wanted to tell someone what had happened, and she did stop by to talk to her mom and dad, but it was Jenny she really wanted to tell. And, as much as she fought admitting it to herself, she wanted to tell Spence.

But she didn't call either one, and her apartment seemed unusually quiet as she ate a heated-up bowl of canned soup, all by herself. Some of her joy from that morning slipped away, but she studied anyway, and then she started on the application. She wished she had a nice IBM Selectric typewriter at home—or the computer that she'd let Greg take to Jenny that night he'd moved her belongings. Instead, she wrote out her answer to a question about her goals, revised it a couple of times, and then decided to type it before she went to bed. Her typewriter didn't have a correction tape on it, so she had to use the white correction slips, but she was very careful to make everything look neat.

At eleven, when she was usually already in bed, she didn't feel like turning in. She'd felt that a lot lately. She was tired, but she didn't like the sounds in the apartment when she was there alone. She didn't think much about the dark, about being alone, when Jenny was sleeping down the hall, but she felt vulnerable now. So she sat up too late watching Johnny Carson on the *Tonight Show.* When she finally did go to bed, she lay awake for a time, trying to rekindle the enthusiasm she'd felt that morning.

Diane tried not to think about Jenny, but she couldn't help wondering whether she would come back for at least part of the summer. Would they never be close again? She knew she had to stop asking that question, but as she lay there, she found herself once again remembering Jenny as a little girl, the two of them laughing and playing together.

In the second week of May the weather turned warm, almost suddenly, and Diane liked the change. Jenny did call, after having failed to do so for a couple of weeks. She was nice enough on the phone, even apologized for not calling lately. Diane made a careful attempt not to seem nosy, and she was purposely upbeat as she talked about the job openings she had applied for. She wanted to sound confident, to give Jenny that sense that Grandma Bea had talked about—that she knew how to be happy. But Jenny volunteered little information, and Diane found herself, in the end, disheartened by the call. She heard the rhetoric of happiness in what Jenny said, but it sounded empty, as though she were worried about something and wouldn't admit it.

On Friday night Diane came home from school thinking about studying, but she didn't really want to. She didn't feel like cooking, either—or opening up her usual can of soup. So she called in an order for a pizza, said she would pick it up, and then drove to a movie-rental shop first. She didn't have a video player, but she rented two of her favorite films and a player as well. She and Jenny had seen *Ferris Bueller's Day Off* and *9 to 5* in theaters before, and now both films were out on video. She and Jenny had laughed so hard about Ferris Bueller, even though the movie had seemed a little too rebellious to Diane, and Jenny had loved *9 to 5* because in it a young woman from a poor background had fought her way up in the business world.

So Diane came home with the pizza and the two movies, telling herself she would have a fun night. She felt a certain irony in doing alone what she and Jenny had once liked to do together, but she told herself she wasn't going to think about that.

It was still early, but two movies would take quite a while, so she hooked up the video player to her television set, picked up the movies, and looked at them. She was trying to decide which one she wanted to watch first when she glanced out the window and saw a car pull up in front of her apartment. It took her a moment to realize that it was Jenny's red Toyota—and then she saw Jenny get out of the car.

Diane felt a flood of joy, and then, almost immediately, an equal sense of concern. Maybe Jenny had just decided to visit, as Diane had invited her to do. If so, Diane would have to be careful. She couldn't probe, couldn't say anything that would drive her away again. But by then Diane could see Jenny's face as she walked quickly toward the front door. She looked upset—looked the way she had as a little girl when she'd fallen off her bike and hurt herself.

Diane hurried to the door and opened it just as Jenny reached for the doorknob. Diane saw that she'd been crying, and then she saw the red mark across her face. They looked at each other for a second or two, and Diane saw everything in her eyes. "He hit me," Jenny said. She started to sob. Diane reached out, took her hands, and pulled her into the apartment and into her arms. She was crying too, and she knew even then that it was perverse to feel joy that this could happen. But at least now Jenny knew.

And yet it hurt, too. Diane knew what this meant to Jenny. She knew how she had felt the first time Greg had betrayed her this way. Jenny had wanted a father so long, had wanted Greg to love her, and now she'd lost that.

Jenny clung tight to her mother. "I should have come home a month ago," she said. "I could see by then what he was going to do to me, sooner or later. I saw how he treated Marilyn. She left today too."

Diane led Jenny to the couch, had her sit down next to her, and held her close again. For a long time she let Jenny cry. Jenny had always been such a self-assured little girl, confident that she could manage anything, and now she seemed soft, pliant in Diane's arms. Diane hoped this introduction of reality into Jenny's life wouldn't break her, wouldn't leave lifelong scars. "I wish I'd never let you go with him, Jenny. I was so afraid something like this would happen to you."

Jenny sat up straight. "You couldn't have stopped me, Mom. I had my mind made up, and I would have done it one way or another."

"Do we need to see a doctor? How bad did he hurt you?" Diane pushed Jenny's hair back, touched her face. There was a deep red mark and a bit of a cut on her cheekbone.

"He hit me with the back of his hand—sort of slapped me. But he knocked me down, he hit me so hard. And he had a ring on. That's what cut me."

"He did that to me once. I know how it hurts. Let's go have you checked."

"No. I'll be okay. But take pictures of me. That's what he would do. We need proof this time, so he can't lie about everything."

"Okay. That's a smart thing to do. But I'll need to buy film. I'll go get some in a few minutes."

"I didn't believe you, Mom. I just didn't believe you."

"Honey, that's because he's your dad. You didn't want to believe he could be like that. I went through the same thing."

"There's something wrong with him, Mom. He doesn't have normal feelings. He just does what he wants, and if people get in his way, he bulls right over the top of them. He can look you straight in the eye and lie without even blinking."

Diane took hold of Jenny's hands. "Tell me what's been happening. What has he lied about?"

"For one thing, he's going to jail. He's been indicted again, and this time it's for things he's done himself. He can't pass it off on his partner. He was taking money from people, telling them that he'd invest it for them and make them a lot of money, and then he was spending it on himself."

"It's the same thing they were doing before."

"I know it is. He doesn't care what he does to people. All those years when he's been saying he couldn't help you, he's been getting anything he wants for himself."

"But do you know for sure that he's going to jail?"

"Pretty much. A while back—maybe four or five weeks ago—he was arrested again, but they let him out, and he came home. He went crazy, screaming about all the lies that people were telling about him. He kept saying that he was going to make a lot of money for people if they would just have a little patience—but they didn't have the brains to give him time. A lot of stuff like that. Then he started screaming at Marilyn, telling her how she was the one who had to take fancy trips and always have new furniture, and that was why he'd spent money from accounts that he should have left alone. I mean, he just admitted what he'd done."

"I'll bet it wasn't Marilyn who wanted to spend the money."

"It wasn't. She told me that after. But she was scared to death. She didn't say a word back to him. And that only made him madder. He started screaming at her that she didn't believe in him, that she was looking at him like she was scared. 'What do you think I'm going to do to you? Hit you?' he kept saying. 'Is that what you think?' And then he looked over at me and said, 'What have you been telling her, Jenny—all the lies your mother tells?' I was mad by then. I told him I hadn't told her anything, and he shouldn't be yelling at us like that."

"I can picture the whole thing. I know how he explodes."

"He told me, 'Your mom's been telling you all those lies, and now you believe them, don't you?' And then he started in with all this stuff about him deserving better than that because he'd done so much for me."

"Oh, Jenny. It's what he always said to me, that I thought the worst of him. And then it's like, when he would hit me, it was my fault, because after all, I had expected it—and that brought it out of him."

"Yeah. That's exactly what he was yelling at us—that if he *did* hit one of us, it was only because we were acting like we expected him to do it."

"Why didn't you come home then?"

"Because he calmed down. And then, after a couple of hours, he came to my room and knelt down by my bed and begged me to forgive him. He kept saying that he had a terrible temper, but that it was all talk; he would never hurt me. He admitted that he hurt you a couple of times, but he would never do anything like that again. He was a better person than that now. He told me there was no chance he'd go to jail. He hadn't done anything wrong. We would still do all the things we'd talked about."

"I know exactly what you're talking about. He would do that with me—beg me to forgive him—and I'd believe him."

Jenny leaned back on the couch. "The stupid thing is, I *didn't* believe him. I'd seen the way he treated Marilyn, always so sarcastic with her, always implying that she was stupid, and I knew he must have done that to you. I was sure he'd been dishonest in his business, too. But I don't know—I felt sorry for him. He begged me, and made me feel bad for him. I think I didn't want to admit to you that I'd been wrong to move down there." She thought for a moment, and then added, "I didn't want to leave Olympus High, either. I liked it there, and I've been dating a couple of boys I like. I didn't like to think about coming back to Ogden right in the middle of the term."

"So what now?"

"I don't know. I do want to come home, if you'll let me."

Diane took Jenny in her arms again. This was life, and Diane hadn't felt enough of it for a while, no matter how hard she'd tried to convince herself. "Oh, yes," she said. "I want you here as long as I can have you. I've missed you so much."

"I've been homesick too. One reason I didn't want to talk to you was that I was afraid I'd start crying. But Mom, I think I need to finish out school down there—you know, the classes I'm taking, and track season. It's only a few weeks until summer. Could I maybe drive down there every day, or something like that?"

"Maybe you could stay with Grandma Bea during the week and come back here on weekends."

"Yeah, I thought of that. I'd like to be with her for a while. But I thought you would tell me just to come home and stay—and go back to Ogden High."

"Jenny, I've always tried to make too many of your decisions. I won't do that anymore. It probably does make more sense to finish out down there at this point, but the main thing is, I need to trust in your judgment."

Jenny nodded. She was crying again. "Mom, thanks."

"But is it the *classes* you don't want to leave behind—or the *boys?*"

Jenny smiled. She wiped the tears off her cheeks. "I'm not, like, in love or anything. I won't mind coming back to Ogden High with my old friends for my senior year. I liked some of the kids down there, but most of the ones I got to be friends with were kind of empty-headed, if you want to know the truth."

"Did you go to church?"

"Not much. Dad always said that he 'normally' went, but then he'd have excuses more often than not. At first, I was just happy not to go. But after he lost his temper so bad that first time, he started going more—like he wanted to prove to me and Marilyn that he wasn't such a bad guy. During that time I got to know my Laurel leader in that ward, and she had some really good talks with me. It was the best thing that happened to me the whole time I was in Salt Lake. She's been telling me that I needed to go home. I'd made up my mind I would come back when school got out, but then, today, everything went crazy."

"What pushed him over the line?"

"I don't know exactly. When I came home from school he was already there, and he was screaming at Marilyn. I heard her say that she was leaving him, and she called him a crook. He had either hit her or thrown her down; she was on the floor when I walked into the kitchen. She was holding the side of her head with one hand, and blood was running between her fingers."

"Blood?"

"She told me afterwards that she'd hit her head on the cabinet when he'd knocked her down. When I came in, he spun around and started yelling at me. 'Are you satisfied now?' he kept saying. 'Did you see what you wanted to see? Go home and tell your mother. You'll make her very happy.' I told him, 'Don't worry, I'll tell her, and I'll tell the judge, too.' And that's when he said, 'Tell him this,' and bam, he socked me with the back of his hand. Then he walked out and got in his car and burned rubber all the way out of that long driveway."

"Is Marilyn okay?"

"I think so. But she was hurting. I helped her tie a bandage around her head. Her mother lives in Salt Lake, and she was going there, and then she said she was going to a hospital. She probably needed stitches, but mostly, she wanted proof of what he'd done to her. She told me, 'Jenny, go home. Get away from him. He's evil.' So I went in and packed up a lot of my stuff. I guess I'll have to go back for some things. I didn't take time to unhook my computer. I was too afraid he'd come back."

"Well, he'll make it tough. I can tell you that."

"Maybe not. I think he gave up today. I think he knows he's going to jail. Marilyn told me that his attorney had called and wanted him to take some sort of plea bargain for a shorter sentence. I guess that's what got him so mad."

"Well, maybe. But Greg always bounces back, and he manipulates every situation to his own advantage."

"That's why we need pictures of my face."

"Okay. Let's get your stuff out of the car. Then you can get your pajamas on while I run to the drugstore and buy some film. When I get back we'll reheat the pizza I brought home tonight, and we'll watch movies."

"I saw the video player. What movies did you get?"

"*Ferris Bueller's Day Off* and *9 to 5*."

Diane saw the joy come into Jenny's face and, just as suddenly, saw her eyes fill up with tears again. "I'm so glad to be home," she said.

"I feel like I can breathe again," Diane said, and she took Jenny in her arms one more time. "But you need to know something. I've grown up a little myself lately. I'm excited about the future. I have a good chance of getting that principal's job, and I'm going to do a good job, if I do. I'm figuring out how I'm going to be happy the rest of my life—after you're not here with me."

"Mom, I'm changing my mind about a lot of things, too. One night I talked with Sister Miller, my Laurel leader, for a long time—all about my future and everything. I just feel different about what I want to do."

"Okay. We'll talk about it. But I won't try to tell you what I think. I'll listen."

"No. I want your opinion."

Diane nodded. "Well, sure," she said. "We have *so much* we need to talk about." And she took another breath, just to feel how good it was to breathe easily.

Chapter 18

Jenny spent the next four weeks living with Grandma Bea. She came home every weekend, however, and she and Diane had lots of good talks. She often reported to Diane the conversations she had had with her great-grandmother and with all her cousins and aunts and uncles, who called on Grandma continually. "I can feel what's happening," she told Diane one day. "They know how frail she is, and every time they come, you can tell what they're thinking: *Maybe this is the last time I'll see her.*"

"I know," Diane said. "I think the same thing when I'm with her. She's getting so she looks translucent—like she's turning into an angel right before our eyes."

"She is an angel, Mom."

"A feisty one."

"I know. She's so funny. I told her that I wish I had known Great-Grandpa—because everyone says how wonderful he was. Grandma said, 'Well, he's gotten a lot better since he died. Back when we had to live with him, he wasn't always so wonderful.' I said, 'Really?' because I kind of took her seriously. But she just laughed and said, 'He was like all of us, honey. He was better some days than others.'"

Diane laughed. "That's true, too. He could be really kind, but he had an opinion about everything—especially politics—and he never stopped trying to straighten us all out."

Jenny was sitting across the kitchen table from Diane. It was a Saturday morning and they were eating Cocoa Puffs with bananas, an indulgence Grandma Bea would have found disgusting. "Aunt Kathy told me the same thing," Jenny said. "I guess she argued with him all the time. But she's sort of the granola queen, isn't she? She's not quite like anyone else in our family."

"Maybe a little like LaRue."

"Well, yeah. But Kathy and Marshall are all into growing their own organic food, and Kathy has quit eating meat entirely."

Diane laughed again. "You should have known Kathy when she was in college, back east. She was pretty much the family hippie in those days—and for quite a while she had nothing to do with the Church."

"What brought her back?" Jenny had finished her cereal and slid back the bowl, but for once, she didn't seem in a hurry to run off.

"Grandpa. Grandma. The whole family, I think."

Diane was surprised when she saw tears in Jenny's eyes. "The Thomases, they're the real thing, aren't they?"

"Yeah, they are. But I haven't always felt like I was one of them—my life going the way it's gone."

"I used to feel like I wanted to do better in life than my cousins, just to show we weren't inferior. But I don't know . . . I don't feel that way now. They really do love me. I got to know Danny at school this year. I could tell he liked me."

"Well, I might as well admit, I asked him to keep an eye on you."

"Yeah, he told me that. But he likes me for myself, too."

"He's like his dad. He's a nice boy."

Jenny finally got up and took her bowl to the sink. "He's got lots of friends, but he doesn't play all the high school popularity games. He's just who he is. He sort of reminds me of Grandma. It's like he knows who he is and he doesn't have to worry about it."

"I think it does go back to her and to Grandpa, and I guess to their

232

parents before them. It's the chain we keep forming when we take the best of what we get and pass it along."

Jenny turned toward Diane, seemed to think for a moment, but she only nodded without saying anything.

Grandma Bea died in July, not quite making it to the 24th of July celebration she had always loved. The family gathered at the stake center in Sugar House for the funeral. Diane watched Jenny carefully, knowing how deeply she felt the loss, but she was glad that Jenny had had those weeks with Grandma. "Sacred weeks," Jenny had actually called them, and Diane could hardly believe that Jenny had grown up enough to think of them that way.

Aunt Beverly read a brief eulogy, and Diane was struck by how little Grandma had done that could actually be listed. She'd served in many positions in the Church, but much of her life had been behind the scenes, just making other people's lives work—especially her husband's. She was mother of a senator, of bishops and stake presidents, grandmother to a whole line of successful people, but she had never been prominent herself—except to the thousands of people, especially in her stake, who knew her and loved her.

Wally was the first speaker. His health had gotten even worse lately. He looked pale and weak, but he was the same man Diane had known all her life, good-natured, funny, and thoughtful at the same time. He talked now about his mother's strength. "Everyone always thought Dad was the power behind our family, but he leaned awfully hard on Mom, who looked every challenge in the eye without blinking. She didn't have to talk about faith—she just *had* it. She knew the Lord about as well as anyone I've ever known, and she talked to Him in her prayers like He was sitting next to her on the couch."

Wally didn't cry, but he took a long pause. "When I think of Mom,

I think of our kitchen table. Our kitchen was like the center of the world, bright and warm in winter, and so full of Mom that when I smell good food, she's the first person I think of. She fussed over us, advised us, chastised us at times—but mostly she loved us. She just knew we were going to be good kids, and I think we tried to live up to that faith she had in us." He chuckled. "Of course, I have to admit, I gave her a few worries before I came around. And LaRue considered her options for a while before she settled on Mom's point of view."

Diane and Jenny were sitting among the Thomases in the front of the chapel, and Diane heard the soft clatter of laughter around them.

"When I was in the Philippines, and later in Japan during the war, I almost died a few times. But certain things kept me alive. I thought of Lorraine, even though I had no reason to believe she'd still be 'available' when I got home. I thought of things Dad had taught us. And I thought of my brother and my sisters. But more than anything, I would picture our house in my mind, remember every part of it and how it felt to be there. And I'd always come back to that kitchen. We weren't fed well as prisoners, so I guess it was natural to think about a kitchen—about the meals I'd grown up with. But mostly it was the smell of the place, the brightness of it. It was Mom, and the way she filled it all up.

"When I came home, finally, I got off the bus, carried my duffel bag, and walked to my house. I savored every second of that walk, and then I stood outside our house and just looked at it for a little while before I walked inside. When I got inside, it was all full of my mother, just the way I'd known it would be. I went in and hugged Mom, and then I sat down at that kitchen table, and I knew it was over—everything I'd been through. I was home. I was with my mother."

He stood silent for a painfully long time, and then he finally said, "Now she's gone home. She'll see her mother. Her father. And her Father in Heaven. And in time, we'll all go home to Mom. I hope heaven smells like that kitchen. I hope it's just as bright. But whatever it's like, it will be where Mom is, and it will be like her. We all know heaven—because we know her." He smiled suddenly. "The one thing that worries me is that she might have to watch what she says a little, up there. She had a great talent for saying what she thought, whether it was what she *ought* to say or not. I hope heaven is a place where that kind of frankness is appreciated. It sure seems like it ought to be. Either way, I have a feeling that the spirit world just got to be a lot more fun, with her arrival."

Diane was laughing—and crying. She loved that her family always knew how to laugh. She thought of Grandma telling her that she was going to go after Greg with a baseball bat. Maybe she would have to repent for that one—or maybe she wouldn't.

Aunt LaRue spoke next. She was almost sixty, but she was still lean and tall, dark-haired. She often joked about dyeing her hair, and Diane supposed she did, but she never seemed to change in appearance, always wearing her bright dresses, her high heels, her slightly reckless smile. She was a BYU professor now, as was her husband, but Diane sometimes wondered how she fit in with the faculty.

"Well," she said, to open her talk, "as Wally already warned you, I was the family project for a long time. I left that home Wally talked about, just happy to get away. I wanted to see what this world was all about, and I took a fairly long look at it. I couldn't find myself a man, and wasn't even sure for a long time that I wanted one—at least one who would cramp my style. But I came home, too. I could fight Dad, rebut all his arguments, and tell him how narrow-minded he was, but I couldn't refute Mom's goodness. It was what I knew was right, no matter how many other approaches to life I tried."

LaRue looked down at the family before her. "Hey," she said, "I didn't ever get *that* far away. I just did things a little differently. I borrowed that smart-aleck side of Mom's personality and tried to develop it into an art form."

Diane thought that was true. She hadn't known Aunt LaRue

during most of those years, but she'd known her cousin Kathy, who had gone east to college and studied at Smith, where LaRue was a professor. They had apparently been much alike, except that Kathy had wandered even farther away for a time. But Diane had always known who Kathy was, no matter how much she challenged the family's sense of what was appropriate. She was one of them. She had Grandma's kindness in her. She had been zealous in her causes, but she had also known that people mattered more than systems or organizations.

"Here's the truth about Mom," Aunt LaRue said. "And most people would never admit it. Her faith was absolute, just as Wally said it was, but she knew the difference between religion and culture, and she didn't buy into some of the outward behaviors of superficial religiosity. That's why she liked to say the 'wrong thing.' It's not as though she didn't know she was shocking people with her little unexpected comments. In her own way, she was always saying, 'Let's remember what real faith is, and let's drop some of the phony stuff we say and do.' I remember one time, Dad was serving as stake president, as he had for what seemed forever, and everyone was always talking about him in respectful tones, as though he were not just a Church leader but a *king* or something. We were coming out of stake conference one day, and mind you, I was a teenager, bored as I could be, glad the meeting had finally ended. A woman came up to Mom and told her how wonderful Dad's talk had been, and started in about the blessing it was to have such a spiritual leader. So what does Mom say? She laughs and says, 'If you ask me, it would have been a better talk if he'd stopped about twenty minutes sooner. He gets carried away sometimes, and he forgets about all the moms with little babies.'

"And you know what? The woman didn't take offense at all. She laughed with Mom, and she said, 'Well, all the brothers go on a little longer than they need to,' and all of a sudden, no one was pretending. I have to tell you, it was Mom's genuineness, her honesty, her *real* faith that I could never quite leave behind, and it was what I came back to.

236

I try to spread a little of that reality around BYU now, and I find that my students don't mind one bit."

LaRue was like a flash of light, her teeth so bright, her eyes so mobile. But she quieted at that point, and she said, "I love the gospel. I love the image Christ holds out before us. He tells us to be meek and humble, kind and loving. He tells us to care about others and not push ourselves forward. I'm not very good at any of those things, but in my old age I want to see whether I can't become a little more like Christ. I read the scriptures to inspire me, and I pray for strength, but when I look for an example of how a true follower should live, all I have to do is think about my mother. I hope you great-grandchildren *felt* what your grandma was, and I hope you let those feelings guide you as you live out your own lives."

The great-grandchildren came forward then and sang "I Am a Child of God," a song Grandma Bea had loved, and then Bobbi walked to the pulpit. "I was just thinking," she said, "how different we brothers and sisters are. I don't know that Dad was particularly happy about that. He would have preferred us to be a little more predictable. I think some of us set out to shock him with our opinions—especially our political opinions. And we could always get his goat. Mom read the newspaper and knew what was going on, but she looked right on past politics and got down to the people who make up our world. When LaRue and I tried to shock her, it was always as though she could see right through our talk. She knew our hearts.

"But I don't want to make Mom sound like a cliché—you know, the sweet little wife behind the scenes, loving and kind and sort of dumb. She just wasn't like that. At funerals we always say, 'This dear sister never said anything bad about anyone.' Mom wasn't like that. She could get really irritated with the things people did, and she wasn't afraid to say so. But all I had to do was start condemning someone I disagreed with, and she would go straight to their defense. It was like she knew the difference between behavior and spirit. She could be disappointed with people, even disgusted with them, but she would always say, 'Well, you know, I'm not perfect myself. What about you?' And that would put me in my place.

"That still sounds like funeral talk, I know. Mom had her faults. I'm sure she did. But I've been trying to think all week what they were, and I just can't seem to come up with any. Is that because she really was perfect? Probably not. But I'm going to think about her that way anyway. And I want to be just like her when I grow up."

Diane was thinking that her mom wasn't quite as soft as Grandma—maybe because Grandma had been ninety years old. But Bobbi *was* like Grandma Bea, whether she knew it or not.

Alex was the final speaker. There was no man in this world Diane had more respect for. He was one of the best-known men in Utah, a senator and a respected Church leader, but she knew him for his kindness and his great interest, always, in her.

"We've known this day was coming for quite some time," Alex said, sounding subdued, not anything like the stump speaker he could become when campaigning. "And I suppose we've dreaded it for selfish reasons, but mostly, today, we're happy for Mom. She's getting the spirit world a little better organized and, as others have said, making the angels laugh. I hope there's cooking in heaven, and good food, because I don't know what Mom would do if she couldn't feed people. Maybe there are other kinds of feeding there, but whatever kind they have, that's what she's doing, making things better by her presence.

"Bobbi couldn't think of any faults Mom had, but she's younger. I was the oldest, and I remember her giving me a few swats across the backside one day, and I remember being convinced that she was a hard woman to punish an innocent man, and to ignore my heartfelt re-*but*-tals for what she'd done to my . . .

"Well, anyway, I can't remember what I was accused of that day, but surely she had ignored the presumption of innocence and sentenced me forthwith. She was a little too quick to judgment, if you ask me, and should have deliberated longer, heard my full defense, and then taken a less retributive approach to my punishment."

Alex stood for a time, smiling, seemingly remembering. "She actually was too quick to make up her mind sometimes, and she often regretted that. It's a quality some of the rest of us in the family are guilty of too. But she didn't make up her mind forever. She could rethink a subject. What I remember best about that day she spanked me was that later on she took me in her arms and told me she was sorry—that she'd been in a bad mood and she'd taken it out on me. I think I was about six or so, and I had certainly been convinced she was wrong, but I never thought a parent—a grown-up—would admit such a thing to a kid.

"Now, Dad, he wasn't as good at that. When he made up his mind, it was like trying to pry a bear trap apart to change his thinking. A rusty bear trap. Sometimes it got stuck in the locked position, and that was the end of it." Alex was still smiling. "I've always tried to be more like Mom in that regard, but I've been accused of being too much like Dad." Now Diane saw light reflecting from Alex's eyes, knew they were filling up. "Since Monday, when she took her last breath, I've had a picture in my mind. I keep seeing Dad, somewhere waiting for her. And I don't know how those reunions happen, but I know for sure that our sadness was his greatest joy. He's been waiting for her a lot of years now. He's only half himself without her. In her own way, she was a little more independent, able to be herself without Dad, but he needed her.

"Dad loved to talk about the pioneers, about our great Thomas heritage, about being noble and strong, and walking with our chins up, like those pioneer forefathers. Mom was the one who would laugh a little and hint that maybe some of them were average folks, just doing their best. At least Dad had a sense of humor, and when she would burst his bubble, he'd chuckle with her, but their two visions worked together. Dad was always trying to get us to see the big picture, to remember who we were, to keep the concept before us—to buckle down and march forward. Mom was the one who would have organized the square dancing in the evening, after the long march of the day was over. She's the one who would have been going from wagon to wagon, finding out how everyone was doing, and telling a family what they could do for this ailment or that one. She was the one who would have cooked a little extra and shared it around. She understood the long trek that was before us in this life, but she figured we ought to enjoy it, and not just focus on the grim realities. When Dad got a little too serious, she could always tease him a little. You would think he would have resented that, and I saw times when he did, but overall, he seemed to know he was a better man when Mom pulled on his pant leg and brought him back down to earth.

"And today they're together."

Alex looked down at the pulpit for a time. "Today they're together," he said again, more softly this time. "You little ones who miss your great-grandmother, will you remember that? You didn't know Grandpa, but remember that he needed her even more than we do, and they're both happier to be together."

After the funeral, the family gathered at Grandma's house, where Grandma's absence was so much more obvious than it had been at the stake center. Diane took time to talk to her cousins, uncles, and aunts, and she watched Jenny move around doing the same thing. At one time, Jenny stepped to her mom, hugged her around the shoulders, and said, "This is how the celestial kingdom will be."

"I know," Diane said. "I was thinking the same thing myself."

Later, as Diane and Jenny were driving back to Ogden, Jenny said, "Everyone in the family thinks it's really important to tell me what a wonderful mother you've been to me."

"Good. Don't you forget it."

Diane had cried enough today. Now she wanted to be as light as Grandma had always been. But she was still feeling that the world would never be exactly the same again. A generation had passed away. How would she feel on holidays when the family no longer gathered at Grandma's house?

"When you're growing up, you never think about whether your mom is being a good mother or not," Jenny said. "You just figure that's what her job is, to look out for her kids."

"But you got really tired of me trying to monitor you all the time—and to question you about everything."

"Yeah, I did. I thought it would be wonderful to live in Salt Lake and have my freedom."

"And you did like it, didn't you?"

"Sure I did. I still look forward to being at college and being on my own a little more."

"I understand that. I was the same way."

"But during that time with Dad, and then with Grandma, it finally started to sink in what you went through. There you were with a daughter and almost no help from Dad. I can imagine you wanted to feel sorry for yourself all the time. But you were like those pioneers Uncle Alex was talking about. You just made up your mind to make the best of things—for me—and you did it. That's what half my relatives told me today. I think they know about me going off with Dad for a while, and they thought they needed to remind me."

"Well . . . I'm sorry for that. They mean well."

"I'm not sorry. I'm really starting to get it. It's like I have to start over now and rethink everything I've been saying about my life."

"And what are you thinking?"

"I don't know. I haven't figured it out yet. I just know I need to. But I wanted to say one thing to you."

Diane glanced at Jenny, waiting.

"Thanks."

Diane couldn't talk for a time, but finally she managed to say, "Oh, brother. Let's not start that."

"Start what?"

"I'm a little too young to be that 'angel mother' everyone talks about once the old lady is on her last leg."

"Well, Mom, if you ask me, you *are* really old. Forty's coming up fast."

Diane stomped on the gas pedal, but the old car only labored a little harder; it didn't really accelerate much. "Then I've got to hurry," Diane said. "I've got to make life as exciting as I can before the curtain falls."

But life actually did look rather exciting to her now. She had been hired to be a principal that fall, and she had lots of plans on how to do the job well. Maybe that wouldn't sound very exciting to most people, but it did bring a new focus to her own life, for which she was glad.

CHAPTER 19

The summer passed quickly and Diane was busy getting ready to start her new assignment at Dee Elementary School on 22nd Street in Ogden. She had been finishing the last of her classes and trying to get ready for the school year at the same time. She had moved into her office, laughing at the idea of herself sitting there when kids were "sent to see the principal," and she was a little nervous now that it was all becoming a reality.

Jenny had decided to run cross-country again that fall. She was working out harder than ever, committed to doing her best in her senior year. Tracy had chosen not to run, but Jenny didn't seem to care about that. She had admitted to Diane that she had little chance of being the best runner on the team, but she wanted to run anyway. She liked the way it made her feel when she was in her top shape.

In many ways, Jenny was as driven as she had ever been, but Diane saw a change in her, too. She was growing up, it seemed, seeing her future as something real that she had to plan for, not just a fantasy she had been thinking about since she was a little girl. She seemed also to be a little more compliant. It was hard for Diane to put her finger on what had changed, but Jenny clearly wanted to get along, not defy Diane about everything.

Diane had been running with Jenny a good deal lately—not for as many miles, and she pleaded with Jenny to slow down when they ran together—but it was good for Diane, and after workouts, she felt wonderful. She had lost some weight and felt the change in her fitness. She could walk up stairs more easily, and she noticed that her clothes felt better on her. For the first time in her life, though, she wasn't asking herself whether she was pretty, but whether she was healthy. She liked that she felt in good shape, and she liked that she was looking forward to the start of school, however nervous she was, rather than dreading it the way she had the last few years. She was also excited about her better paycheck, which would take away one of the biggest pressures she'd had over the years.

Greg's circumstance was still unclear, but it seemed very possible that he was going to jail. Either way, she didn't ever want to take any money from him again, and she wanted him to stay away from Jenny. Diane had always liked to think he was actually sorry for what he had done to her all those years ago, but now he had hurt her child, and Diane was not about to trust him again.

On a hot August morning, the day before Diane was to take over her job officially, she and Jenny decided to take a hike instead of a run. They got up at five o'clock, drove to the foothills below Malan Peak, and hiked up to the waterfall in Waterfall Canyon. That was an easy hike, but from there they hiked on up through a narrow, steep passage, all the way to the top of Malan Peak, which was below the majestic Mount Ogden. From the top of Malan they could see the whole valley. A little haze was hanging over the city, but they could see out across the Great Salt Lake, see Mount Ben Lomond on the north end of the valley, and see south into the Salt Lake Valley. They had brought some sandwiches with them. After they had taken in the sights, they moved back out of the sun, sat, and ate, resting in a grassy spot surrounded by patches of scrub oak and quaking aspen.

They talked as they ate, mostly about Jenny returning to Ogden High. Jenny was worried about fitting back in. That was one of the reasons she had decided to return to the cross-country team. "I'm sure

Heather will be excited to see me back at school," Jenny said, laughing. "What's ever happened with her dad, anyway? Did he just disappear?"

"Mostly. He calls me once in a while."

"What's he doing, just stringing you along?"

"I don't know. He's worried about his kids, and he talks to me about that. Heather seems to get a little worse all the time. Anyway, we seem to be 'just friends' now, as far as he's concerned."

"That's okay with you, isn't it?"

"Sure."

"Hey, that didn't sound very convincing." Jenny was sitting on the grass with her long legs straight out in front of her, angled away from Diane. She was smiling, looking rather impish.

Diane tried to think what to say. "Well, you know, I do like him. I almost wish he wouldn't call. He's more interesting to talk to than almost anyone I know—but then it's always, 'Well, nice to talk to you. See you around sometime.'"

"See you around?"

"Not really. But it amounts to that. It's okay, though. I made up my mind while you were gone that I couldn't wait for anyone else to make me happy. I'm just glad my life is changing right now—and I'm excited about it."

"Are you scared about the first day?"

"Yeah, I am. I've got all these plans in place, and all these ideas from graduate school, but it's kind of scary to face the real thing."

Jenny laughed. "When I was in grade school, I never would have thought that the principal was scared."

"Most of them aren't, I'm sure. But the first day—you know how that is with anything."

"They're just little kids. And they'll all like you because you're so pretty."

Diane had just taken a drink of water from a canteen she had carried. As she was putting the cap back on, she looked at Jenny. "What does that have to do with anything?"

"I don't know. Kids get used to adults who look stern and grumpy. They'll think you're more like a mom. The little girls, especially the sixth graders, they'll be dazzled by you. You're looking like a movie star now—so thin and tan and everything."

Diane laughed. "You know what? I don't want the kids thinking I'm pretty. I want them thinking that I care about them. I want them to feel that school is a place where they can feel comfortable and do their best."

"They will. That's exactly what they'll feel—because you're nice, and not stuck on yourself."

Diane was tired of sitting cross-legged. Her legs were actually a little sore from all the running and the hike this morning. She lay back now on the grass, stretched her legs out straight, and laced her hands under her head. "So tell me what you're thinking lately," she asked Jenny, "about school and everything. You told me your goals are changing. In what way?"

"I don't know exactly. Ever since I found out I was poor, way back in about fourth or fifth grade, I've been trying to prove something to the world. I was going to have houses and jets and fancy clothes, and people would know I was *somebody.*"

"Don't you feel that way now?"

"I still think about stuff like that, but I saw what money—or actually, the lust for it—did to Dad. He's such a miserable person, and I don't think he even knows why. But he's got it in his head that if he can just be filthy rich, he'll have everything he wants."

"It sounds like he's *had* everything he wants."

"True. But he always spends more than he has—trying to *look* rich—and that's what makes him so desperate. That's why he cheats people. He takes their money, and I really think he intends to make money for them, but he has to pay his bills, so he uses their money and ends up in a trap. I don't think he *planned* to cheat anyone, and I actually think he doesn't think he *did* cheat them. It's like he was just *borrowing* their money until he hit it big, and then he was going to pay them back with big-time gains. It's just unbelievable to hear him explain how he hasn't ever done anything wrong."

"Something is missing in Greg. He's like a little child who wants a toy. If he has to hit another kid to get it, that's what he does."

"I know. I saw that when I was living with him. But there's a nice side to him. I really thought he loved me. When I crossed him, though, that was the ultimate sin. He's all charm, and if you buy into it, he's happy, but once you see through him, he lashes out at you. It's almost like he knows what he really is—a fraud—but he can't stand to have anyone else know."

"That's exactly right."

"That's what you were trying to tell me, wasn't it? Back when I decided to go down there."

"I guess so. I was mostly afraid that you would get into all that—and become like him."

"There's too much of you in me for that."

Diane laughed. "Well, I suppose. But I was seeing a lot of him come out in you, there for a while."

"I know."

"So let's go back to my question. What's changed? What are you thinking that you want to do now?"

Jenny was staring out toward the valley. They were sitting back far enough that they couldn't see the city now, but they could see where the sky and the Great Salt Lake blended together, only slightly different shades of gray-blue. "I'm thinking I want to go to BYU, for one thing."

Diane sat up. "BYU? Are you serious?"

"Why do you say that? You loved it down there."

"I know. But you've always said you didn't want to go there."

"Well, Aunt LaRue is there, and every time I talk to her, I realize I want to get to know her better."

"Wasn't she talking to you about going to Smith?"

"Yeah. And I might do that later. Go east, I mean. I still think I want to go to law school. But I want to be an advocate for abused women and children. I'm over that whole thing about needing lots of houses and everything. That's just so selfish in a world where so many people have almost nothing."

Diane laughed hard this time. She watched Jenny, who was smiling, obviously not surprised that Diane would find this funny, but still apparently not convinced that the idea was all *that* funny. Finally Diane said, "I thought you were going to get rich first, and then use your money to help the poor."

"I know. But rich people who help the poor just write checks most of the time, and they still live in splendor."

"Who said that to you, Kathy or LaRue?"

"Why do you ask that?"

"Because I've never heard you use the word '*splendor*.' And it sounds like something LaRue or Kathy would say."

"Well, they both came to see Grandma a lot when I was down there. Kathy came down once a week, every week, all the way from Heber City. And LaRue was there even more than that."

"So which one said that 'living in splendor' was wrong?"

"Both, probably. I don't know. It seems like I thought of it myself, but maybe they said it."

"So, after all my talk, you end up listening to my cousin and my aunt."

"I don't think that's exactly what happened. I had just come out of Dad's house, and I was already thinking I'd been looking at life all wrong. They came along at a good time."

Diane stood up. She walked a few steps forward, so she could see more of the valley again. It was strange to think how opposite she'd been from Kathy and LaRue as a young woman, and how they would have been the last people she would have listened to. "You always said BYU was too goody-goody. Have you changed your mind about that?"

When Jenny didn't answer, Diane turned around. Jenny was still on the grass, sitting with her legs in front of her and her arms back, bracing herself. She looked beautiful with her dark hair falling back, her eyes so pale and blue, but there were tears in her eyes. "Something happened to me at Grandma's funeral," she said. "I've been getting up in testimony meeting all my life, reciting my little speech—mostly because I liked to be up in front of everyone, all of them looking at me. But sitting in that funeral, it's like it hit me for the first time, 'This stuff is really true.' When that thought came into my head, suddenly my whole body filled up, like I was going to float off my seat, right up in the air."

Diane had waited so long for this moment. But she didn't say anything. She couldn't.

Jenny was sniffing, swallowing. She finally said, "One of the things I thought that day was that the best people I've ever known in this world are Grandma Bea, Grandma Bobbi, and you. I'm the next in line. I want to be like you three."

"Don't put me on the list, honey. Just model your life on your grandmothers."

"No, that's not true. You basically gave up your life for me, Mom. When I try to imagine myself in your situation, I wonder what I'd do. If I had to give up all my goals and think more of someone else, I don't know if I could do it."

"But it's what parents do—at least, what they should do."

"It's so weird to grow up thinking only of yourself, and then, just when you start to fulfill some of the things you've dreamed about, you have kids, and you have to give up a lot of the things you thought you wanted," Jenny said.

"Well, it depends. Sometimes the goals and the family life mesh together just fine. That's why you have to think about life the right way."

"Yeah. I know."

"Do you still want to wait for a long time before you get married?"

Jenny smiled. "I don't know," she said. "But I'm thinking I want my own kids—especially a little girl I can teach to be like you and my grandmas."

Diane laughed. "She'll fight you all the way—and want to be *herself.* That's how it always works."

Jenny nodded. "But it's more important to be a good mom than to make a lot of money. Don't you know that, Mom?" She was smiling now.

"No. I had no idea. You're teaching me some interesting new concepts."

Jenny got up. She walked to her mother and put her arms around her. She didn't say anything, just held onto her for a long time. Diane was wondering whether it was possible to be any happier than she was at that moment.

Diane's first week at school was busy and satisfying. She had learned the names of all the teachers, and she was getting to know them. She was also working on a project to memorize the names of all the children in the school. She had some ideas about "school atmosphere," and when she met with the teachers, she wanted them to buy into certain changes she planned to make, without feeling that the new principal was some amateur, just out of school. Overall, the faculty seemed to like her, and Diane was putting in long days, but enjoying them.

She was sitting at her desk one afternoon after school when Beth, her secretary, came to the door, even stepped inside the office. "There's someone here to see you. He said it would only take a minute."

"A parent?"

"I don't know. I don't think so. He knew your first name."

"Well . . . have him come in."

"He has a very nice smile—and no wedding ring."

Diane rolled her eyes. "I'll bet he's a textbook salesman."

So Beth left, and a moment later, Diane looked up to see Spence standing in the doorway—smiling. "I've been bad. My teacher sent me to the principal."

Diane stood up. "I have no doubt you've been bad, but you're a hopeless case. I'm just going to suspend you."

"It's what I deserve. But do you have a minute first? I want to plead my case."

"Maybe two minutes—not more."

Spence sat down in the chair by the door. It was not a big office, but he seemed to fill it up with his height, his big shoulders. He was wearing a red polo shirt, and his skin looked very brown against the brightness. She thought maybe he'd been outside a lot this summer. "Wow, you're looking good," Spence said.

"For a principal?"

"For anyone."

"I've been running this summer with Jenny."

"How's she doing?"

"Really well. What about Heather?"

"Well, that's one of the things I stopped by to talk to you about. Not long after I talked to you last time, everything hit the fan. What was that, a month ago?"

"Something like that."

"Well, she came home one night really late, and I could tell she'd been drinking. She got mad and told me what she thought of me, and admitted she'd been taking drugs, too. So we've been through some hard times together. But I finally put my foot down, and I think that's what she was waiting for. And yes, I know—it's what you told me I needed to do a long time ago."

"You knew it too."

"I did. But it took something dramatic to get me to take a stand, and I started clamping down on her. At first she revolted—at least verbally—but I've kept her away from some of the people she was running around with, and I took her car away from her. The best thing is, we've had some really long talks lately, and I think she's coming around a little. She's growing up, for one thing, and she's starting to realize that she's messing up her life."

"Jenny and I have had some good talks too. Being with her dad was the best thing that could have happened to her."

"I read in the paper about him. He's going to prison, isn't he?"

"I don't know. His lawyer is appealing his case, but he's in really deep trouble, that's for sure."

"Couldn't have happened to a more deserving guy."

"I know. But it still hurts me to see it. I loved him once, and it's sad to see him ruin his life. He had everything going for him at one time."

Spence nodded. He was watching her, and once again she could see that he liked what he was seeing. She wished he wouldn't come around and get her interested every now and then. She had felt better lately, not having to think about him. "Well, that's good about Heather," she finally said.

"The other kids are doing a little better too. Last night I got everyone together and I told them that I was thinking that it might be good for me to start thinking about getting married. Heather wasn't in love with the idea, but the other kids told her she was being selfish—that it was just what I ought to do."

"It sounds like you've met someone, Spence."

"Actually, I have. That's why I came over. It seemed like I ought to tell you."

"I appreciate that. I hope you'll be really happy." But Diane was actually *not* happy about it, and she wished he hadn't come. Spence never had seemed to understand that he was making her miserable with all his drawing near and pulling back.

"Well, don't jump to any conclusions. Nothing has gone that far. She's just someone I really like to be with—and I think she likes me. We need to spend more time together before we make up our minds."

"I'm sure she'll have no trouble falling in love with you. You're quite a catch."

"Actually, I haven't treated her the way I should have, and I'm not sure she'll be willing to forgive me for that. I *am* in love with her. I'm just not sure how she feels about me."

Diane had heard all she wanted to hear. "Well, good luck." She stood up and reached out her hand.

"Thanks." Spence stood too, and he shook her hand. "You've been a big help to me when I've been going through all this stuff with my kids."

"You've been very helpful to me too."

"Good. Are you still interested in helping me give my money away?"

"Well . . . I don't know. Maybe someone else could do a better job with that. I've talked to a teacher friend of mine about getting something started—in a small way."

"Okay. But it's still something I want to do. I think we could work together really well." And now he was smiling.

Diane was getting more annoyed every second. She wanted him to leave. She looked down at her desk so she wouldn't have to look in his eyes. "Well, anyway, it was nice of you—"

"Would you consider going to dinner with me Friday night?"

Diane's head popped back up. But she didn't answer.

"And then I was thinking, maybe we could spend some time

together Saturday. Maybe go for a ride on a bridge. I just want to start spending a lot more time with you, if you're interested at all."

Now he was really smiling, and Diane felt her breath coming fast.

Spence stepped closer to her desk. "I'm sorry for the way I've handled this whole thing," he said. "But I think it's time we see whether we can move ahead."

She stood still for a long time, telling herself to be careful. At last she said, "Maybe we could go to church together on Sunday."

"Yeah. I'd thought of that, but I was a little hesitant to take your whole weekend."

He was looking at her like he wished the desk weren't between them, and Diane had no idea what to do. "Did you say you love this woman?"

"I did say that."

"Or do you feel sorry for her? Maybe you just want to beat up all the bad guys in her life and be her Superman?"

"No, it's not that. I'm in love with her. I have been for quite a while, but I thought the situation was too complicated."

"It is complicated. It could turn out to be a mess."

"I know. There's a lot to figure out."

"But your theory is, this woman needs a lot of time to get to know you better?"

"I think so."

"Maybe not as much time as you think."

His eyes were glistening now. "I'm wondering," he said. "Does the school have a rule about kissing the principal?"

"You know, that's something I've never checked on."

She was coming around the desk by then. And Spence was coming around the other way. When they met, he took her in his arms, and he did kiss the principal.

Diane tried not to think. She let him hold her for a long time after they had kissed, but all the while she was wondering how things could

ever work. She had no answers, but she knew that life was always complicated. Why should she expect anything else?

It occurred to her, however, that life was also good. She hadn't
always felt that way about it, but life really was good.